MW00942978

Prodigal's Blood

By

Mark Herbkersman

Mary Kay,
Thanks for the
support,
Mark

Cover design: Jeffrey Dowers

This book was previously released in 2014 with the title Battle for Yesterday. In this new edition, mistakes have been corrected and the new title applied. It also has been made a part of a series.

See these other titles in the Henry Family Chronicles:

Book 2: Revenge on the Mountain

Book 3: The Branding of Otis Henry (available autumn 2015)

Acknowledgments

Publishing a first book is a true learning experience. I believe it to be true, at least in my case, that there is much more learning to be gained from mistakes. I made several with this book the first time around. The original title, Battle for Yesterday, lacked something and was even confused with being a philosophical treatise of some sort. Far from it! Also, many errors had escaped detection and needed correction. To make it even more difficult, I realized that the cover needed much more of a western flair.

So a renewed journey began to remake the book. In the process, I realized that it is not the writer alone who experiences the journey. I wish to thank all the following who also shared this effort with me.

My friend Jeff Dowers gave of his time to masterfully create the new cover. We dealt with dpi, jpeg, pixels and a host of stuff!

I gained a new friend in Joni Murphy, who gave of her time and masterful skills to edit this manuscript.

To my dad, Bob Herbkersman, who shares a love for the Western and, like me, has read all of the good ones. Louis L'Amour tops the list.

To Zig Ziglar, who never knew me, but who always urged people to follow their dreams.

To Bill Craig, my new friend and fellow writer, who made a difference.

To my daughters, Cora and Joy, who too often saw my nose in a book with eyes glazed and elsewhere on some adventure.

I give thanks to my wife of many years, Marilyn. She tolerated my preoccupation and determination to write. I love you.

Above all, I give credit to God, who inspired me to write and who gave His Son for me.

Follow Mark on his blog:
markherb.blogspot.com

And feel free to email him at
askmherb@yahoo.com

Prologue

A tapestry can be an exquisite work of art. There is beauty in the colors and the choices of weaves and the way the colors blend. Yet, when a tapestry is turned and the underside exposed, the colors seem more random, there is a roughness in the build, there are frayed ends and the construction is obviously less refined than the final product that the viewer sees. So it is with the history of man. We look back and we see the beauty of the final tapestry, yet miss the roughness, the frayed ends and the less refined aspects hidden underneath.

The migrations of man in the American west, as with migrations elsewhere around the world, show the weavings of a tapestry, with the strands woven in various colors and textures.

Throughout the history of man, there have been migrations where, for whatever reason, masses of men sought something that seemed to be on the horizon. Always, there were those of individual spirit who, traveling in contented solitude, created the trails that others followed. Then came groups of few and many, venturing together for safety and companionship. They all sought land, fortune, freedom from oppression - a multicolored interweaving of reasons - and maybe just to get away. In all ways, they sought something better than what they had, or which seemed better than what they had. It is said that Daniel Boone complained of "no elbow room" when there was someone within a mile.

As usual with these migratory trends, there were those who came to prey off those who came before, to take a lawless hand in a land in which formal law was limited and often based solely upon the speed of a gun or the power in a fist or the strategy of the moment. Their strands are also woven into the tapestry. Throughout the history of man, there has been a branch of humanity filled with brutality and lack of conscience, seeking power and control. Men and women of education have often tried to tie this to some occurrence in their early years, but there are some instances that defy all explanation, where the cruelty morphs into a brutality that defies all explanation.

Some men found it impossible to settle. In many, the war had disturbed something deep within. They were broken.

A few turned violent, which had been so needed for survival in battle, and became first rather than second, nature. Feeling was lost and humanity stunted. These became predators.

Then there were those who had been unstable already, due to whatever quirk of being, and the war ignited in them something ruthless and terrible. They were men whose only happiness - if such it could be called - was through the domination of others. Not infrequently, it became brutal.

These individuals migrated also, for purposes base and disadvantageous to the lives of others, like coarse black threads interwoven not so much for color as for texture.

Thankfully, the less desirous element was a minority and, like all men, life was fleeting in the sands of time. Their lives ended and their actions ceased and their bones rotted in the soil of the land. Yet there were always those to follow the same weave.

One of the many migrations of men, and women, who were always a part of the migrations, either by companionship with a man or by seeking advantage over men - occurred immediately following the Civil War, as men who had given their all for a cause and found themselves without homes sought solace in the golden opportunities of the American West. They packed up wagons or saddlebags and ventured out into a new land, a new life, facing danger, privation and tragedy as they settled and carved lives and futures out of the wilds. They formed the backbone of a new society, and their wandering, adventuring days became a thing of the past and were relegated to the memories of their youth.

Another, different kind of migration came a generation later, as the sons and daughters of those earlier veterans and settlers came of age. Typical of new generations, they were not all satisfied with continuing the work of their parents. Some sought adventure themselves and to see what was around the bend in the trail. They traveled north, south, east and west and some found new lives, others disappeared forever and some...well, some found that what they were seeking was something they already had - so they returned to that land of their youth. They settled and became part of the fabric of the land.

Others traveled a route that led to their being woven into the fabric of another life altogether, yet something within them remained tied to the past. When life came to a proverbial bump in the road, they turned their hearts once again to what had once been forsaken, saw the beauty of it, felt the pull and their hearts drew them homeward.

Some returned to find home was changed from their memories, or they themselves had changed too much, or home had disappeared in the sands of wind and time.

Others returned to find more than they ever dreamed...

The man screamed. It was more of a croak, as a grip of incredible power squeezed the man's vocal cords and pinned him to the moss-covered bricks of the old jetty. The terror in the man's eyes was wrought of failed desperation. His hands clawed desperately at the muscled arm holding him. The other arm of his assailant grabbed both wrists with his free hand and squeezed. As bones cracked, the man whimpered.

"So…you miserable wretch…" The words were filled with venom and dripping with morbid pleasure. It was the pleasure of a man who was getting inordinate delight in wringing the life out of another. It was a pleasure wrought of brutal triumph. "You thought you could get away."

The man's eyes began to fade. Boss Carter eased his grip enough to bring clear sight back to the eyes. He wanted the man to suffer.

"You talked to that lawyer! You thought I wouldn't find out." The hand squeezed again, then released when the man was turning blue.

"There's somethin' I want you to know before you die." Eyes wide with the pleasure at another's misfortune, Boss spoke. "I killed your sons this morning and your wife, well, we'll take care of her, too."

The man's eyes bulged, Boss Carter laughed, and the grip tightened and the man's head fell forward. Lowered to the ground, hands quickly tied a rope to the man's legs and kicked him over the edge into the swirling water. Then, the large rock was hoisted and slipped over the edge, carrying the man to the bottom.

Chapter 1

The rider emerged as a shimmer on the horizon, a shape wriggling and dancing out of the joining of the earth and the sky. At that time of day and at that distance, movement looked surreal, and at first glance to distinguish the shape as human – or even real – would have been impossible. The image wiggled and wavered, seemingly caught in time until it burst forth. It was almost as if the rider were leaving one world and slowly merging into another. In a sense it was true…

Ike watched as the shimmer became more distinct, emerging as a rider in the distance, yet there was something about him. He didn't ride with the slouch of a saddle tramp. The colors of the evening sun shown on him as he rode in from the east, giving him a sort of magenta cast that almost seemed to radiate from within.

Ike spat into the dust and squinted his worn

but experienced eyes as the distant figure neared and details became clearer. No, this one wasn't like most of the usual riders around. He rode differently, with a confidence and purpose. Nobody'd believe he could tell the difference. He used to talk about it, but they'd just chuckle and cast knowing glances at one another and say, "Ike's a little off." It used to annoy him, but now he accepted it. He kept his thoughts to himself. Just did his job. Let them think he was just a "dumb hostler," It made no never mind to him.

As the rider neared the edge of town, Ike stood and leaned against the stable doorway and worked through the recesses of his mind, piecing together a puzzle based upon years of observation and experience. So Ike looked toward the shimmering, glowing rider, working all his thoughts, seeking clues – not for any particular purpose, just because.

Yes, there was something about this rider...he was dressed different. Nicer, somehow, but not like a dude that was all show. No...this one looked like.....Ike squinted more carefully....something vaguely familiar. His mind ranged thru his storehouse of memories of people seen thru the years, stopped, looked again at the approaching stranger.

He went back to his chair and leaned against the wall on two legs. This was where he spent a good part of his day, musing over this and that in his mind and philosophizing in the way that only western men and especially those with time on their hands can do. He didn't have to rush. He never was prone to rushing. He remembered as a kid when he heard some traveling preacher tell about each day having enough worry of its own. Ike realized that, and each day turned into another day and each year into another year. He didn't like change. The only regular change he experienced was when he bought fresh secondhand clothes. He rarely left his spot. It was a good spot, with a view of all that went on in town, all that came and went. They thought he was crazy, but he knew more that was going on than any of the others. Yet, this simple man - and he himself acknowledged his simplicity - had more time to think than those of more earnest occupation, and this resulted in a great deal of education of the practicalities of life and the ways of men, women and horses. Yet, he chuckled to himself, others saw him as some sort of village idiot. They didn't approach him or take the time to know him, judging him solely by his clothes and occupation.

Well, almost all the others. There was Marge.

Now that was a nice lady, Ike mused. She had come from nowhere a couple years back, settled into town and opened a little eating-place across the street and down a ways. She had always been kind to Ike. She never looked at him like he was crazy, and had actually stood up for him once when somebody was making fun of him. Nobody bothered him anymore in her place.

Hers was a safe place. It made him wistful of times when he was a kid back in Virginia.

He spat again into the dust. At first the townsfolk were all stand-offish of this attractive, busy young lady, and wondered why she chose their town and where she got the startup money. The code of the day prevented them from asking about her past. Yet, when they tasted her food and learned that she was here to stay, there was a change that took place. They found themselves seeking her food and her advice. She was gracious, looked straight at you in a way that made you feel like you were the only person in the world that mattered. She was mature beyond her years, and the advice she gave was good. Her place became a clearinghouse of information. And she always had a kind word for Ike. He felt special when she was around, and she always had a nice sliver of pie for him that appeared on his plate with no extra charge. Sometimes she seemed to press for more information about going's on in town and who rode in when, and he was inclined to give it. After all, every man has his price.... and her pie and kindness made all the difference to his sometimes-lonely life. He was a good judge of people and he knew that she would have been kind to him whether he had any news or not. So when he had a hankering about something he just sort of moseyed over to Marge's. He walked something like the short, choppy steps of a banty rooster, and his head moving in a curious back and forth motion. He heard the kids make fun of him, but he didn't give it no never mind.

He looked again towards the rider. The livery stable was always the first stop for travelers. A man always takes care of his horse first, and his was the only stable in town. So Ike just had to sit and wait. Business came to him.

On a wooded outcrop on a hill not far west from town, another set of eyes evaluated the rider as the heat waves released their hold upon him. They were eyes experienced at judging men, and eyes that held a veritable catalogue of names and descriptions. He squinted in the evening light, pulled out a small brass telescope and trained it on the rider. The telescope was tarnished to a smudgy black-gold color. Only a greenhorn or a fool kept their brass polished in this country. Polished brass reflected sunlight and revealed one's position. The duller the better. His preference was to stay in the realm of wondering - not certainty - in the minds and eyes of others. His brow wrinkled and his eyes squinted as he found the recognition he was seeking and hoping.

Mel Stacker smiled, a genuine smile that revealed straight but tobacco-stained teeth. Spending much time riding alone, Stacker had been unable to get away from the chewing that helped wile away the hours. He was a long-faced man with intelligent, piercing eyes. Dark hair tangled with his shirt collar. A natural tracker, even in his youth, Stacker had learned to follow a trail in a way that only Indians could understand. He not only looked for tracks and signs, he calculated the thoughts and actions of the person he was tracking. If one understood the habits of the human mind and the peculiarities of the target, then often a predictability arose.

Try as he might, he could not build up a strong familiarity to this rider. The rider was good on the trail, excellent at leaving little trail and no patterns of behavior. He remembered his mother, standing beside his horse many years ago as he left to find his way in the west, reminding him to stay on the right side of the law. He had, and the Rangers had taught him well over the years. Now, of course, he was not on Ranger business, but a private job, and paid well for it by some group of lawyers in Boston. They had said he might need all his skills to track this man, and they were right. He had finally waited outside this town toward which his employer had told him Henry would head. He raised his eyebrows. His orders were simple – follow the man, make sure no others followed and watch over him.

He rolled his chew around to the other side and spat at an ant on the rock. As the ant fell, Stacker wiped his mouth and he began to ponder the job. He was a close-mouthed man and known for few words. One old Ranger Captain used to joke that he spoke exactly 100 words per month and no more. He really didn't see the need to say much. Most people just talk to hear themselves talk, and waste words talking about nothingness. He just preferred not to say anything unless there was something to say. After all, there was a reason God gave two ears, two eyes and only one mouth. He believed in using them in the right proportion and his life often depended upon it.

Of course, being on the trail as much as he was didn't leave much reason to talk. There was a girl back down the trail a few years back who he took a bit of a shining to, but he couldn't abide her talking so much. I guess, he thought, you need to talk about nothingness to be someone's sweetheart. He chose not to have a sweetheart. Sometimes he wondered whether that was the right decision, but then he was quite content to be alone.

He turned his eyes back to the trail and watched the rider head into town. From his position he could see much of what happened at that edge of town. He sat back…maybe he'd head into town early and get a cooked meal. Jerky and coffee was great for the trail but got old after a fashion. Maybe he could find a place where he wouldn't have to talk. He grinned, wiping the dust from his face with a faded yellow bandana.

Chapter 2

As the rider pulled up in front of the livery, he looked down at Ike and a smile crossed his whiskered jaw. He was a man of average height, lean and strong, with muscular shoulders and arms. He was muscular in the legs, indicating a man who did not - or had not - spent most of his hours in a saddle, but a man used to walking and doing whatever a man does when not on a horse. Yet, he did not look like a farmer, nor did he have a farmer's work-hardened hands.

Ike, like many a western man, noticed the details. Fairly new shirt, jeans, and hat with no sign of the wear of a cowhand. Boots the like of which you'd never find out here, but tough and obvious quality. Custom made, no doubt. He also noticed the saddle and the horse. The horse was a dun, one with apparent spirit and stamina. Not many around could match either. The .44 Russian top-break on the right hip seemed to fit the man. The hammer spur was filed off. That spur had been good for the first shot's accuracy, but was known to slow the hammer pull for the second shot. It also tended to catch on things, and a catch could be fatal in this country. He seemed like he was at home in the clothes, but not long at home. Or maybe it was the clothes that seemed out of place on the man, like he was used to wearing something different. Didn't matter, really, Ike said to himself. Out here what a man - or a woman for that matter - looked like on the outside wasn't important. It used to be more that way. Times was changin' a might. Some people got all a'shiver with fancy clothes and such, but Ike still judged men and women and horses by their character. Too many people dressed to try to impress someone. Ike had seen some pretty nicely dressed scoundrels and some real gentlemen wearing rags.

This was a man accustomed to comfort, but without the signs of those of such ilk who rode the hoot owl trail.

He looked more like someone used to the complicated things of life. It shown in his eyes. Ike pegged him as eastern. Not a dandy, but used to importance. His was a face that women found pleasant and men found strong and invited wariness. The eyes showed deep intensity and awareness as they settled on Ike.

"Hello, Ike."

Ike squinted....could it be? He spat and wiped his mouth to gain a moment to remember. Hazy memories became sharp and clear. A wry, wistful look came to his eye and the corner of his mouth rose with the faintest trace of a smile. He wasn't known to smile.

"Billy? Billy Henry?"

The stranger nodded, "I'm glad to see some things never change, Ike. You're a breath of fresh air."

"First time I ever been called that. Usually, I'm called the opposite. Had a hunch you'd be back someday. This country seemed to grow on you."

"I'm back. If it's alright with you, I'd settle for Bill as my short handle." Bill responded. It was a strange sound since back east he was always addressed as William.

"Your folks know you comin'?"

"No. Are they ok?"

"Fur's I know. Your pa, he taken a bullet helping his neighbors with some rustlers a few months back, was laid up for a spell, but seems to be coming along. I 'spect they'll be right glad to see you."

Bill glanced around the town. He was an expert with a poker face, but inside his heart was pounding. Pa had been shot? His every urge now was to kick into a trot and go the last few miles to the home place. But he knew his horse was tired. Matter of fact, so was he. No, he'd better wait till morning.

"Changed a lot around here," he ventured, glancing down the street.

"Yup...keeps growin."

New Haven lay nestled in a valley between the foothills and the lower ranges. Like many towns, it began with part of a wagon train, tired and weary of travel, deciding to put down roots and forego the push over the Rockies to Oregon territory. It helped that a storekeeper's wagon had busted a final spare axle and none of the others heading over the range were willing to part with theirs. So they had a store. Another was a blacksmith, and yet another an old trapper who knew how to treat bullet and arrow wounds and how to make good imitation rotgut out of whatever was to hand, so they had a doctor and a saloon. A few farmers settled to set out crops and they suddenly found themselves a community. They had stood by each other through some Indian troubles and some white men who got too pushy. Through it all they stood strong, shoulder to shoulder and came to see one another as family. They saw to each other's needs and knew the same would be done in return. Over the years, necessity and proximity resulted in some marriages that further melded the families together. Then came the war, and they heard rumors of all the going's on, but no one paid much attention to it. It was miles away and there were crops and cattle to care for. After the war, there were soldiers of gray and blue who wandered through, liked the sense of community and settled in to stay and raise families of their own. Yes, there were a few who tried to push themselves around, but they quickly found that the town stuck together and they were ridden out...after a burial or two.

When Bill left those years ago, New Haven was just a bump in the road, with Wilson's general store, the ever-present Tagget's saloon that doubled as a hotel, the blacksmith, a few cabins and a couple clapboard cottages and, of course, Ike's stable. As he looked around, he saw the sprawl. More buildings and more people. And a little white church. Yet, it was still a bump in the road compared to Boston.

"Is there anything that hasn't changed, Ike?"

"Well, let's see..." Ike scratched his chin like he was chasin' a flea, which he might have been, considering cleanliness was not a strong suit for him. Many townspeople avoided him for that reason, but he didn't care....his ma used to say that cleanliness was next to Godliness, but he didn't reckon he was close to God, so being clean didn't matter. Besides, washing was a waste of time for a hostler. Mucking out a stable took the edge off clean real quick. In fact, if he wanted to get rid of someone being a bother, he'd just a set to scratchin' with a vengeance and the person would look bothered and hurry off.

"Wilson's still here - solid as always, just got hisself a bigger store. Must be doin' pretty well. He's got a picket fence and such round the house. 'Spect his missus had a say-so in that. You remember Ernie, owns the smithy? He's still here, but hurt his back a couple years ago.

Both his boys is growed and bigger than he was...they do most of the work now. We got a sheriff. I reckon you remember Walt...Walt Larimore. He done took the job and does it well. Ain't had no real problems here in a coon's age. Some of the others is still here. The town's quiet-like nowadays. Some of the new folks ain't of the same mold as those as came first, but most'r decent. One feller tried to open a crib, an' you shoulda seen the happenin's then. It was the women what drove him out! The wild west done left us....good riddance, I say. All that mess of shootin that used to go on of a Saturday night. It seemed like they was a funeral every month."

"You haven't changed, Ike."

"And I ain't never goin' to."

"What's that fancy lookin eating place over there? Good food?" He had noticed the building set by itself a ways up the street. Checkered curtains stood out amongst the more practical business storefronts.

"That's Marge's place. Good food, place to go." His attempt to hide a smile did not go unnoticed by Bill.

As he glanced down the line of buildings, he had a sense of being watched. Did he see the curtain move at Marge's place? Something to think about. It was one of those things that he didn't really focus on, but which by nature he filed in his mind.

Bill Henry already noticed a change in himself in the 3 weeks he had spent heading west. A horse out of Boston, a train ride under an assumed name to Philly, then another horse to a railhead west of Philly, and a train to St. Louis. Through the change and the travel, Bill had felt some of the intensity of his life fall away. He was sleeping better since leaving St. Louis, and well remembered that first night camped with some other travelers out of St. Louis. It was a ragtag bunch, headed to seek their fortune in the west. Like so many, they seemed to think that there was a pot of gold at the end of every rainbow and silver in every outcropping. He kept quiet, as that was part of the plan to keep his exodus from Boston secret and safe. He was wise enough to know that his education and refinement might be conveyed to others who might be asking questions. Besides, there was nothing that he could say that would bring these dreamers back to reality…they were enamored with the fantasy and he would be looked upon with distaste if he said anything.

But he had slept better than he had in months, with the brightness of the stars reawakening a wonder in his mind. Now, here he was, back from whence he came. It seemed like a long time ago.

"It's good to be back, Ike."

"Reckon on stayin?"

Was he?

"For a spell anyways. Take good care of my mare, would you? I'll be by in the morning."

Ike spat in the dust. "I'll give her an extra

bait of corn. Looks like she's had a long ride and is used to good care."

Bill smiled, ignoring the suggestion of more information. It was a habit he had learned. The less others knew, the better. He handed the reins to Ike.

Ike smiled, too. This wasn't no kid anymore, but a seasoned man. Hard, seemed like, but still decent.

Chapter 3

Taking his bedroll and saddlebags and heading across the street he saw the "closed" sign slipped into the window at Wilson's store. Guess I'll pick up supplies come sunup, he thought to himself. Better rustle up something to eat.

He was used to eating in fancy places, but they really held no interest to him anymore. Same with the crowds. Bypassing Tagget's, he headed towards the smaller, well kept "Marge's." He paused and looked down the street - and gave a quick look in the window. He had learned the way of wariness in his early years in the west, where life often depended upon a full awareness of people, animals and the environment. In Boston, he found the skill refined further in the detection of clues in challenging cases, in the reading of the actions and statements of opposition lawyers and troublesome clients. He also was sure his life had been prolonged by being constantly observant. Walking in, he saw a nicely dressed couple in one corner, but otherwise the place was empty. From the back, in response to the jingle of the bell over the door, he heard a pleasant shout.

"Have a seat and I'll be right there."

He picked a table in a corner with a view of the street in the waning light. Things were picking up at the saloon. A nicely dressed couple walked across the street, and a few cowhands loitered at the walk outside the Express Office. The town had changed, he said to himself. Dragging at his memory, he tried to remember the town as it had been all those years ago. Still, he sensed a peace here. They say you can never go back home, but he was gonna try.

"You look hungry."

He looked up into a quite pretty face. Her hair was pulled back, sleeves rolled up, apron smudged with flour. A few wisps of hair hung down from her forehead. Yet nothing could hide the refined yet down-home quality of this woman.

He stood up out of courtesy, and saw the amused look in her face.

"You must be from back east," she said with a smile. "Thank you for the kindness." She poured him a steaming cup of coffee.

"You're welcome, ma'am. I suppose it is near closing time, but I was wondering if there's still any dinner left? Ike speaks highly of you." He saw her smile.

"Ike's a good man, I don't care what others think. And it just so happens that I have some dinner left. Ever had a Hungry Jack?"

"I don't think I ever have, but if you made it, it's going to be good." He saw her smile. Genuine and sweet. It'd been a long time since he'd seen that in a woman.

As she returned to the kitchen, she looked back, but he had already turned his glance back to the window. A handsome man, seeming out of place in a sense, but not in others. Her eyebrows knitted in deep thought.

Before he left, he complimented her on the Hungry Jack. "Ma'am, that was a meal fit for a king. Thank you."

She blushed. She could feel it and was ashamed of it and saw him notice it, which made her blush even more. "You're welcome. Got a good breakfast, too."

"I reckon I'll be by in the morning. Good night, ma'am." As he left, a tall, lanky man with smiling eyes came through the doors.

"Howdy, sir."

Bill nodded in response and headed for Tagget's, both weariness and relaxation in his eyes.

Far away, in the refined area of Boston's wealthy and privileged, a door opened and a simple servant girl hurried down the manicured lawn. It'd been a long day, made more so by the fact that there was nothing to do. Nevertheless, she and the other servants were made to go about normal routines and to give the impression that all was as usual. But word had crept among those of the household staff that something was amiss. They had been told that their employer, William Henry, was ill and that he needed rest and only essential staff were to go upstairs.

News had spread that they were all to receive a bonus to go about business as usual and to keep their mouths shut. There were no complaints, as Mr. Henry was well loved and always treated his staff with respect. Yet, as often happened in staffed homes, there was a backstairs romance and in the midst of an embrace the downstairs staff found that Mr. Henry was not really in the house.

As the servant girl reached the hedge separating the estate from the road, a set of grimy arms grabbed her roughly and drug her into the bushes. There, with a knife to her throat, she was forced to speak and tell what she knew about her employer. Because of the backstairs romance, she had something to tell, and an equally grimy thug was seen running towards the waterfront. He had a message to give. A message that he was not excited to give, but he had no choice in the matter. His was not a position of wealth and privilege. It was a position of subservience to power...a power vicious and merciless. The thought of not doing what he was told elicited a shudder. Even those of his caliber and vocation who knew they were in trouble with Boss Carter would rather cower at his feet than receive what came to those who ran from him.

Chapter 4

His room that night was not the best, being near the main saloon, but he was tired and slept reasonably well. He was up before the sun and headed to breakfast. He wasn't the first one in. A trail-hardened man with a long face sat in one corner, focused on the plate in front of him. The man wore a faded yellow bandana and looked to have just come in from the trail this morning. Several days' growth of whiskers and dusty clothes. There were many such men in the West, Bill thought. Men with no real home. Of course, any person could be fresh off the trail, but this man had a wary look about him, and something about him told Bill this man could take care of himself. He obviously was relishing the meal, indicative of many days on the trail eating catch as catch can.

Marge came into the room.

"Good morning, Ma'am."

"That makes me feel old when you call me ma'am. Unless I mistake my reflection in the mirror, I think I've got a few years yet before that fits, so please just call me Marge."

"All, right, Marge. That's a pretty name. Suits you better." He also noticed that she wore a newly laundered apron and had her hair done nicely.

A few minutes later he was wading thru a pile of eggs and bacon when the door opened. The sheriff paused, looking over the room. His eyes met Bill's, and a wry smile brought the wrinkles to the corners of his eyes. He walked over.

"Hello, Bill. Been a long time."

"Hello, Walt," he smiled as he stood and offered his hand. "I heard you were sheriff."

"Yep. Been at it about 7 years now. Guess I started 'bout the time you left. You're probably a bit shocked to see me with a badge."

Bill chuckled. "Not really. You were a bit rough around the edges, but you weren't mean. You were always fair to me. Have a seat?"

"Thanks. Guess I had to make a choice and I think I made the right one. Married Sally Wilson, got 2 kids now. You come home to settle down, or just here for a spell?"

"Like to stay a while. We'll see."

Walt had not changed much, Bill mused. A little thicker around the middle. His wife must be a good cook. Walt was shorter than average, but thick and with a neck like a bull. He used to love to fight, and it didn't matter whether he won or lost. A good-natured man, he didn't hold a grudge and would give anybody the shirt off his back....after a fight! He had been involved in some questionable activities, bordering on the edge of the law.

"Looks like marriage suits you, Walt." He grinned. "But I don't recall your shirt being that tight."

Walt laughed in the free and easy way that only he could. It was very easy for him to laugh at himself. "Yep. Sally knows her way around a fry pan, that's for sure. And she seems to think I'm gonna waste away. One look at my britches and it's easy to see I ain't gonna disappear anytime soon!" He laughed again, and it was a laugh that relaxed Bill and made him lean back in his chair and laugh along. "My," he thought, "been a long time since I laughed like that."

He'd forgotten how much he enjoyed Walt. He leaned forward.

"I heard my pa had a bit of trouble a while back. Can you fill me in?

It was the sheriff's turn to chuckle this time. "Seems like these rustlers decided to drive off some of Old Man Slater's cattle. Your pa, being the right neighborly sort, decided that he couldn't abide this happening to his friend - your pa and Slater being thru the war. They never sought no other help, figuring they could saddle this bronc by themselves. So's your pa and Slater takes after the bunch of them, come across their camp one night, injun'd themselves right into camp, got the drop on ‘em and offered the chance for them to give up peaceably. The rustlers decided not to take that offer, and the lead started a'flyin'. Your pa took one hard and low, but they got the cattle back, and your pa refused to go to the Doc until the cattle were back home. Parson Weaver showed up whilst they was on the way back and helped out.” His mood lowered, “Your Pa almost bought the big one, Bill. It was touch and go for quite a spell, but he's been up and around. Still a bit gimpy, and not workin' overly hard yet. I 'spect your folks will be mighty glad to see you."

"The rustlers?"

"Didn't need me...but the undertaker had a bit of business."

Bill nodded. He looked around. "It's been a lot of years."

"I heard you been out east, lawyerin'."

"That's right, Walt. Many folks know that?"

"I reckon not. Your pa mentioned it off hand to me when he was 'bout killed by the rustler's, thinkin' I might need to contact you." He sensed a slight concern in Bill about how many might know. “Been no call for anyone else to know. You in some sort of trouble, Bill?"

Bill, ever a good judge of men, sensed the sheriff was one who could be trusted. His friends back east had always told him that he could sense a rat quicker than anybody. That was why he was so successful at what he did.

He leaned forward, casting a glance at the long-faced man in the corner. Seeing Bill's glance, Walt cast a glance towards the man also. The man rose to leave, giving no greeting as he passed. He walked through the door and Bill could see him casually pause and glance all ways before crossing towards the store. Both men watched him.

Walt noted how his friend watched the man.

"Know that hombre, Bill?"

"No. Never seen him before."

"You were sayin'…"

"I don't think there'll be a problem, Walt, but I'd just prefer that nobody knows what I've been up to. Might be some unsavory characters trying to locate me." He saw the look in Walt's face, and decided he needed to fill in some blanks. He knew that Walt used to be rough, but he was always trustworthy. He needed someone in town, and Walt was the sheriff. He'd know if strangers showed up in town, and he'd be able to sense the type they were. Besides, Walt needed to know if there was possible trouble coming.

"I was involved in a big trial. Put some men behind bars, one hung. There were some threats. I'm trying to get away and lay low for a while."

"I'll keep my eyes and ears open. Anybody know where you're at?"

"Just a couple, and I don't think anybody followed me west."

Marge came by with coffee and to bring Walt breakfast. The sheriff turned to her as the door opened.

"Hello, Parson," Marge said to the newcomer. Bill noticed her glance lingered for a moment, and her smile appeared brighter.

The Sheriff said, "Marge, this here's Bill Henry. Used to live round these parts, and his folks still do. His pa's Otis Henry, from out south of town. I suspect you've met Otis. Wouldn't back down to a rattlesnake if it already had aholt of his leg."

"I know who you're talking about. Ella must be your mom. She sure is the opposite of your pa. I think he'd back down to her."

Bill chuckled. "I suspect you're right." He took a last sip of coffee. Daylight was wasting and he wanted to get to the ranch. Been years since he'd seen his folks and this talk was making him more homesick by the minute. He pushed his chair back. As he did so, he noticed a plate placed in front of Parson, but he didn't recall Parson ordering. Must be right regular, he thought.

"Thanks for breakfast, Marge."

As she headed back to the kitchen, he turned to the sheriff. "Time for me to head to the ranch, Walt." Lowering his voice, he said to him, "By the way, there'll be a trunk coming along soon. It'll be addressed to Bill Henderson. I'd appreciate it if you might watch for it and pick it up from the express office when it arrives. And Walt, I'd appreciate that information being kept between you and me."

"Sure thing, Bill."

Gesturing to the man referred to as Parson, “That the man who helped my pa?” Walt nodded.

Bill walked over to the Parson. "Parson, I’m Bill Henry. I hear you helped my Pa, Otis Henry, a while back. I appreciate it." Parson stood and shook Bill’s hand.

"Glad to help. I heard he and Slater were headed out and thought I'd give a hand. Didn't make it in time for the fireworks."

Bill lifted an eyebrow. "I always heard of parson's trying to stop trouble, not get in the middle of it."

"Well, sometimes the peaceful way ain't the way to get it stopped. Sometimes you got to 'smite them hip and thigh.’" He grinned. "I probably ain't the average parson...I've rode the river before, shall we say."

"Well, I appreciate it. If ever I can do something for you, let me know. Good day." He walked out the door, pausing to look around. This did not go unnoticed by the parson. His eyes wrinkled at the corners as he sipped his coffee.

Bill’s first glance was to see where the strange rider had gone. He glanced towards Wilson’s and saw the man lounging on the boardwalk. In any town in the west the same thing could be seen. Someone lounging outside, legs stretched out, dozing.

Chapter 5

As he approached the stable, he heard a sound like distant singing.

He paused, ears alert and eyes searching. It sounded like singing, but different somehow. He turned as the sound came nearer, and saw large man on a scraggly buckskin start into town from the trail west of town. The rider was unlike anything he had ever seen: hair beyond the shoulders, wild and mostly gray and untamed, with here and there a leaf or small branch where head had rested on the ground. His clothes were buckskin, stained and worn, with a mass of hair protruding where the shirt was unlaced to mid chest. He wore knee-length moccasins and carried a Spencer carbine diagonally across his back.

As he came nearer, Bill could see, barely visible under the edge of a battered derby hat perched precariously and miraculously atop the wild mass of hair, a pair of piercing eyes, one pointing left, the other right, making it all but impossible to tell which way he was looking. It was hard enough to see the face, peering as it was through a long and out-of-control beard. Out of control except for a long braided section hanging down the left side.

And the singing! Out of tune, nonsensical and loud. It was non-stop and the tunes changed continuously. Bill looked on in amazement and incredulousness, his actual emotions hidden behind the straight face of his legal training. As the man came abreast of Bill, he pulled up his horse. Bill heard a voice behind him. It was Ike, still leaning against the wall in his chair.

"Don't make no sudden moves, Bill." Bill perceived that Ike was talking with a wry humor. Even so, he made no moves, for this was something to make a man stop in his tracks. Bill had seen acrobats and contortionists and magicians in Boston do amazing things, but never did they match this apparition here on this street for sheer jaw-dropping amazement.

The stranger was waving his hand in circles, still singing at the top of his lungs. Suddenly he shifted to poetry, with a poem by Tennyson:

"Half a league half a league,
Half a league onward,
All in the valley of Death
Rode the six hundred:

'Forward, the Light Brigade!
Charge for the guns' he said:
Into the valley of Death
Rode the six hundred.
'Forward, the Light Brigade!'
Was there a man dismay'd ?
Not tho' the soldier knew
Some one had blunder'd:
Theirs not to make reply,
Theirs not to reason why,
Theirs but to do & die,
Into the valley of Death
Rode the six hundred."

He looked again at Bill, put his hand down and looked again at Ike. Bill thought he was looking at Ike, but the only indicator was the direction of his face. The eyes made it impossible to be sure.

"I'm outa tobaccy, Ike! Can you spare a man a mite?"

Ike brought his chair forward, heaved himself up and reached into the front of his bibs. He came out with a wrapped plug of chewing tobacco and carefully walked within long-reach of the man and extended his arm with the coveted item. He snagged the plug and pulled a massive Bowie knife from its scabbard and made as if to cut off a piece. He paused and turned his face to Ike.

Ike smiled. "Keep the whole thing, Dooley."

Dooley grinned, sliced off a piece and

quickly shoved the rest inside his buckskin shirt amongst the hair. Bill grimaced at he thought of the result on both man and tobacco.

"Thanky kindly, Ike. Nice day to you." With that, he rode off out the other end of town, singing and alternately reciting the remainder of Tennyson. The voice made Bill cringe inside, being such a noise that might take the bark off trees.

"Cannon to right of them,
Cannon to left of them,
Cannon in front of them
Volley'd & thunder'd;
Storm'd at with shot and shell,
Boldly they rode and well,
Into the jaws of Death,
Into the mouth of Hell
Rode the six hundred.

Flash'd all their sabres bare,
Flash'd as they turn'd in air
Sabring the gunners there,
Charging an army while
All the world wonder'd:
Plunged in the battery-smoke
Right thro' the line they broke;
Cossack & Russian
Reel'd from the sabre-stroke,
Shatter'd & sunder'd.
Then they rode back, but not
Not the six hundred."

"That was Dooley. Crazy man lives in the hills. Showed up nigh onto four year ago. Keeps to hisself, but rides through once'n awhile. I keep a spare plug stashed for him."

"He always sing like that, and yell like that?"

"Yup. Top o'his lungs mostly. Harmless though. Don't want no friends – I tried. Just wants to be to hisself. I wonder if'n he wanders through town just to see people. I hear tell he wanders through ranches hereabouts. The womenfolk or the cooks hear him comin' and meet him with a piece of pie or some other such and hand it to him as he rides by. He just nods his head and keeps riding. But he seems to know who makes the best vittles and when they's fresh." Ike chuckled and plodded back to his chair, promptly leaning back on two legs against the wall.

Interesting, Bill thought as he saddled his horse. He could still hear the man yelling in the distance, the sound seeming to echo across the distance:

"Cannon to right of them,
Cannon to left of them,
Cannon behind them
Volley'd and thunder'd;
Storm'd at with shot and shell,
While horse & hero fell,
They that had fought so well
Came thro' the jaws of Death,

Back from the mouth of Hell,
All that was left of them,
Left of six hundred.

When can their glory fade?
O the wild charge they made!
All the world wonder'd.
Honour the charge they made!
Honour the Light Brigade,
Noble six hundred." *

* Alfred, Lord Tennyson, Charge of the Light Brigade.

Chapter 6

"Lost him!?" The big man came out of his chair with a speed belying his immense size. The eight men in the dank, smoke- filled room all startled backwards, though they were merely bystanders and the anger was centered on one sorry, trembling excuse for a man cowering at front and center.

The big man was red, fists clenched, and all those present knew that the poor hapless wretch standing wringing his hat in his hand was close to death. You didn't fail an assignment given by Boss Carter. If you did, nine times out of ten it was lights out for you. They had seen it happen over and over. At times, Boss Carter dispatched the victim with one blow to thc back of the neck, other times he seemed to take deeper pleasure in prolonging the issue. Other times, the victim was sent away seemingly reprieved, yet was never seen again. Boss Carter was a man oftentimes possessed - his anger, cruelty and ruthlessness were enough to keep others from threatening his territory or operations. Even authorities cowed at his name.

Boss Carter slowly worked himself back into control of his emotions. He was immense, with arms hard and thick, a build that some saw as fat, but it hid immense power. He was a man who could turn on the charm and have others eating out of his hand one moment but, if riled or crossed or, in this case, defeated, he was deadly and the hate seeped out of him in emotional torrents. He did not strike out at the poor hapless mutt of a man who had been charmed in a past life by Boss Carter's free drinks and now had become a trembling mess over what had become a nightmare of a job.

Carter held himself in check, but was still red and trembling with pent up anger. "What happened?"

"We was watching the house like you said, Boss. We think he was never even there in the house." The man was almost crying, knowing the precipice upon which he stood.

"You THINK he was never in the house," the words were spit out with a disgust that would make a fighting dog cringe.

"Yes, Boss, sir" his voice quavered as he struggled not to cry, knowing the potential of a shortened life span. He had, after all, just taken this job to help feed his family. "We had all the ways watched, but then this morning we nabbed the maid as she came out of the gate. She was afeared of getting roughed up, and begged us not to hurt her, and said that it was all a trick, that Henry'd been gone for two weeks. She said she didn't know where."

"Blast it all! I can't count on anybody not to make a mess of things! So help me "- he glared at the trembling soul in front of him -"If I find that he was really there and he got away, I'll not rest till you're a whimpering mass of what used to be a man! Jonesy!"

"Yes, Boss? " The new man stepped out of the group that had sought to escape the angered man, though perhaps this particular man didn't really step back out of fear but rather to not stand out. For this was a man who was not afraid of much. Boss Carter knew this.

"Get down on the wharf, see what you can find out. With all that scum somebody musta seen somethin'. " He reached into his drawer and pulled out a small leather bag of jingling coins inside. He tossed it to Jonesy. "This may bring back some memories. If they try and lie for money, kill 'em. If someone says they won't cooperate, make them cooperate. I want information and I want it quick! We can't let Henry get further away! And get some men to check all the towns around for word of him. Finnegan!" Another man stepped forward. He was a pinch-faced man with a scraggly mustache that nobody laughed at. Finnegan was efficient...in all ways.

"Yes, Boss."

"Check the telegraph office and the trains. See what you can find. Somebody has to know something." Boss Carter sat down, heavily, as a man deeply disappointed and ready to break.

"You! You low life!" he yelled at the trembling has-been standing as if awaiting sentence, "Get out there and see what you can find out from the other house help! If you're not back in 24 hours I'll hunt you down and squeeze the life out of you."

The man, with the sense of a last minute reprieve from a death sentence, quickly left the room.

Boss Carter puffed heavily on the fat cigar held between his teeth. His mind was already calming and focusing on this new challenge. William Henry was a man he hated and despised for what he had done in court. A man who had caused the collapse of a whole wing of his empire. He thought he had him trapped in his own home. But it was Henry who had the last laugh, and that did not make Boss Carter happy. So be it, he would eventually locate him and then they'd see who had the last laugh. He grinned with a look that could not be misunderstood. Boss Carter did not forgive, but took deliberate pains at revenge.

Chapter 7

After he'd stopped at Wilson's and picked up a few things, Bill headed out of town. Probably an hour's ride to the ranch, he remembered.

He looked around as he rode, remembering parts of the landscape that he hadn't thought of in years. It all came back to him, and he found he could recall almost the whole trail. Funny, he mused, how certain details are with you for life. He glanced into the distance and noted Tully's Peak, recalling the many times he and his brothers had climbed its slopes and surveyed the country around. The bluffs and hills seemed unchanged, with maybe the trees a little taller, but otherwise timeless. He had often mused how man grows old and dies, but the same hills he was riding had been ridden or walked by many before him and would be so traveled long after he was gone. He recalled a certain bend in the trail to the ranch was punctuated by a lightning-struck and stunted ponderosa pine and, sure enough, it was still there, though now almost limbless in the stages of decay, a haven for birds and the nests that marked the beginning of life. Life seems to beget life even in death, he thought. Trees grow and reach maturity, and then some natural event takes the strength out of the tree and initiates the dying process. Yet, even after it dies, the decaying process of a pine takes many years and through that time, the trunk becomes a haven for life, hosting nests of birds and rodents in its hollows, then termites and other insects until the wood breaks down and it falls and slowly becomes part of the soil which then nourishes the younger trees nearby, and the process continues over and over on through time.

As Bill walked his horse along the trail, he felt again the calming of his mind and heart as he left the wariness and constant vigilance of Boston and the East behind and slouched more in his saddle with the slow, rhythmic steps of his horse.

Always a skilled man at details, Bill had chosen this horse from the corral of a horse-trader a hundred miles or so west of St. Louis. He had chosen a horse that, though broken to saddle, still had fire in its eyes. He had learned early, from his father, that a horse and a man were partners. Treat the horse right, Otis would say, and the horse would be loyal in return.

Some men broke horses and others gentle broke them. The former often lost their spirit, and became subservient. Gentle broke horses still retained the spirit and some were still more wild than broke, as if merely allowing a cowboy to ride.

In looking over the circling and nervous horses, Bill had bypassed the horses others might choose, ignoring classic colors and blazes and those with obvious breeding. Instead, he was drawn to the dun. Smaller than some of the others in the remuda, it showed a spirit and power that belied its size. Knowing he had a long ways to travel and needed a long-haul horse, he dickered with the trader, manipulating the interchange with his lawyer's mind so that he got a fair deal, and the trader felt even better. Never know when you'll need help again, he thought. The dun had been just the ticket, taking the miles and the trails with effortless grace and stamina. Bill discovered he was ground-broke and readily stayed near when he dismounted. Bill mused why the horse, of obvious quality, had been in the sale corral. Was the previous owner dead, down on his luck, or what compelled or forced him to part with such a horse? Such was the way of this land that so many things could happen.

As he rode, his mind continued to transition back to the range, back to the days of long ago, and he began to take in the details of the trail, such as erosion, the tracks of animals and the effects of wind on the branches of the trees. Details surged from deep recesses of his mind as he rode and observed, welling up in a flood to his trained and calculating mind. His training as a lawyer had brought organization to his mind, much like a formal parlor with everything in its place.

It was not the best of circumstance when he left years ago. He had become unsettled, tired of the seeming dreary sameness of his life. He well remembered the hurt and anger of his father when he told him he planned to leave.

"A man's got to find what he's lookin' for, Billy. But sometimes a man's gotta open his eyes and see – really see – to find it. Sometimes, like the Good Book says, they's scales on our eyes and we can't see till they fall off. You been unsettled for quite a spell, and I can't talk any sense into you. A man's got to ride his own broncs and use his own saddle."

His father reached into his vest pocket and handed bill a poke.

"Trail money. You let us know when you find what you're lookin' for. Your ma will be waiting." There was a moistness in his eyes.

Parting with ma had been the hardest thing he'd ever done. He remembered her tears and her parting admonition:

"Billy…you stay right with the law, give a man a days work for a days' pay and stay away from loose women. And write your ma." Her voice cracked and he felt choked inside. All he could do was nod and hug her. He had mounted his horse and rode away. It'd been 10 years now.

Something had happened over those years.

He had changed and was somewhat startled to be feeling that it was good to be back. There was simplicity to life here. Oh, the ballrooms and parties in the east had their allure, but he never felt the peace that he now felt riding quietly over the trail hearing only the birds and the sounds of his horse, feeling the breeze with a hint of wildflowers. How did he ever get used to the east? There was none of this sense of space and self back there. All was business and pomposity and clutter and appearance. Here a man was his own man, and there was genuineness, and a man stood or fell on what he really was. Of course, the women were different, too. Here, a woman may not turn every man's head, but the inner qualities, the ability to stick by their man, to stand in the face of all that this life on the frontier stood for and demanded - these are what marked a woman. Back east he first had to tell what was real and what was just a put on by some very lovely ladies. Their world often demanded that they flatter and tell a man what he wanted to hear. One's standing depended upon connections and invitations to events focused upon pretense. That's why he never formed any lasting relationships back east. Oh, there were a few with whom he had been enamored, but they eventually showed themselves for what they really were - all fluff and no substance. Not any that he would want to "ride the trail with" as they said out here. No...he needed someone solid, someone genuine, someone with whom he could build a life and raise sons and daughters with character. He smiled. What was he thinking about anyhow? It was a thought that he had lost in the fluff and nothingness of the society ladies of the East.

This western land bred a different type of people than did the east. His parents were an example. Married young in Pennsylvania, they spent their first months of marriage putting together an outfit to venture into the west. Settling in Colorado, they worked themselves to the bone to make the ranch pay and they had prospered, though the first years were tough, what with Indians, rustlers and other riff-raff, all bent on taking what another man builds. Then his father had left for the war, and was gone for 4 years, leaving his mom to carry on. When he returned, she had improved the place and they picked up where they left off and built it into an impressive operation. They were a well-matched pair.

The movement of the land dictated that each succeeding generation take the progress a step further than the parents generation. His father had broken the land, planted grain and raised some of the best cattle around. People just coming to the land rarely understood all that a previous generation had gone thru to make this land a place to raise children and grandchildren. They didn't understand the droughts and disasters, blizzards, the Indian troubles, the rustlers and the just plain bad men who wanted to prey off the success of others. They just saw what they saw and didn't realize it hadn't always been so.

He remembered when he was just a sprout, maybe 4 years old, when his pa was confronted by two men in town who were part of new bunch of roughs coming through. Otis Henry had spoken to others about running them off, and word got to the leaders, who sent the two who faced Otis by the livery.

The two were a ways apart, obviously ready to brace and remove Henry from the situation. One of them, a square-built man with a blind eye spoke.

"Henry, we's been told you ain't likin' us. We think that's a bit unfriendly-like. You said we's trash. I say you's a liar."

Otis Henry had sensed danger when the men were approaching, and had slipped the thong off his hammer and tilted his Spencer a bit in the right direction.

Not taking his eyes off the speaker, Otis spoke to his son, "Billy, go off to the other side of the horses. Now." Billy had obeyed and watched, entranced and scared as the scene played out in front of him.

"Calling a man a liar is just baitin' me to fight. You ready to die?"

The man drew and Otis Henry tilted his rifle up and shot the man through the chest. The man fell like a rock and the other man looked aghast. Suddenly there was the sound of a half dozen hammers cocked and the man still standing looked around to see several townsfolk focused upon him and he faced several angry gun barrels.

"We'll see your friend get's words spoken over him. But you'll be too far away to hear. Understand?"

The man looked around again, gulped and nodded. He was of the type where courage stopped when advantage stopped. His type of courage was born of group support, and easily waned when faced with it alone.

They had guided the man out of town with a strong urging never to show his face again. As Billy and his dad rode home later, Otis Henry said few words.

"Boy?"

"Yes, pa?"

"Don't' ever be like those men. Stay on the right side of the law, and don't put up with those that are on the raw side. Don't be a coward. Live and die with pride. Make your loved one's proud."

"Yes, pa." He gulped with emotion. He WAS proud of his pa.

Chapter 8

That was years ago and times had changed a mite.

Newcomers looked upon some of the old timers as harsh men. They didn't see the reality that it took guts to make and break the land. In years past there survived only two types: those who were naturally harsh and those who chose to be harsh when needed, like his father and Slater. There was a difference, and then the two types clashed, one because of selfishness, the other in principle. Over the years principle had won more battles because it was from a deeper well than what drove those who sought only their own way and wanted to ride over anything and anybody. His father was a man of deep principle, and of that tough breed, and the need to be on guard and wary at all times had created a toughness that the softer newcomers did not understand - couldn't understand - because the west had been changed in many ways and the breeding ground of that toughness had been all but lost to understanding by the natural changes. Yet, all was not totally changed, as evidenced by Slater's rustlers and the response of the two war veterans and the parson. Wherever people congregated, there would always be those who sought what others had and those who would respond to principle and seek a better society.

Even back east, referred to as "civilized" in these parts, there was the presence of both elements. Those such as Boss Carter and other such criminal machines were ruthless seekers of what others possessed, and stopped at nothing to get it. Well, he had taken Carter down a couple of notches….he shook his head, trying to clear his mind of the mess he had left behind.

He mused. The west was also a place of building from the ground up. People out east didn't understand the lack of any organized society in the west of not too long ago. There was a need to work, and work hard, day after day after day. Survival dictated constant vigilance and attention to making it better and improving the situation.

Turning a corner in the trail through the foothills he naturally turned in the saddle and glanced along his backtrail just before he lost sight of it. A lifelong habit that he first learned as a boy out here. Part of that life that the newcomers didn't fathom. Landmarks are a key to any journey, and many men in traveling towards a desired destination, looked only to the landmarks in front and lost their way upon returning because they neglected to look behind as they traveled, to line up landmarks for the return journey. He grinned as he realized that was an analogy that could apply to life itself.

He guessed he really didn't understand all that till just recently, when he'd thought long and hard about returning. He'd left years ago just wanting to get away from the wearying cycle of labor that seemed so non stop that it was often hard to tell when day ended and night began. Day after day, season after season it went on and on. Yet, now, with maturity and time and experience, he saw there was a steadiness, a straight shooting way of living that was attractive after the artificial life of the east.

Oh, he'd known some good men, genuine men, back east. He'd forged friendships that would last a lifetime. They were few, but they were solid. He'd found men, and women, he could count on, who lived by a different code – who lived by the truth in their hearts and held to that code despite all the temptations around them. Then there were the others -those who manipulated and preyed on others and relished in their power and control.

It was a lack of control, perhaps, that in part contributed to his leaving the ranch years ago. He well remembered the build up of the frustration over the seeming repetition of the days and seasons, and the lack of any break from the pattern. He still despised patterns. He used them to trap criminals, but he tried to avoid patterns in his own life, realizing that predictability could be his enemy. He had become naturally suspicious of the motives of others, and rightfully sensed their desire to eliminate him.

He'd done well in the east. In fact, he had a goodly amount of gold with him, and an open draft on a bank back east run by one of his solid friends. He'd not been idle these years. He was not short of funds or reputation or ability.

He'd started without much direction, but all that had changed around a campfire in Kansas when he'd come across some cavalry officers buffalo hunting. They'd invited him to share their camp. He'd talked with them that evening, just a 17-year-old kid seeking his way. One officer in particular kept asking him questions about the land and the settlers and the movements of the buffalo. Bill had always been good at noticing details and telling the real from the false. He hoped some day to be able to properly thank the officer. He remembered his name....would never forget it - Colonel Bart Taylor. He remembered that he had been at the edge of the camp that night, listening to the night, when Colonel Taylor had approached.

"Anything unusual out there?" The Colonel had spoken softly, not wanting to disturb Bill.

Bill was faced away from the fire, so as to be able to see into the darkness. So many sat staring into a night time fire, and when sudden action was needed there were precious seconds lost as eyes adjusted. The officer noted this detail.

Without looking, Bill paused, looking towards a copse of trees. "Coyotes just picked up a rabbit near those trees. Otherwise all is quiet." He looked at the Colonel, a wry smile showing through his week-old whiskers. "I guess it may seen strange to say it's 'quiet.' There's actually a lot of sounds to hear, from critters to insects to men. It seems that the reality is that danger is sensed through the lack of sounds. When the natural sounds are all there, a body can relax. It's when the birds stop, when the coyotes are quiet, when the insects are not heard that the senses sharpen and a smart man reaches for his rifle."

"You've lived out here all your life?"

"Yes, sir. My ma and pa carved a ranch out of a Colorado valley. Ma held it together while pa fought in the war. Been there all my life."

The Colonel was quiet for a moment. "I sense some dissatisfaction with ranch life, young man." He said it as a statement, in the way of that time and place, not to pry into one's past.

Bill paused. "I'm tired of living the life of my parents, Colonel. I want to live my own life. I can't abide the sameness day after day."

Colonel Taylor thought a few moments, listening to the night. "Might I ask your father's name, Bill?"

"Otis Henry."

"Otis Henry. I have heard of him. Distinguished service in the war. The 49th Cavalry, I believe. A name to be proud of, Bill. Perhaps for your father the sameness, the routine is calming, compared to what he experienced in the war."

Before they parted early the next morning, Colonel Taylor gave him a letter of introduction to a friend in Boston. He told Bill that he saw in him great ability, and suggested he'd one day make his mark on the land. A casual and passing moment that was to have incredible dividends in his life. One readily hears negatives, such that a positive becomes magnified in importance.

From that encounter he had not gone directly to Philly, but had meandered a bit, working some in a gold mine, then some work herding cattle, a short stint as a store clerk. He learned how to bare-knuckle fight and to play poker. He found himself with natural skills. All these added to the man that he was becoming, but he didn't reckon he'd reached all he was to be yet.

Chapter 9

He eventually rode into Boston, not too clean or impressive looking. He'd gone to the home of Colonel Taylor's friend. Russell Long was a distinguished attorney who took an instant liking to this rough-edged kid from the west. Long liked to hear the stories Bill told of life in the "wild west." Bill never embellished - not too much anyway - and he suspected that Long was living another dream vicariously through him. Bill saw that Long had the character that would have done well in the rough west. He'd been an officer of cavalry in the war.

Long taught him law, taught him all he knew, and Bill was a ready learner and was not afraid of hard work. It seemed that law was a natural use of his observational talents. He loved the give and take sessions that Long would hold with him many evenings, going over case after case and talking of laws of evidence and how to piece together a rock-solid case so it wouldn't unravel in court. Long hated to lose a case - and it didn't happen too often. His preparation for a case would daunt most attorneys. He taught Bill all the in's and out's.

At the same time, he insisted that Bill live in his home, and he continued his education in the realm of society. Bill became comfortable moving in circles that would daunt many, but he had a self-confidence that made people seek him out. He met and interacted well with people from both sides of the track, as they'd say. He was respected by quite a few of the rougher element because he was always fair. He never built a good case on lies and hearsay. He defended both sides of society. Yet, if someone were in the wrong, no matter what side of the tracks they came from, he'd nail their hides to the wall.

He was extremely busy. Long made him a partner in the firm and they fought many high profile cases side by side.

It was the last case that got him. He had defended an innocent victim of a swindle played out by one of the crime "bosses" of Boston, Hook Logan. Throughout, he and witnesses were threatened and attempts were made to bribe him into throwing the case. He fought doggedly on and, against long odds, Logan was convicted. Another crony of Logan's was convicted and hung for murder. Someone, they suspected Boss Carter, had a hit hired on Bill, which failed due to the hit man being unaware that Bill had grown up on the frontier and not only carried a gun, but knew how to use it and use it fast.

After that failed attempt to get rid of him, his friends met with him privately and suggested that his life was short, at best, if he stayed. He needed to get away till things cooled off. He had disrupted the kingdom of Boss Carter, whose ruthlessness was almost legendary. It was rumored that he had once torn a man to pieces with his bare hands, leaving the mutilated man whimpering plaintively for his mother as he slowly died. Carter did not take kindly to his enemies.

Bill's friends suggested he head back to the frontier for an extended time. He had to admit to himself that he was tired, too. He was mentally worn out, and needed a break - a break that would not come if he stayed in Philly, because his reputation brought numerous requests for his service.

Only a select few knew where he came from, and them only in a general sense. They knew he came from "the west," that area some knew only by the name, sort of like "the great beyond." Only Long knew the exact location, so he decided the familiar was where he would return. He'd slipped out of town thru a series of ruses concocted by his friends and had, as far as he could tell, achieved total secrecy in his departure. There had been deliberate rumors spread that he had suffered a breakdown and needed extended rest and would not be taking cases or visitors. By the time it was found to be a ruse, he would be long gone. It'd been 2 1/2 weeks and the ruse might yet be working. He had deliberately avoided the telegraph, as many offices had persons of the questionable element hanging out trying to get information. He wanted no hassles here and, most of all, he wanted his family to be left alone. Nobody out here, including his parents, knew he was coming. That was part of the plan – leave no trails.

He felt relaxed. After watching his back trail carefully and giving fictitious names where a name was required, he felt very confident that he was safely away. Yet, there remained something in him that would not let loose of the watchfulness, so he continued to be aware, his senses keen. It was just a part of the way he was. There was one point where he seemed to have a sense in his heart that there was someone back there, but he never saw anybody. At one point a few days back he sat in the brush for an hour watching his back trail. The closer he got to home the more careful he became. Though he saw nothing, his natural wariness and his experience with the rougher side of life kept his senses alert. His intentional lack of communication with Russell Long or others back east had the effect of also keeping him in the dark as to whether his ruse had worked and if his leaving was undetected.

He knew that he had caused a serious ripple

in the underworld back east when he convinced one of Logan's thugs to turn states evidence and it led to Logan heading to prison. The real power was in Boss Carter, and Bill knew that Carter was incensed by the breach and had put a price on the lawyer's head - a significant price. Yet, though a couple attempts had been set up, Bill had been able to thwart those efforts. He knew, however, that the law of averages indicated that somewhere along the line he might be caught unawares. He agreed with his handful of close friends that it would be best if he dropped out of sight for a time. Especially after the thug who testified, as well as a juror, had been killed. The cruelty of their deaths was a trademark of Boss Carter. One had been tied to a railroad track and the other had been tied to a rock that was thrown into the river and placed at such a depth that death occurred slowly as the tide came in. Who knew what other tortures these men experienced before their demise. Boss Carter was absolutely evil.

So far Boss Carter had been able - through cruelty and a second sense - to avoid the arms of the law. Little did he know that Bill had meticulously prepared much evidence, and witnesses had been carefully and securely sequestered, such that Boss Carter might soon be toppled. But that would all depend on others now, as he was out of the picture, and had turned the files over to Long.

A ways out of town, he turned from some

deep memory through an almost unnoticeable gap in the rocks and headed down a trail that was invisible before you actually were on it. The secret family trail. Well, kind of a secret. A few others knew of it. He and his brothers had called it the Sneaky Trail as they grew up, as it led through the hills to the bluff above and behind the ranch house. He smiled as he rode the almost overgrown trail. Never much used, it likely began as an animal path but was used by his family and a few others to avoid the regular trail. In the now more peaceful times of the West there was little need for secrecy and the trail was seldom used. From the looks of it, probably not used for a year or more. He wondered about the other places he and his brothers had discovered as boys.

So, here he was, riding the familiar trail, smelling again those scents that once were a part of his daily life, seeing the familiar landmarks and making turns in the trail seemingly from some habit buried deep within that was emerging anew. He felt a newness of spirit, a freedom and a happiness, such as he imagined would be felt by someone released from prison.

Yes, there was something awakening within him. He saw...his senses were coming alive. Yes, in Boston and the courtroom he was fully attuned to what was going on around him. He could read men like the back of his hand - but this was different. He somehow sat taller in the saddle; he saw the trees, the bark, the bugs, the wide-open skies and the myriad patterns of the clouds - details he'd forgotten about. The mountains in the distance were larger than he remembered, and the colors as they receded in the distance were breathtaking and wondrous. He remembered how he'd just sort of grown up with the awareness of all around him. It was the way of the land, to learn the landmarks, to notice the details of the trail so as to be able to find the way back. It was a skill that just happened, as a way of the land and the people. Probably, he thought wryly, a way that was being lost to a new generation, as the west became tamer.

He looked around as he rode, noticing the diversity of the trees. There were pine, spruce, cottonwood, aspen, juniper and fir. He drew deeply of the air, smelling once again the varied scents that so differed from those of Boston and the east, which were mostly deciduous wooded hills that became bare and grey in the winter. The needles here stayed on the trees for the most part, though some, such as the White Pine, had significant loss of needles each year, replacing them with new growth. The forest floors were replenished and nourished by decaying needles and trees, and then life began anew as lightning ignited dry needles, burning off the undergrowth and in the process released seeds from cones, beginning the cycle of life once again.

Riding in and out of the forested ridges, in view of the high rocky peaks in the blue distance, he was awed. He'd forgotten what open country was like, without someone always rubbing shoulders with you or jostling you. And the quiet! He could hear the birds singing and the creak of the saddle and the breathing of his horse and the rattle of leaves in the breeze. He was lost in his thoughts for some time, until he jarred himself back to reality. He was startled at himself. He was always aware. It was his trademark and saving grace. It kept him on top in the courtroom and helped save him lately from those who would love nothing better than to throw dirt in a hole that contained his corpse. He stopped and turned to look down his back trail once again, listening intently for any sound not fitting with the surroundings.

Chapter 10

He emerged from the trees and came to the edge of the bluff overlooking the Henry ranch. Pulling up, he sat there for many minutes, awed and thirsty for all that lay before him. The valley of his youth. The rolling foothills seemingly fading into the distant blue mountains. There it was. The memories flooded over him as he took it all in. The house and the barns - a second barn had been added, as well as a couple other buildings. He saw once again that which used to be wearisome to him but now was like the taste of a clear mountain brook – refreshing and energizing and soothing all at once.

Home.

Did he actually feel that? It had so easily come to his thought. Home. Nestled in the valley below, it seemed from this distance that not much about the valley had changed. He used to know every nook and cranny of the surrounding hills, with his father encouraging he and his brothers to know the land. Why did that warm his heart? Perhaps deep inside he wished he could take back the years and pick up where he had left off. Perhaps he now had a greater appreciation of what once set him on an unsettled path.

His father had chosen well. With an eye for beauty that would please his wife, as well as the practicality of a commander, he had chosen an extensive ranch with natural boundaries. With the ranch buildings tucked near a dense wooded canyon leading steeply upward to the crest of a rocky ridge known as Sampson's Porch that formed an unusual up-thrust of the foothills, there was a view over miles and miles of valley, lush with watered grass. The stream thru the middle of the range was treacherous in bad weather, but its presence assured the prosperity of the ranch, for without water the land was worthless. As with all western lands, water was the focal point of any claim. Yet, Bill could not deny, the miles and miles of foothills leading to the Rockies were beautiful unto themselves, with lush canyons and bluffs that served as shelter to the cattle in rough weather. There was a peace and rest to the mind and the soul in the lay of the land.

Above the ranch in a high valley beyond Sampson's Porch, and feeding a spring above the ranch, was Whispering Lake. Many hours had been spent exploring the reaches of the area, and the water that came from that lake was crystal clear and cold. Many were the times when a drink either from the lake or the spring back home had been his goal and refreshment after a long days ride or a hard day around the home place. Wherever he'd been over the last few years, a drink of water always paled in comparison to that of Whispering Lake and the spring.

What about his brothers? Were they married? Buck, the oldest, and Chad, next in line. And Matt....Matt would have been 10 or so when he left. Why, He'd be a grown man by now. And ma...There were tears in his eyes. He urged the dun forward.

Chapter 11

Otis Henry slowly straightened his back after digging the post hole. He took his bandana and wiped the sweat from his eyes. It was slow work, what with the wound still healing, but he was taking care. He wasn't ready to be planted on the hill yet.

A strong man, Otis was the son of a Pennsylvania side-hill farmer. His youth had been rough, with barely a subsistence taken from the land. It grew more rocks and red clay than sorghum. He learned to shoot early in life. His Pa, Hiram Henry, had an uncanny eye and taught Otis all the skills of hitting what he aimed at. Otis had, if anything, a better eye than pa, and it was noticed by many through the years. He could not only hit what he aimed at, but he was a good judge of the quality of the game. He became a skilled judge of men also. Later, after joining the cavalry at the start of the war, he rose rapidly through the ranks, being mustered out as a Colonel. His ability to take in a situation and move swiftly and surely gained him immense respect among his men. They knew each move was carefully viewed regarding effectiveness and protection for his men. He was seen in tears when men of his command fell in battle. His men loved him, and the Fighting 49th, as if it were their own family. He still kept in touch with a few of the men, and occasionally a fellow veteran would come by the ranch.

He had built this ranch with the same intensity that characterized his military command. He planned for defense, and did not falter at hard work. He had no use for laziness, and he smiled inside as he realized he had solid, hard working sons who would continue to build the ranch when his own building days were done. Already, he was becoming more of a guiding force, as he entrusted more of the work on the ranch to his sons. Just like military command, he thought: to build capable leaders, they must be given rope to try ideas and own their mistakes and successes. His sons had learned well and he was proud of them. The ranch continued to prosper. The land had been peaceful. He had heard rumors of some trouble over towards Royton, a 3-hour ride by a non-lazy horse, but nothing nearby. It was peaceful here - a far cry from the old days, when danger and wariness was the price of life.

He scanned the hills – a lifelong habit. He had learned in the war that it was best to see the enemy comin' before they could get a bead on you. Then, out here it also did a fella good to have some warning. In the early days at the ranch it was critical to keep a watchful eye for marauding Indians and ne'er do wells. There were others he had known who let up on their vigilance and they wound up pushing flowers. Those without warning rarely had a second chance to change their ways. Things were relatively peaceful and civilized in these parts nowadays, but you can't easily drop old habits. They were reminded of this when Old Man Slater was hit by the rustlers.

He grinned to himself. Even though he had been abed for a time after that skirmish, he had to admit that he had felt alive and permeated with an excitement that he had not felt since the war. There was something in the focusing of all the senses in the pursuit of a goal that only a soldier could understand.

He scanned the hills and squinted through the sweat. He saw movement.

Rider comin' down the mountain trail. Single horse, looked like. A ways off yet. He scanned the hills around. Looks to be alone. Don't normally get any riders from that trail. It was a trail known to only a few. He looked across the pasture and saw Buck glance his way. Otis pointed toward the rider and Buck nodded. It may be civilized, but Otis still felt for his gun and felt the comfort of old habits as he slipped the thong off the hammer. He was still stronger than many men, but not what he used to be in the old days when they called him "Bull." He hadn't heard that since the old days. He moved to pick up the shovel and felt a twinge.

The recent fight with the rustlers had left him out of it for quite some time, and he was feeling his age. He didn't heal like he did when he was young. And it took longer to get the kinks out in the mornings or when he sat too long of an evening. And he wanted to sit more than he used to.

He'd earned it though, he reckoned. He'd built this place from nothing and it had prospered over time and now he had 3 strong sons - actually 4 but...

He pulled himself - with as much determination as strength - astride his horse and headed to the main house where the trail would lead. Hope Ella has some extra grub on, he said silently to himself. She was particular about guests and got all fired out of sorts if she was surprised with not enough food for a guest. He chuckled. That didn't happen very often. She was quite the hand with the stove.

As Otis Henry came up to the main house, he hollered to his wife,

"Ella!"

His wife came to the door.

"What is it, Otis?" After all these years

together she knew his call was more than just wanting to see if she could whistle Dixie.

"Rider coming down the hill trail. Set an extra plate for lunch."

"Oh, my," she said, dusting off her apron. Old habits were hard for her to break, too, and she mentally calculated the distance to her Winchester over the kitchen door. Ever since the incident of Slater's rustlers she'd been aware that old habits had awakened that had not been needed for a long time, at least since the country had built up. She smiled wryly to herself, chuckling at her caution, but at the same time glancing out the window toward the hills. Yep, one rider in the distance, off the hill trail now and coming at a canter.

Ella Henry was a woman to ride the river with, as some would say. She was a slight woman, but not to be mistaken for soft. She'd cut her teeth on the prairie and stood with her man thru all that life sent their way. There was iron in her will, and yet she could also be tender. She had met her man in the hills and had followed him everywhere, and the ranch was as much a home as it could be. She could down a running deer, fight Indians, pull an arrow out of a man without a second thought, yet she also knew how to comfort a child and bake cookies and make a house a home. No visitor ever left her home hungry. She pushed the coffee pot back over the fire. Practicality reigned in her home, from the positioning of the rifle to the placement of her pots and pans. She wanted things right to hand when necessity was upon her. Not much wasted effort in Ella Henry. Too much to do, and she was determined to do it.

Chapter 12

Bill cantered across the meadow and stopped a few hundred yards from the house, a lump in his throat. It had been years, and now he was home. There...he'd said it. And he really felt it. Home. He walked his horse towards the house. There was his pa...getting down off his horse, on the opposite side from his unexpected guest. Old habits die hard.

He moved forward and stopped his horse thirty feet or so away from his father, but his face was shaded and his pa didn't recognize him.

"Light and set, stranger. Welcome to our home."

"Hello, pa." He watched his pa's eyes squint. Otis Henry took a step towards his son.

"Billy?" He whispered. Bill lifted his hat off

so his pa could see his face.

"Billy!" He hollered. "Ella! It's Billy!" Then Otis Henry strode to his son as Bill dismounted. It was the biggest hug either had ever given or received. Old Otis Henry had tears in his eyes and saw the same in his son. Ella Henry came running out of the house, hand over her mouth, and the tears coursed down her cheeks like a summer rainstorm.

"Billy, my son!" She cried as she jumped into his waiting arms.

That evening was an evening to remember. There was a realm of emotions - from tears to laughter - wrought of years of separation and wondering and hope and fulfillment of hope. The conversation flowed non-stop and if there were a fly on the wall they would have seen the frequent glances of all parties at Bill, just drinking in the reality of his return and the man he had become. On Bill's part, it was the same, as he not only noticed the age of his parents, but also the growth of his brothers.

Land's sake, he thought, these boys have become solid men - men of both strength and character. They had a look of confidence, of men who were used to succeeding. And they were successful. The ranch had blossomed. Pa's influence was evident, with well-kept fences and herds of beautiful cattle. Not just scrubs, but well-bred beef. Everything was neat, with obvious care taken for appearance as well as production. That was ma's influence, he realized.

The talk went on until Buck pushed back his chair and excused himself to do the evening chores. The other boys almost simultaneously did the same, as if they'd had the same thought. Bill started to rise, but Buck waved him back. “You’ve got a reprieve for 24 hours, but no further.” He grinned at Bill as they grabbed their hats and went out.

Pa pushed back his chair; Ma reached for the coffee and filled their mugs.

Looking at Bill with the love of a mother, Ella Henry asked the question that had been in the back of her mind all evening that she didn't want to ask, probably for fear of what the answer could be.

"How long are you stayin’, son?"

"Hard to tell, ma, but it could be quite a spell." He smiled at his mother's obvious pleasure that he was not rushing off.

Otis Henry looked at his son. "Son, it does my heart proud to see what kind of a man you've become, and to have realized the blessing of seeing it myself. It is all-fired good to have you home, son." There were tears in his eyes. Ella Henry leaned over to her husband and rested her head on his arm. Tears coursed down her cheeks.

None of them could speak for a few moments, as the emotions rippled thru their hearts.

Finally, it was ma who spoke up. "Lands sakes! I'm forgettin' my manners! You must be tired, Billy. I'll get your bed ready."

Chapter 13

Otis Henry got up and refilled their cups. “You didn’t write to tell us you were comin’. Then you show up traveling light.” He looked steady at his son. "You in any kind of trouble, son?" He was a man with unusual senses.

Bill grinned wryly. "I don't think so out here, pa. There was a case I prosecuted, and the opposition seemed to think they could intimidate their way to an acquittal. I proved them wrong. One man hung, the other will be sitting behind bars for a few years. Their friends didn't like it and think I should be dead. My friends decided that I needed to get away for a spell. "

"Good friends. You can express my appreciation to them. Think anybody will follow you?"

"Not likely. Elaborate plans were made to get me out of town unnoticed. They may still be watching the house in Boston." He said nothing about his sense on the trail that someone was there. No sense in getting things riled here for undo reasons.

"Anger like that'll die slow. Sounds like you may be here a spell" His pa grinned. Then he frowned again. "I gather you've learned to handle yourself well, Bill. You sure you ain't been followed?"

Bill paused, and Otis' eyebrows lifted perceptibly. "You saw something?"

"No. It's more like I felt it, but everytime I checked, there was nothing and no one. I think I've just been so keyed up I'm over reacting."

"Maybe…maybe not. I can remember being rather skittish after I got home from the war." He chuckled. "I jumped at every little noise and every time I heard someone pop a cork, I wanted to duck for cover!"

"How are things here at the ranch? Sure looks grand, pa"

Otis Henry visibly swelled with pride. "Things are going real well, son. All the hard work and the years have paid off. Cattle prices have been good, the last few years have been good weather, and we got money in the bank. Of course, wouldn't take but 2-3 bad years and we'd be set back to where we started. That's the way of this land."

"Looks like you got three solid ranch

hands."

Otis Henry smiled. "Yep, I got reason to be proud. All three ain't any stranger to hard work. They got the old Henry spirit." He swelled again. "Buck'll be ramrod someday. He is a lot already. He's got solid sense, Bill. Chad - well, he's a bit impatient at times, but it serves to get some things done that might otherwise suffer from too much thinkin'. Matt, he's growing up strong. All three are mighty handy with a rifle, but Matt's the best. Steady eye. They all get along well, with a few rough edges now and then, but I can sure be proud. And you, son. I got four boys a man can be proud of." Tears showed again. "You forgotten all I taught you, or can you still ride and shoot like you used to?"

"I may be a bit rusty, but I think it'll come back quick! Anyway, whatever's rusty will get smoothed out here."

His pa chuckled. "I imagine you'll be a bit sore for a few days. We better get some rest. You might remember that morning comes awful early out here."

It was Bill's turn to chuckle. "I suspect I'll need all the rest I can get. But remember Buck gave me 24 hours! Night, pa."

He lay for what seemed like an eternity in his bed. His mind traveled back as he looked around his room with the aid of the moonlight. His old battered work hat still hung where he'd left it all those years ago. He ran his fingers over the logs at his head, feeling for the old piece of chinking that he had worked out years ago and used the space behind as a sort of secret hiding place. He found it, worked it out, and then reached in to find his old battered work knife with a half-broken blade. He smiled. It seemed strange to be laying here. It was like he'd been gone, yet like part of him had never left. How many nights had he lain in this exact spot, dreaming teenage dreams of the future and what he would become? He chuckled to himself...Colonel Taylor and Russell Long had shifted him to a path of which he'd never dreamed. Then a wry smile came to his face as he got up and pulled a .32 six shot S&W top-break out of his saddle bags and put it in the log cavity, then replaced the chinking. He'd carried it in a special holster in Boston. A sort of grown up version of the knife. He slept the sleep of a man totally at peace.

Chapter 14

The first days were rough, building and repairing fences, forking hay and straw, mucking out the barns, riding in the old familiar hills and drifting cattle to better grass. He found muscles long forgotten and unused, and he slept the sleep of the dead. Then his body toughened and remembered the old movements and responded to the ministrations of his mother's ladle at mealtimes. He'd forgotten what long ago he'd taken for granted about his mother's ability to revive a worn and hungry man with her simple but sumptuous meals. He thrilled at the taste of simple food he had dreamed of while sitting in fancy restaurants eating off fine china. There was no comparison to the hearty meals of his mother. She noticed his delight and her pride glowed on her face. Ma had cooked on trails, on cattle drives, in the midst of Indian attacks, right after birthing her boys. Pa said she'd stir the pot, then turn and shoot her long gun at the Indians. She took both duties seriously and knew how to feed an army or just a few. She made sure the garden was plowed first and she could work miracles with both beef and produce.

As the days passed, then a week or two, his thoughts relaxed and his heart melded with his new surroundings.

It seemed that he had changed, and his brothers had grown, but so much was still the same…there were the ranch hands – aside from a couple younger, newer hands – Brewster and Gimpy, there were those he remembered – Isaac, who loved a good joke; Tetch and Sim, former slaves and as good as members of the family; Gard and Shorty, who had served with his father. All good hands. None of them shirked work, nor gave him any leeway in his first few days!

His father was one of the first he knew of to hire former slaves. Some looked askance at Otis Henry, especially when it was discovered that he paid them the same wages as his white hands, but Otis Henry was unfazed. He paid a working wage and he didn't give a rat's hair what color their skin was. The other hands quickly accepted the black men and their color became a non-issue on the ranch. There were issues that arose in town, but the other hands made a statement in the early days by refusing to drink in the saloon.

They would buy a bottle at the mercantile and take it out back of the stable to drink together. When Mitch Tagget realized the loss to his purse, the town grudgingly accepted the changes and now, all these years later, the ex-slaves were accepted by the community in most ways. Oh, there were some holdouts, but it was cemented among many when Tetch happened upon little Wally Hudson freshly snake bit and saved his life.

The Henry hands were not the usual drifting cowhands, but were long-timers. They were part of a family and the entire ranch ate together on holidays, with both Ella and the camp cook, Gus, applying their skills to a memorable meal. Black and white sat together and such a thing built unity and loyalty.

Otis Henry had built a dream, had built it strong and built it to last. Most men only dream dreams, but somehow are unable to apply themselves to fulfilling that dream. In fact, most men went to their graves with their dreams unfulfilled.

What a man achieves is the result of work; hard, back breaking work. So many seemed to feel the world owed them a living. Bill knew many of that type. He had seen other dreams attained, but for every dream attained there were so many others that never came to be, due to the dreamer sort of figuring that something should be handed to them. Anybody who expected to be given a free ride usually wound up poor. Poor in many ways: poor in money, poor in relationships, poor in health.

How is it that a man is born into one or the other ways of thinking? A man born of someone expecting from others tended to turn out that way himself. Those born to hard working men tended to grow into solid, hard working citizens.

His pa was a solid man. All his sons were hard workers, expecting nothing but what came from the work of their own hands. Even himself, he realized. He had wanted to get away so bad all those years ago, but the lessons learned and the ceaseless toil had paid off in his own life.

There were times when Bill's thoughts drifted back east and he wondered about what might be happening, but he had yet to send any letters. He didn't want any slips and he knew that his enemies in Boston likely knew by now that he had slipped away and would be looking for information. He didn't want to open any doors. Besides, he was working too hard. His trunk had come - Walt had collected it and brought it out to the ranch the day before. It sat at the foot of his bed, still unopened.

Walt had ridden up to the ranch house in time for the noon meal, bringing a big smile to Ella's face. She had always liked Walt and appreciated his timing. He brought the latest news from town. Ernie's son was to marry Wilson's youngest daughter, how there was a shipment of fancy cloth come to Wilson's and the talk was that Mrs. Wilson wanted her daughter to be the finest looking bride the town had ever seen and that prices were going up to pay for it. They all chuckled at his insights.

Walt paused at one point, and just a flicker of concern crossed his face. Bill picked up on it.

"Walt, is anything wrong?"

Walt glanced hurriedly around the table. These were dear friends as well as solid citizens and they could be trusted.

"Something's going on south of here. Just little bits and pieces, but it appears that folks over t' Royton have been having a bit of trouble. Seems someone is trying to ride roughshod over them, demanding payments for safety. A rough element is moving in."

"Walt, if that's in Royton, why do you have that worried look? Seems there's more to this than you're letting on." Bill eyed his friend carefully.

"Couple rough-lookin' feller's showed up at Marge's couple days back, spoke unkindly to her and suggested she might need some help keepin' safe. She told them she rightly figured she could take care of herself. They tried to argue with her, but they didn't notice Parson Weaver off in the corner. Parson reared the hammer back on that big Spencer he carries and they stopped mighty sudden. Seems Parson had his gun naturally laying on the table facing their direction. They laughed at her and left. Got me kinda wonderin' if they's gonna try and horn their way in."

"Any idea who's behind it?" Otis asked in a

tone that left no doubt anyone named would receive a serious visit soon.

"Not yet, Otis, but as I was heading here this morning, I run into a feller from the Circle-O. He was driftin', but said that some of the ranches over thataway had been threatened and some were payin' protection money."

Bill interjected, "Extortion! Pa, isn't Mike Nettleton over that direction? You'd think he would step in and run them out."

"Bill," said his pa, "You been gone a while. Mike started that spread some 50 year ago. He's not as young as he used to be, and he lost his two boys over the years. He's got no one and he's up in years. Still a working ranch, but he doesn't carry the clout he used to."

"The Ladder-N was one of the ranches mentioned," said Walt.

Otis Henry rubbed his forehead, "Was a time Mike would take on anybody. He was tough. Came into this country couple years after us. We fought rustlers together. He still has a tough galoot for foreman – name of Hansen. Hansen was like a son to him and I wonder what's happened."

"Hansen was found three weeks ago up in the breaks above the ranch, on the trail to one of the line cabins. Dead. Shot in the back." Walt saw the shock in the eyes around the table. Hansen was respected and well thought of.

"Who would want him dead?" asked Ella Henry

"Don't know, but maybe he was in the way."

Bill sat back in his chair. He realized that somehow he had been living a dream, thinking that by coming out here he was coming to some sort of fairyland, where all was peace and contentment. Here he was now faced with the grim reality that the tentacles of crime extended to even the remotest locales.

"Who would stand to gain from this?" Bill mused, partly to himself.

"Nobody seems to know any answers so far," said Walt.

Chapter 15

Bill found time to head to town every few days, usually under a pretense of needing something for the ranch. But really he still enjoyed some sense of society and town did it for him. In town, he usually spotted the strange rider, same yellow bandana seemingly just lazing around. From a distance he could see at times that the man seemed to be looking his way, but the shadows prevented Bill from noting where he was looking.

Bill, like many others, took to Marge's for the food and the variety of conversation.

Marge was a mystery to all, but respected. No one, save possibly one, knew her past and her determination.

She watched and learned and listened. As she wiped down tables and ladled out sumptuous portions – she knew men liked their food piled high – she also was a quick study of character. It had been a trait built of necessity.

Her father had been a drunk, and took little notice of his daughter, except to act important around her and demand respect. His weakness was gambling, and every little bit he earned as a swamper in the dancehall he gambled away, always seeking his proverbial pot of gold. Marge – her name was different then, grew up hungry and learned in the ways of those at the bottom of society.

At age 16 her father, sure of a winning hand, placed her as collateral in a poker game. It was a low end game, in the low end of town, among the low end of society, so no eyebrows raised at this action. She was brought forward, a skinny, half-starved girl. The other hand in contention was held by a two-bit gambler they all knew as Ace. Ace looked her over, and nodded his assent. Her father had a full-house to Ace's Royal Flush, he got drunk and she headed out of town with Ace, her father too drunk to care.

She traveled with him for a year, used by him and treated as a half-person. He occasionally gave her to other men, then treated her worse. She learned to survive, never losing her humanness or femininity but becoming strong and determined.

One night on a trail outside St. Louis, they

linked up with 2 other men at dusk and agreed to share a fire. The two men kept staring at her, and she knew what was on their minds. She cringed inside and, as the men began drinking and plying the bottle to Ace to get him drunk, he lumbered around and began to stagger. She feigned to hold him up, and slipped his derringer out of his coat pocket and into hers. Ace fell into a stupor and one of the men felled him forever with an oak limb, and then turned to her with lust.

As both approached with obvious intent, they misjudged her innocence and stopped, startled, when they faced the gun barrel. She was wise to take hold of opportunity and the men died there on the trail, with coyotes howling in the distance. She rummaged through all the men's belongings and took money and valuables, found Ace's "grubstake stash," and gold watch, and headed down the trail. Heading into the bustle of St. Louis, she found work cooking for Hazel's Boardinghouse, in exchange for food and a room.

A friendship developed as Hazel learned the character, the strength and determination of this new girl, who now referred to herself as Marge. Hazel could see early on that Marge would move on – she had that in her being, and after 3 years Marge told of her intent to join a wagon train headed west to Colorado Territory. One evening they stood on the porch as the stars twinkled overhead.

"It's in you to go west, Marge. But always

know you'll have a place here if you need to return." It was a statement of kindness possibly mixed with a bit of wistfulness, but they both knew she would not return.

"It's been wonderful here, Hazel. I was lost when I came here. Your care and trust saved me. But now I feel like I have to make my own way."

"I know. And you'll do well, girl. You find a place and set to cooking and don't forget what you've learned, and you'll have all the business you can handle. You're a natural." She had then reached into her apron and brought out five gold eagles. They clinked as she placed them in Marge's apron pocket. "For your new start. May God guide your steps."

The next day, as she rode her horse in the van of wagons, she pondered her provision. She had carefully hoarded what she had taken off the bodies so long ago, and kept all wants in check. She had $500, a veritable goldmine to many, and knew she must carefully guard that this remained unknown. She paid a gold eagle to a Mormon family to join their camp for the trip.

She parted ways with the others at the edge of Colorado Territory and eventually made her way to New Haven. She made a deal for the building and paid cash – gold money – for supplies, creating a bit of a stir, and started feeding. Business came quickly and she eventually overcame the angst of the women and became a part of the town.

She felt a belongingness unknown in her

past. The town had given her that.

And Parson Tanner.

Chapter 16

It was on the third time to town in as many weeks that his desire to stay out of the limelight took a hit.

He was coming out of Marge's, where he always seemed to find his way to lunch, when he saw a commotion up the street by Wilson's store. There were several horses with a strange brand gathered at Wilson's hitch rail, and inside were laughing and yelling. Bill knew that Wilson's young boys often helped in the store and, with a mixture of curiosity and concern, he quickly crossed the street.

As he approached the store, he simultaneously heard a scared whimper from Wilson's son, Josh, and had his path blocked by a big man who stepped from the store. His anger surged. He disliked defiance and disrespect.

"You can't go in there, pardner," the man said, chewing on a broom straw with his thumbs hooked in his gun belt. Bill feigned to turn away, then suddenly turned back, slipped his gun out and laid the man cold with a barrel to the head. Bill looked down and saw the gash already bleeding. He walked into the store, stopping quickly to let his eyes adjust. He saw Wilson, bent over the counter with a hand twisted behind his back by a large, muscular man. Around him stood other strange riders, all looking and grinning at what was happening. The boy yelled, "leave my pa alone!" It was a cry of fear and anger. "I'll get the sheriff!" He was held firmly by one of the roughs.

"The sheriff's out of town, boy. Besides, we just want your pa to show some manners. He doesn't seem to think that we should get credit. We think that's rude." The other men were grabbing supplies.

Nobody noticed Bill enter, so intent were they on their humiliation of the storekeeper.

Bill Henry, always a friend of the underdog, grabbed an ax handle from a barrel and took a step forward.

"Hold it, my friend. There seems to be some confusion as to who's manners are unrefined here."

The man straightened from twisting Wilson's arm and slowly turned to face Bill Henry. Bill noted a somewhat strange looking flattened face with an unusually large nose placed like a centerpiece on a table. The others turned toward Bill, at the same time spreading out. Wilson slid to the floor.

"Mister, you're all alone. Where's that army you think is gonna help you tell me what to do?"

Bill had learned over the years, both in the courtroom and out, the element of a surprise revelation often was the winning move. With a practiced hand, he whipped the ax handle into the gut of the man with the big nose, and stepped sideways out of line of the pistols being pulled. In the instant they were distracted he had his gun out and covering them. Their hands relaxed when faced with the dark barrel of a Colt. It was like looking into the face of death, and many a man acted and talked tough until they faced a barrel of a gun, at which time they often changed their tunes.

Nose slowly came to his feet, holding his gut, no longer eager for a fight, yet far from tamed.

"You made a bad move, stranger."

Bill looked at the man. Yep, his friends out East said he could always smell a rat….this was definitely a rat.

"We don't consider it appropriate for our townsfolk to be roughed up."

"We was just wanting a little credit till we came back through. We'll have money then and we thought it right unneighborly that this fella didn't think we were to be trusted. By the way, what'd you say your name was?"

"I didn't, and I think that this is a convenient time for you and your flunkies to mosey on out of town."

"Certainly, stranger." Most smart men didn't argue with a gun barrel, but one of the fellas at the side was making a slow move for his gun.

"I wouldn't think of it, if I were you," Henry said. The man stopped.

As Bill stepped aside, they moved slowly out of the store. He stepped into the doorway, gun still in hand. The man on the ground slowly stood up, holding his bloody head in his hand. He'd need attention. By that time, there was a small group of townsfolk approaching with guns held at the ready. The toughs realized their fun was over and their only focus was to ride off.

Nose gave him an unpleasant glare. "Boss won't like this meddling."

"Tell your boss we don't like his meddling, either. This is a quiet town and we prefer it stay that way."

They slowly mounted their horses and rode out of town, Nose looking back frequently.

Wilson came out to the walk, rubbing his arm and shoulder. His son stood beside him.

"Thanks, Bill. They surprised me with how quick they moved when I turned down their credit. They weren't up for discussing it. Those are mean men. I'd watch your back if'n I was you."

Bill looked at the boy. "You ok, son?"

“Yessir.”

"Know anything about them, Wilson?"

"Not much. 'cept they been coming through every week or ten days, buying supplies and trying to push me into giving them extras for free. I sort of figured we'd eventually have a run-in, and I'm sure thankful that you were here. You handled them like a pro, like you'd done that before.” Bill ignored the lead-in.

"Where do they go?"

"Dunno, but I heard one of them mention something about over by the North Fork. Seems like I hear about a lot of riff-raff over there.”

North Fork, that was just a few miles east of Royton, and there used to be a small canyon over that way where trappers had gathered in the old days of the land.

His mind turned this over. Out here a man saddled and rode his own broncs most of the time. And he desperately wanted to avoid any recognition. However, if this was the precursor of the Royton trouble spreading…could it be ignored? Not likely. His experience told him that the best way to take care of trouble was to deal with it head on.

Chapter 17

Cigar smoke filled the room as Boss Carter puffed furiously. For a man who took pride in being unpredictable, smoking was a habit that revealed much. If an observer had been allowed, they would have noticed that the man had billows around him when deep in thought.

At this moment the room was filled with smoke almost as impenetrable as the fog of the waterfront.

His mind was totally occupied with the issue of last night. He puffed and puffed, oblivious of the smoke being so heavy his eyes were watering. It didn't matter, for when Boss Carter applied his significant concentration nothing else mattered.

He had been summoned by Finnegan at a

very late hour, being told that there was something that needed his immediate attention. He despised being interrupted late at night, and came from his rooms angry, to find his loyal hand leaning casually against the doorway, with one of his informants sitting cowed in a chair.

"This better be important," he fumed.

"It is, Boss." Finnegan was not easily intimidated, which irritated Carter. Yet Finnegan's strength made him valuable. There would be much use for him with the new plans unfolding in the West.

Carter glared at the seated man. "O'Halley, isn't it?" The man nodded, knowing that for the Boss to know an informant's name could be good or bad.

"What is it that is important enough to keep me up?"

"I.....I.....I..." The man stammered.

"Speak, you!" Boss glared at Finnegan.

"You're not in trouble, O'Halley...just tell the Boss what you seen."

The man lowered his head. "I seen sumpin today."

"What?" Boss had little patience.

"I seen some strange men on the wharf."

Boss spluttered, "There's always strange men on the waterfront!"

"These was different somehow's. There were two of them, and they was askin' questions about you."

"And?"

"They was snoopin' an askin' questions and they was seen later by Callagan talkin' to some other men uptown."

"Where uptown?"

"The Boar's Head." The Boar's Head was an upscale tavern in the business district.

Boss was getting impatient at the little bits of information trickling from the man. He was turning red. He glared at Finnegan. Finnegan held his hand up, indicating Boss should be patient. Finnegan turned to the man.

"Tell Boss who they was talkin' to."

"They was talking quiet with some men from one of the lawyer's offices."

"Which office?"

"The one we's watchin' the house."

"Long and Henry?"

The man nodded. Boss' mind began to focus. Agents on the waterfront, investigating him, meetings uptown.

A few minutes later he dismissed both men and lit a cigar.

He knew that Henry and others had been building a case. He knew he was a target of the authorities, ever since they nailed Hook Logan, yet he took great pride in being a step ahead. The recent court battle showed he wasn't as far ahead as he thought. A week earlier, an important informant in the courthouse disappeared. He, Carter, had nothing to do with it, and he speculated that some rival had tried to get the man to turn. Boss figured a body would be found somewhere, but none had.

Could the authorities have him hidden somewhere as witness? He had had some difficulties lately in getting information, as his informants were disappearing or losing their jobs. If they were holding witnesses, then Henry and others might be closer to trying to topple his empire. But Henry was gone. He must've gotten the information together and left it with the others when he vanished. So now the others were preparing to close the noose on him. Probably just a matter of weeks…

It was time.

Carter never had been one to be caught without options. He had been working for months on this eventuality. He stood and fought his way though the blue billows, bumping his hip against the desk and cursing.

He walked to a faded and yellowed map on the wall. He placed his finger.

Yes, it was time.

Chapter 18

She rode into town as she always did, as a blur on the horizon and not slowing down till she reached the hitch rail. Skidding her horse to a stop, she jumped off in a fluid motion and up onto the boardwalk. She was recognized hereabouts as a wild, free spirit, but of good stock and with a solid sense of decency. She just had a mind of her own. People frowned at her boldness, but usually with a smile at the corner of their lips. She was loved by everybody, and she had a figure and a smile that naturally had the most wayward man thinking of hearth and home. Yet, she could ride and shoot with the best of the boys and sometimes let them win on purpose to preserve their pride. Other times she took great pleasure in showing them up. She knew it was a man's world, but she planned to make a few tracks of her own. She liked her horses on the wild side, with the energy and spirit to go all day. She was known to range far and wide, rode fast wherever she could, carried a Winchester on her saddle and a short-barreled Colt in a holster strapped to the saddle horn. Many suggested she had another gun hidden on her person.

As she hit the boardwalk and was about to enter Marge's she looked a few buildings down to the store across the street where there seemed to be some commotion. Being naturally curious she leaned against a post and watched, noting the retreating horsemen and the man on the porch of the store.

There was something about the man on Wilson's porch. A stranger, she thought. Down the street Bill turned away from the riders fading in the distance and glanced up and down the street, his eyes seeming to rest briefly upon her.

From a distance she thought he grinned, then he began to walk her way. That walk...now why did that ring a bell?

He came onto the boardwalk and smiled as he approached. "I suspect you might be little Becky Trapp."

She hadn't been called that for years, and it sparked a fire in her, but she just stared. Recognition dawned and her eyes widened.

"Billy Henry?"

"Hello, Becky."

Becky Trapp grinned. "Well, I'll be a flop-eared mule! The prodigal boy returns. But you sure have turned into a man!" She whistled and walked boldly around him.

Bill said "Well, you've turned out mighty fine yourself, Becky. A lot different than that little pert thing I remember."

"Well, I still don't put up with no guff, but I 'spect I've got a reputation for being a bit more refined than I used to be. What brings you back to our quiet community? I never 'spected to see you again."

Becky had an incredible way of looking a man directly in the eyes and holding that eye contact until the other person looked away. Even seemingly confident men or women seemed unable to meet her eyes for long. Some said later it was like she was looking deep inside and seeing truth or falsehood. As so many had falsehood hidden beneath the surface, many looked away with a sort of inside shame. There were several in town, however, who met her gaze confidently, and it was these she gravitated towards. She looked long at Bill. He held the contact until finally she looked away. It disconcerted her for a moment. Yet her spunk recovered instantly.

"I came for the quiet. But I suspect," He glanced at the men riding away, still visible in the distance, "that things aren't as quiet as I had anticipated."

Becky looked troubled. "That was unusual.

What was it all about?"

Bill related what he knew. Becky looked thoughtful, then he noticed a troubled look flicker briefly on her face.

"Do you know something about this, Becky?"

"They've been havin' some troubles south of here a ways. Some peaceful folk bein' roughed up. Wonder if this is part of that same problem." She smiled suddenly, all concern disappearing. She faced him and clasped his arms. "You're lookin' healthy and like you've been busy whilst you been gone." Her brow furrowed. "But there's tiredness in your eyes, Bill."

"Nothing time won't cure. Say, how about lunch? Marge serves up a mean spread."

As they sat in Marge's, it seemed to Bill that there was something in Becky that made the years roll away, and they were kids again, chatting about everything. Recalling childhood antics, they both laughed until Bill held his stomach.

"Stop! I can't take it any more!"

Becky laughed harder. Recovering her composure, she gasped, "I ain't laughed like that in so long…." She looked long at Bill, holding his gaze this time until they both looked to the window and back at the same time when the boardwalk creaked. After that it didn't matter to her anymore. There was something different about this man. A deep confidence and ability that she did not remember in the boy who rode off those years ago. The aimless, unsettled youth was gone and before her sat developed and solid manhood. The years had worked miracles.

Both had grown up when the town was still an extension of the older, wilder world. Becky had been some years younger than he, but still knew the edge of the wild past.

"How long you stayin, Bill?"

"Not sure. Taking some time away." Becky sensed a wall rising, peaking her curiosity. But she knew better than to pursue it right then.

"People tell me out East is really something, with fancy stores and lights in the streets and dances. You seen all that?" There was a touch of wistfulness in her voice that Bill perceived. The girl who loved the West still wondered about what else was out there.

"Yes, and it is nice – to a point. It's hard to judge character there, Becky. First you have to get past the appearances. Things that matter there are different than what matters out here. Don't get me wrong, there are some fine people out East – some who would match with the finest here – but there is more of a focus on what one looks like to others, to officials, to society. Things may be falling down around someone's head and they would smile and claim all is well. Many will do most anything to maintain the illusion they have so carefully built. I've seen men who have lost most everything still scrimping to buy fine clothes and act like nothing is wrong – even to the point of spending money needed to feed wives, children and even themselves. It's all about climbing the social ladder, about getting ahead, about marrying 'right.' That means matches made for financial consideration. It's a life of ego, a life of fear of losing face, a life that demands much and pays little real reward. It's a busy life, too. No long rides in the saddle to give time to think. Life was constant busyness and one society engagement after another. Constant go, go, go."

Thoughtful, she noted his philosophical answer. She sensed refinement, deep thought, and even a touch of sadness in his words.

"Do you have a home there?"

He hesitated. "Yes, a physical home." She noted the far off look in his eyes. He shook his head, smiled, "It's a different world, Becky. Not like this out here, where a man makes his tracks and character is judged by action, not lifestyle." He caught a look from her and grinned. "A woman here makes tracks, too! You seem very content and happy."

Becky noted Bill's expert shift of focus.

"I am, Bill. I love this country. Yes, I guess there's a part of me that'd like to see the East, experience some of the things I read about. But this is the country I love. I love the foothills, the mountains, and the quiet of the trail. I love to ride this country, Bill. I guess you may have figured that!" She grinned. "I love a fast horse."

He looked across the table at this vivacious

young woman. Here was a woman unlike so many in the east: self-assured, strong, intelligent, with simple and pure motives. Along with that, she had an energy and vitality that was refreshing. She was more than a match for any woman he had ever met. Along with that, Bill mused, she was very attractive. She had filled out in all the right directions and certainly must have half the territory dreaming about her.

Becky must have sensed some of his thinking, for she paused and gave him an appraising look. "You got yourself a girl back east?"

"No. They don't make them the same way back there."

"What's so different?"

"There's a lot of lace and giggles and sometimes what is behind that is either very manipulative or just not much at all."

"What kind you lookin' for?" Then she turned red and that saucy look came back to her face.

"I suppose I really haven't seriously looked. Too busy doing other things and no good prospects around."

"Well, while you're back home, maybe we could do some riding – go to some of the old places you'll remember."

"I'd like that, Becky."

"You goin' to the box social next week at the Martin ranch?"

"Hadn't planned on it."

“Well, I think you’d better plan on it...if’n you plan to make any friends,” she said. “Besides, how can you buy my box if’n you ain’t there?” She looked boldly at him.

He grinned, “I may have to reconsider my plans.”

“I reckon so,” she looked him straight in the eye and said with finality.

Bill glanced out the window and watched Walt Larimore ride into town. Bill waited while Walt saw to his horse and, sure enough, he made a beeline to the diner. As he came in, he glanced quickly around and, seeing Bill and Becky, grinned and walked over.

Becky beat him to it. “Light an’ set, Walt!”

“You two hashing over old times?” Walt was grinning and eager to talk with his old friends. They chatted about some of their antics of the past, growing up on the range, and of the happenings of the years Bill was gone.

Bill finally glanced outside. “Well, I better head back before my pa sends out the troops to look for me. I suspect he may be a bit perplexed at me wanting to come to town so much.”

Becky looked at him thoughtfully. “I bet he understands. Your world is bigger than the ranch now. You been out in the great big world and town gives you a feeling of that. A small feeling of it, but you’re used to being with lots of people.” She looked deep in his eyes.

Walt glanced from one to the other. “Hate to break up the reunion here, but I got things to do, too."

Bill filled him in on the happenings at Wilson's and Walt looked worried and scratched his head.

"Some rough outfit has settled in around Royton and the North Fork. Blacksmith over to Royton turned down the offer for protection. Disappeared 3 days ago. Kids fishing a few miles east of the Fork found him yesterday morning. Weren't a pleasant sight. Strange."

"There's more here than meets the eye, Walt."

"It gets stranger, Bill. I never heard the like, but this feller had a burlap bag of horseshoes tied around his ankle and was thrown into a deep pool near the bank. The kid saw his hair floating on the surface. What a way to go."

Bill's mind reeled. Weighted and thrown into a deep pool. That sounds like an eastern thug method! He shared his thought with Walt and Walt just looked at him.

"That sounds like terrible cruelty! Treating him like he was an unwanted puppy," added Becky. "That ain't the way of the west."

Bill glanced at her, his mind miles away, remembering the cruelty of Boss Carter. It was a method that Carter would have approved.

"You're the local sheriff, Walt. What has you riding out there?"

"I know I ain't got no jurisdiction outside of town, but this here has got my curiosity up, not to say my anger. That blacksmith was my wife's cousin."

"I'm sorry, Walt."

"Sally wants me to go fetch his wife and the kids and bring them over here for a spell." Walt looked concerned.

Becky spoke up. "Walt, ya better not go alone. There's some strange doing's all around that part of the country."

Walt looked at Becky and read her eyes. He knew she covered a lot of country. Becky often knew what was happening before anybody else.

"I'll go along," said Bill.

"No, Bill. I think I will go it alone. I'll be ok." Walt knew his friend's desire to keep a low profile.

Later, Bill walked Becky to Wilson's. Before they reached the steps, he said, "It's been great seeing you, Becky."

"I'll see you at the social" With a flick of her hair and a twist to her hips, she strode into the store. Bill grinned and crossed to his horse.

Chapter 19

Box socials were prized events. Word spread quickly, almost mystically, about any sort of gathering and the great mass of western settlers would drop everything to attend such an event. Sometimes it seemed as if the prairie dogs themselves spread the news - it was that fast. In the vast open spaces of the west and amidst ranches that might range in size from miles to hundreds of miles, any chance to get together and socialize created unparalleled excitement. There was guaranteed entertainment, from little gatherings behind the barn to sample the latest quarts and fifths, to the occasional fight, good-hearted teasing and the spectacular event of the bidding on the lunches.

People gathered in from miles around, often

hundreds of miles. Ranches left only essential hands at the ranch, and those unhappily; stores such as Wilson's did extra business, with cowhands and others seeking to spruce themselves up a bit with new shirts and collars. Everybody seemed to be bathing, washing the grime off and putting themselves in stiff new clothes and willingly suffering the collars and starch. Barbers anywhere close had sore hands and shoulders that day, as men came in to get the best shave available.

And for the young men of the region, box socials were a rare opportunity to gaze upon the girls who caused their hearts to flutter and kept their thoughts occupied in the long, lonely hours and days riding the range.

The ladies tried their best to outdo each other in making lunches. Boxes would be packed, then auctioned off with the highest bidder gaining the privilege of eating lunch with the girl who created the lunch. It was a rare time to have alone with a girl. Supposedly anonymous in the bidding, there were frequent hints given by the ladies to the men they preferred, or through intermediaries who sought to give appearance of anonymity. Bidding at times became furious and exorbitant amounts often were paid for lunches. It was great for whatever cause benefitted, but not always good for the now-broke cowhand.

Bill, his ma and pa, Chad, Matt and all the hands but Tetch and Sim rode over. It seemed best to leave some at the ranch, in light of the recent happenings, and both ex-slaves wanted to avoid any trouble with strangers, so they and Buck stayed behind. Otis Henry had spoken to the former slaves beforehand.

"You sure you don't want to go?"

Tetch looked him in the eyes, "Colonel, they's gonna be some strangers there who ain't used to us. Some un' will pick a fight. Used to I'd go to it, but I ain't young as I once were." He chuckled. "No, sir, I don't feel like nursin' myself on purpose. Don't get me wrong. I ain't shirkin' no fight that comes to me, but a man's got to save hisself for the important fights."

Sim shifted his weight, took off his hat and rubbed his wooly hair. "B'sides, we's fine in town, people know us an' such. But we still cain't look at no white women. Be nobody we can dance with."

Otis nodded. He had deep respect for both as hands, but he realized some of their dreams so far were limited, especially in terms of wives. He wondered how he could help.

Buck had volunteered to watch the place, knowing that there were stirrings in the country around. Most likely the other ranches would leave the home places manned in some way. Buck wanted to see the girls and dance, but the ranch was his responsibility. Work before pleasure.

Ma and pa rode in the spring wagon and the others on horseback. Pa looked fine in his Sunday-go-to-meetin' suit, but complained of the tightness of the whole shebang and tugged often at his collar. Ma shushed him repeatedly and told him he looked fine as the day they were married and as how he hadn't complained then about being dressed up. As they covered the country to the Martin ranch, they saw in the distance other wagons and riders heading in the same direction. As they neared the ranch there was an excitement in the air and even the horses seemed to sense something new and to step livelier. Wagons and riders who were off in the distance an hour ago drew close as they all converged upon the same point, like the spokes of a wheel drawing close at the hub. There were smiles and greetings of people who had not seen each other sometimes in years. Joy and excitement were the dominant emotions.

Bill was recognized by some and there was backslapping and the harassment began. One hand from the Martin place yelled across the crowd at another arriving hand from a distant ranch:

"Hey, Rowdy! You's just as ugly as when I seen you last year! When you gonna get your face fixed! You remind me of the north end of a southbound range bull!" The men chuckled, knowing the fun was starting.

The other hand grinned. "Fred…We ain't even danced yet. Can we fight later?" He looked around at the hands nearby, then over at a cluster of girls at the food table. "I gotta keep my lips to kiss me a girl!" At that the men around began joshing him. Rowdy grinned from ear to ear, showing a couple teeth missing already.

Red Bowen, from the Cummings ranch, was known for his humor that usually had no bounds. "Oh, we all know you two love each other! Whyn't ya just kiss and make up!"

There were loud hoots and hollers. The men both looked at Red and they knew there was a score to settle. Red laughed loudly.

Already the men were glancing at the ladies. Women of quality were rare and the ratio of men to women was depressing and guaranteed loneliness for many. The men were excited and hopeful that they might catch the eye of a young beauty. Some of the men were there not as prospects for the box lunches because they were a bit older, but there were still some older widows and spinsters to meet that might have prospects. It was a lonely country at times.

Bill recognized some of the Trapp ranch hands, as he had ridden over recently for dinner at her invitation. He had been working on a section of fence and saw a rider approaching at a walk. Removing his hat, he wiped his face with his kerchief and felt for his gun.

The other man approached, grinned.

"I been sent by Miss Becky. I been told to give you this." He grinned wider as he held out to Bill a folded paper. He opened it.

SINCE YOU AIN'T LIKELY TO HAVE

ANYTHING ELSE TO DO, IT WOULD BE
NICE TO HAVE YOU JOIN US FOR
DINNER AT THE RANCH THURSDAY EVE.

It had been a delightful evening. Becky's father was a refined man of sorts, but a solid western hand also.

Bill remembered that Becky had walked him to his horse later, and deliberately brushed her hand lightly against his as they walked. He reached and grasped her hand, but she pulled away.

"Why, Bill! Such liberties! We hardly know each other."

Bill realized Becky was strong-willed. He grinned as he mounted the dun. She seemed bothered that he had not tried again.

"See you, Becky." She came close to his horse and touched the stirrup.

"See, you, Bill." And he rode off into the darkness.

Chapter 20

The dancing began with a sudden burst of excitement from a fiddle. At first there were few dancing. Most of these men, Bill thought, would tackle a she-bear before they'd get up the courage to ask a woman to dance. But slowly the men sheepishly sidled up to the ladies and requested a dance. Before long the energy increased and the dancing went into full swing.

Hearing a murmur in the crowd to his left, Bill glanced over to see a handful of strange hands ride up and dismount. There was a bit of serious enmity expressed as shoulder bumping as some of the old hands realized the interlopers were of that outfit over to Royton. It was noticeable to some that none of the people of Royton rode in for the social.

There seemed to be an unspoken understanding that there would be a fight, but also that there was dancing and the box lunches were to be finished before other issues.

Later, as the bidding began for the boxes, Bill hung at the edge of the crowd, enjoying the antics and seeing who was interested in whom. He was gathering much information as was his tendency and training. He knew Lucy Alvarez was sweet on Wally Gardner, and that his own brother, Chad, had a thing for Gretchen Willings.

One of the boxes went for near $30 for a cowhand who obviously knew his favorite girl's box. Bill had to chuckle at the friends who bid the box up, knowing this hapless cowhand would be mooching tobacco for weeks after paying a good month's wages. Yet they enjoyed the matchmaking. Ella Henry had been set up to take the money.

Occasionally, 2 men would be bidding furiously and the winner would be triumphant while the loser would slap his leg and look like the world had ended....but only for a moment as jocularity and other antics brought them back into the fun.

Bill felt a hand at his elbow and looked over. A cowhand he recognized from the Trapp ranch passed him a note and disappeared into the crowd. On it was simply written: BLUE BASKET - PURPLE RIBBON.

He grinned. Obviously "somebody" wanted him as a lunch companion. Be careful, he thought to himself - you didn't come west for this. He easily carried enough gold to outbid any average cowhand. Even his family did not know that he was well off.

Why not, he chuckled to himself. A nice conversation and lunch might be nice.

One young lady frowned briefly as her box was bought by a lanky, buck-toothed galoot from an outlying ranch who looked like he had been bred too close to the tree. But the frown disappeared as the spirit of the day took over. No one was obligated to marry – it was just a lunch.

One box after another sold to the highest bidder, with the couples rushing off to find shade and some sense of privacy. Each winning bid was accompanied by fun-filled catcalls and comments that had both parties blushing and grinning.

As the bidding progressed, some of the Triple-C gathered in a group. The message was passed by eye contact and nod of the head. Men touched their hips, but most had left their weapons hanging from the saddle.

The Triple-C had no idea what was going on at first, unaccustomed to the ways of wide West. But then they began to throw in bids. None continued to the point of winning. Perhaps, Bill mused, they were wary of causing a dispute. They hung more on the fringes of the crowd. As the bidding continued, it became clear which girls still had not been claimed for lunch, and they huddled and giggled in a small knot.

Finally, there was the blue basket with the purple ribbon. An unfamiliar man with narrow eyes and a sly look started the bidding at $20! This was no simple cowhand, Bill realized. He also didn't care much for the man's looks. His years had taught him many skills and this man was not a man who made an honest wage. His eyes were devious. He was not the kind that a mother wanted a daughter to bring home. He glanced at Becky through the crowd…she looked pale and stressed. So the mysterious note writer was Becky. It was her basket.

Another disreputable hombre bid $25. Bill looked over at the knot of girls at the end of the bidding table and saw Becky. He caught her eye as the bidding went up. She was a brash, pert girl, but her look to him was one of concern. Her looks conveyed a pleading to him.

"$30," he bid, seeing the look of relief on Becky's face, even as he noted the mean, cold look on the faces of the two bidders.

"$31," narrow-eyes bid.

"$40," Bill countered.

"$45!" Narrow eyes really wanted this bid. Why? Bill sensed there was more to this than a box lunch - but what? Whatever it was, it was time to shut it down.

"$100." The crowd gasped and all eyes turned to Bill. Becky was wide-eyed. Otis Henry watched and smiled. "My son's turned into quite a man," he thought.

There was a move of the rough-looking

bunch towards Bill but, as if on cue, a number of solid ranch hands "accidentally" stepped in the way, blocking their move.

The narrow-eyed man gave Bill a look that could not be misunderstood, then turned and walked through the crowd.

Becky's eyes showed relief and gratitude. She came to him as he paid. Ella Henry took the money and looked Bill in the eyes and said, "That was a good thing you did."

Becky said, "Thanks, Bill...you don't know what this means."

He grinned from ear to ear. "It means I get to have some time with a beautiful woman...how about under that oak over yonder." Becky looked into Bill's eyes and her gaze lingered. She had been called beautiful by many, and some had tried to win her heart, but she always felt like she was the senior partner. She wanted a man who would make her feel like a woman. As she looked at the genuiness in Bill's eyes and felt the gentle grasp of his guiding hand on her elbow, she felt something, and saw something that quickened her heart. Never one to be prone to submissiveness, she now let herself be guided to the shade of the oak.

Chapter 21

After a wonderful lunch, and laughter, Becky realized that, despite her independence that was on the verge of legendary in the area, she had enjoyed the time with a man and, most startling, wanted it to continue. Usually, a short time with one of the locals cowhands and she was itching to get away and to ride off, which she had done before and left cowhands gaping.

They talked of many things, of her dreams, her family, the rides she so enjoyed. It became clear to Bill that Becky knew more of the going's on in the area than many, due to her propensity to ride and explore. She was sharp and intellectually superior to many women he knew. No wonder the local cowhands had trouble courting her - she was out of their league.

To Becky, it was clear that Bill had become a fine man, had accomplished much, and was a confident and capable man.

Yet, his was a mind always seeking to know, to learn, to put together pieces of the puzzles that surrounded him.

"Becky, tell me about that character who was bidding for your box."

"I.....he......," she stammered. He'd never seen Becky without the confidence and brashness that was her hallmark. Here was another side of her – hurt, needy, scared.

"What is it, Becky?"

"I was threatened....if I tell anybody they said they'd hurt daddy."

"Who threatened?"

"Some of those men....the Triple-C men."

"Becky, what can you tell me about the Triple-C and what was the threat?"

Tears welled up in her eyes as she spoke. "The Triple-C is a new outfit over by Royton. I was over that way a couple days ago trying to find out more about the doing's over thataway – you know, Bill – the way I am." A slight smile shown through the tears. " I was in the mercantile and these men came in the door and started to make comments. When Mr. Blick – he's the owner – tried to intervene, they shoved him aside and held a gun on him."

Bill was alarmed. "Did they harm you in any way, Becky?"

She shook her head. "No. I think they would

have, except that a man came in and they stopped and he told them to leave me alone. They all had a look in their eyes and never argued with the man. He excused himself and tipped his hat and left."

"Did you learn anything about the outfit?"

"Most of them seem to be Easterners. They act tough, and seem like they could handle themselves pretty well in a scrap. I haven't been able to find out who's behind it."

"This man who stopped them…what can you tell me about him?"

"He was dangerous. You know, Bill, there are just some things you see in a man's eyes. His was pure poison. The men stepped back and obeyed without question."

"Do you remember a name?"

Becky squinted as she thought. "Finnegan. They called him Mr. Finnegan."

Bill found his enjoyment of the day curbed by his preoccupation with all the going's on and the trouble Becky had experienced. He surveyed the crowd, trying to gain any information on the Triple-C. He could easily see the Triple-C men hanging together at the edge of the crowd, ogling some of the ladies and laughing amongst themselves. He was getting irritated and he could see that he was not the only one so bothered. Over in one corner, several of the local ranch hands were talking in low voices and casting glances at the Triple-C. Bill could see it was like

a powder keg ready to blow.
Even Rowdy and Fred stood together, looking irritated at the easterners.

He watched carefully, wary as the tension in the air was very palpable, with unabashed glaring going on between the Triple-C and the local cowhands. Off to one side, Bill noticed the man with the yellow bandanna. He had appeared alone, and stood aloof at the edge of the crowd. He was obviously seasoned, with peering eyes that seemed not to miss much. He had a bulge under his coat, and Bill surmised he had a holster under his arm. Bill sidled over to him.

"Strange doin's here today."

"I think all hell's about to cut loose."

"I see you around. Where do you stand in this?"

The man in the bandanna looked at him. "I'm a peace loving man, but I ain't afraid of a fracas. I ain't likin' the way those men are lookin' at the womenfolks." He spit into the dirt.

One of the local hands threw down his drink and stepped out towards the Triple-C bunch, who to a man stopped laughing and glared at the hand.

"You challenging us, cowboy?" It was a man in a slouch cloth hat. His arms bulged with tattooed power.

"You ain't got no right to talk about the women like that!"

"I aim's ta talk as I please."

The cowboy swayed with drink, but stepped

forward. Tattoo stepped forward to meet him. On both sides men stepped forward. Who threw the first punch would never be known, but suddenly the fight was on.

A few hours later, men trailed slowly away from the day's events. Some slouched in the saddle, some with remnants of blood around their mouths and their knuckles.

Bill had stayed out of the fight at first, aside from watching for any pulling of weapons. He saw one of the Triple-C men reach under his jacket. Bill moved up behind the man and suggested strongly that the man leave whatever it is alone. He punctuated the suggestion with the barrel of a short gun he kept in a special holster in the small of his back. The man complied and no one else appeared to see the interaction. He looked over and saw Becky. She was looking at him with brows furrowed.

Chad had jumped into the melee and had held his own, seeming to relish the spontaneous bursts of energy. He smiled until he took a blow to the side of the head from a man who still wore a derby. Chad turned and laid the man out with a wicked blow to the jaw. Chad half-crouched with the pain to his hand. Bill suspected he had broken a bone. He smiled inside as he realized his brother could handle himself well.

Bill saw an eastern man raise a bottle to hit someone. He stepped in quickly and gave the man a staggering blow to the kidney. The man gasped and staggered to his knees. Another stepped in and Bill turned his head with the blow, barely touched. He stunned the man with a solid blow to the chin.

He fought well. His training in the east had given him an ease with bare-knuckle fighting. That, combined with the knock-down, drag-out fighting he had done on the frontier, gave him an edge. He received scuffs, but no solid blows.

As they fought. Bill noted an easterner slip back away from the crowd. He slipped back himself and caught a glimpse of the man as he went to the barn. Bill quietly went from buggy to buggy to keep from sight, and walked to an outside stall door. As he peered in, he saw the man bend over and there was the sound of sloshing. Bill walked in and came around the corner as the man was preparing to pour what was probably oil on a pile of hay in the corner. The man turned and Bill hit him. The man was startled with Bill's presence. He started to rise and Bill hit him again, with anger that such a man would burn another's barn. The man fell, unconscious.

Bill dragged the man outside. Matt was approaching, having seen Bill slip away. Bill reached over and hefted the can the man had dropped. He sniffed – lamp oil!

"What was he doing, Bill?"

"He was intending to burn the barn down. Caught him getting ready to pour oil on the hay. Give me a hand and we'll take him to the sheriff."

They both grabbed an arm and dragged the man back to the crowd.

Back at the fight, the Triple-C had fought with skill and power. The fight had been brutal and with deep feeling on both sides. There had been some severe injuries to both sides as they fought wildly until Old Gracie Martin shattered the noise with the blast of a shotgun. She yelled out and officially called off the day's activity and told everyone to go home, then stood glaring at the Easterners as they grudgingly turned to leave.

Bill called out to Walt. "Sheriff, this man was planning to burn down the barn." The crowd stopped and turned back to where the man lay at the sheriff's feet. To burn a man's barn down was sacrilege. To lose the hay, the tack, the supplies could ruin a man beyond recovery. Men began to mutter and seethe with anger. Gracie Martin hurriedly reloaded her shotgun from the shells she habitually stashed in her apron.

A few of the ranch hands had been to their saddles and retuned with weapons. Others pulled hideout guns. Old Edgar Martin, realizing how close he had come to losing his barn, grabbed the shotgun from his wife and snapped it shut with a vengeance and strode to the man on the ground. The man was beginning to stir and, as his eyes opened, he was aware of all eyes upon him and the shotgun pointed his way. His eyes opened wide.

Walt stepped between the man and Martin.

"Edgar, that ain't the way to solve this. We'll take the man to jail and he'll get a trial."

"He don't deserve no trial, sheriff. He deserves what I want to give him. Or a necktie party."

"Edgar!"

"You take him, sheriff! But if'n nothin' happens, I'll take care of it. And I don't want none of them Triple-C on my land!" He looked around. The eastern bunch had fallen back in the crowd and were riding off.

That had now been two days past. Bill worked on a fence near the farmhouse, still nursing sore knuckles. He had to admit, with a smile to himself that, despite the circumstances, he had felt confident and the physical release of taking the man down had not been entirely unpleasant.

He did see, however, that the Triple-C men were cruel fighters, not against biting and no holds barred tactics. He had seen them attempt to stomp men who were down and grab bottles to use on the locals.

All in all, looking back, he felt both sides held their own. Perhaps the Eastern thugs realized that this was not a pushover and that they would not get their way around here.

Still, he did not feel that they were going to back down, and that there was a more significant battle ahead.

He smiled. After Walt had intervened, Becky had appeared suddenly at his side, checking for injuries. Aside from the knuckles, he had no injuries. It almost seemed to disappoint her, as if she was hoping to do more doctoring.

Chapter 22

Parson Weaver was a happy man, though a curious sort for a preacher. The townsfolk just knew him as "Parson." Raised in the hills of Tennessee, William Jefferson Weaver cut his teeth on fatback and knew the value of a bullet. In his neck of the woods boys learned to provide for the family, and Will's dad taught him to hunt by counting the bullets he brought back and requiring results for each bullet used. It wasn't cruel - it was necessity, shot and powder not being cheap. But Mal Weaver taught his sons well, and Parson generally hit what he shot at - dead center. His life changed when, at the age of 16, he found himself in the middle of a feud ambush and was trapped and barely escaped death. He made a decision that he wanted a different life and left the hills and headed west, helping on cattle drives and doing odd jobs. Having been raised on the Good Book and being prone to quote it, he gained the nickname "Parson" on a drive down the Chisum Trail. Definitions blurred, and it naturally followed that word spread for "the Parson" when death reared it's head. Perhaps he should have explained himself, but the need was there and it was enough for him and the authorities and next thing he knew he was officiating weddings and baptizing babies. He took his role seriously, but ran a few cows on his small spread and the rest of the time wandered the hills. He was quiet on the trail and handy with any gun.

He was a right neighborly sort, ready to give a hand where it was needed, and serve the needs of the people in what he had come to see as his extended congregation.

He had not been at the box social, but had spent the afternoon with Marge. He had heard of the fight. The peace of the area was fraying. He, too, wondered who was behind all these new happenings.

On this particular morning he rode with haste and care on a mission. Word had come that a cowhand on the C bar C was near death from a gut shot and was asking for the Parson. He had seen the agony of gut shot men before, and that there was nothing that could be done other than to wait through the agony and reach the welcome rest of death.

As he swung into the ranch yard, he naturally pulled up to the bunkhouse where a cluster of hands were gathered and the agonized groans of a man could be heard inside. The cowhands nodded, with looks of pain and anger on their faces as they heard the end nearing for a riding partner and friend.

Inside, Dorta Cummings sat wiping the man's brow as he groaned, her apron soaked with blood. Already the fever of death was upon him. Dorta and Eston Cummings had been in the valley many years and she treated the cowhands as her own sons. She had tears in her eyes as she looked up at Weaver. She nodded to him.

"Thanks for hurrying, Parson." Her voice was strained. She was a strong woman with sharp features and gray hair knotted at the back. The passage of years showed in the lines of her face. This happening after many years of peace to one of her "boys" had taken a toll. As she continued to wipe the man's brow, Parson knelt by the man's bedside.

It was Red Bowen. The peaceful young man known for his humor. A favorite at the dances and roundup and any time hands gathered. His long red hair was his pride and joy. But today it was matted with sweat and blood. Parson grasped Red's hand and the dying man squeezed with the need to alleviate the pain. Nothing would cut this pain, Parson knew.

"Pray for me, Parson," Red gasped.

"Are you ready to meet the Lord, Red?" He

asked gently.

"It hurts bad! I wanta die! I'm ready."

The hands present removed their hats and Parson began to pray. "Dear Heavenly Father, we bring to you today our friend, Red. We know he's gut shot and all, and we ask that you would ease his pain and…" There was a shudder and spasm and all eyes opened to see Red take a last breath and his eyes stare vacantly.

Dorta Cummings began to sob and went to the arms of her husband. The other hands wandered off, tears showing despite the code of the range, for Red was a favorite and had brought much joy to a rugged life.

"What happened?" Parson asked quietly as he looked at Red's now painless features.

One of the older hands spoke. "He was on his way back from the line cabin south of here. Said he met a pack of sour-lookin' riders who stopped him and told him he wouldn't be ridin' this range so easy 'afore long. Red made some comment and said the next thing he knew they was drawing and shootin.' He thinks he got one, maybe two, and they left him layin' on the grass. His horse came back a few minutes later and he came in, holding his guts in with his hands." Anger showed in the man's grief.

"Any idea who the men were?"

"He said never seed 'em afore. But he said a couple was wearing strange hats – them rounded kind we hear about now and again."

Bowler hats. Eastern style. Parson turned

quiet with thought.

An hour later the man was buried, Parson reading from the Book and trying to give comfort. Yet, to these men, only the passage of time and the bringing of frontier justice would do anything to ease the pain.

He spoke to Dorta and agreed to pass on any information he might find as to the identity of the men.

The seasoned woman looked to the bunkhouse and hollered, “Donson! Tipper!” The men came instantly to her. “You two go see what you can find out with the trail. Don’t mess with the outlaws, just see iffn’ you can locate ‘em. Then we’ll roust up some men and go in with strength. I want no revenge actions until we get there, understand?”

“Yes, ma’am.” They went to gather their necessaries and saddle their horses.

Chapter 23

Boss Carter was getting a bit perturbed. He paced the room seeking answers from the depths of his intellect, which had always served him well. Nobody could say he wasn't smart. He had planned and connived and outmaneuvered others to get where he was today. Why was it that things were not working well on all fronts? He was a man used to success, used to men doing his bidding and he took pride in all things being thought out well so that there were no glitches. Now, he'd gotten a telegram saying that they had run into trouble with some stranger in some little town called New Haven. His men had been on their way to Royton to make some preparations. Now they had had to stop and get patched up. Jackson, who had been leading the bunch, said he had sent a man back later to find out who the stranger was. Word was that his name was Henry, from a ranch back in the hills. Henry! Why did his opponents have to have the same name? Why, he'd give his eyeteeth to get a hold of William Henry. He had his feelers out all over the eastern seaboard and had come up empty on that fancy attorney. He desperately wanted to get his hands on him. And when he did, he'd.... He stopped in mid-pace. Wait! Could it be? Could it possibly be? His heart beat faster as he went to his desk and opened the top drawer and brought out a telegram.

PROBLEM IN NEW HAVEN STOP FANCY TALKING STRANGER NAME HENRY STOP WHAT ARE YOUR ORDERS?

Boss Carter folded the paper, puffing furiously on his cigar, thinking just as furiously. Two days earlier he had asked for more particulars, and awaited a response. Why did the blasted telegraph have to be so slow! Smoke billowed as he puffed viciously.

There was a knock on the door.

"Come!"

The man from outside looked down as he walked in, arm extended with a telegram. Boss Carter took it roughly, opening it and shifting his cigar.

MAN NAMED BILL HENRY NEW HERE.

Carter puffed even harder as he dismissed the man. His mind reeled.

In some conversation after a court win, somebody had referred to William Henry as, “a bull - just like his father.” Could this be his enemy? Was his family from Colorado? His heart leapt with morbid delight and evil cunning.

He’d have Bill Henry killed! Then it will be done. Wait, though. How to make it hurt more? He puffed harder and a smile - if such it could be called - came to his face. Yet nothing could mask the quivering rage in his eyes.

It had to be him! He’d gotten away and run back home to mommy and daddy! How quaint! Evil surged in his cold heart.

Bull Henry - that’s the target! Kill the father and watch the pup cry! Then wring the pup’s neck.

Boss Carter took time to write a note clearly.

He hollered, “Boy!” The door opened quickly and a teenage boy entered, one of Boss Carter’s eyes and ears. He often learned more from the boys, as they moved in and out of crowds and adults talked as if they weren’t there.

“Take this to the telegraph right away!” The boy left and his running steps were heard fading in the hallway.

He needed to just wait for final confirmation. He puffed.

What was going on here, Parson thought! Strange men riding in and threatening and people dying. There was something deep going on here. He was on his way home, but came to a bend and took a different trail, a trail leading to the Henry Ranch.

Otis Henry was a strong man with strong sons. He was a leader and known for his judgment. He might be able to shed some light on these happenings.

It was early evening when he reached the Henry ranch. Despite the grim situation at hand, he grinned to himself at his impeccable timing. How many times he had arrived on ranches at dinner time. Here it was, nearing that time, and Ella Henry had a reputation for prime grub. The code of the west dictated that those traveling through be fed and given a place to put their bedroll for the night.

As he cantered into the yard, Parson sensed someone in the shadows. Otis Henry stepped out from the lee of the barn, rifle in hand.

"Expectin' someone, Mr. Henry?"

"Not in particular, Parson. Heard your horse and can't be too careful lately. Things are happening. Light and set." There was a bond between these men, having shared battle together. "What brings you out our way?"

"More strange doings, Mr. Henry."

"Call me Otis, please. What strange doings you referrin' to?" It was a sign of the respect for

Weaver's reputation that Henry would offer his first name, but Henry would never venture to call Weaver by anything but his title. Weaver had noticed over the years that deference was paid to clergy, at least to those who earned the respect.

"These strange riders I keep hearing of. First they were south and East of here, but that's changed. I just left the C bar C and buried a good hand. Gut shot by a tough-talking bunch near one of their line cabins."

Otis grimaced instinctively. Gut shot. One of the worst ways to die. Constant unbearable pain, no relief, lingering for hours. Men gut shot often begged to be put down. The one time it wasn't considered murder was when putting down a gut shot man.

"Which hand?"

"Bowen."

"Red? Dear God…he was just hereabouts for grub not long back. Everybody liked him. Good hand."

"It wasn't a pretty sight. He said a group of men said they wouldn't be riding so easy now. Said all at once they was shootin." Thought he nailed a couple."

"Was it bad for him, Parson."

"Most of his guts were outside….it was bad as I've ever seen."

"Dear God…"

Ella Henry came out the door, wiping her hands on a towel and patting her hair.

"Hello, Parson! You'll stay for dinner, of

course?"

He touched his hat brim. "My pleasure, ma'am."

Ella Henry looked from Parson's face to her husband's, reading the sign. "What's happened, Otis? Someone hurt?"

Otis and Ella had ridden many miles and years together. She was a tough frontier woman, and he pulled no punches.

"Red Bowen bought it, Ella. Gut shot by a rough bunch up by one of the C bar C line cabins." The shock showed in her face. So many years of peace and then this. And such a fine young man – one welcome at any ranch hereabouts.

"Any idea who the men were?" Ella asked.

"Not yet, ma'am," Parson answered, "but there's been some strange doin's down t'Royton and some ranches south and east of here."

"Whatcha mean by strange doin's, Parson?"

"Rumor has it that some of the ranchers are paying protection money to these toughs."

"Walt was by the other day and spoke of that. Told us Hansen had bought it."

"Hansen….a good man. I heard the blacksmith disappeared and they found him in the lake."

"Well, Otis Henry, better get your gun oiled and load all the cylinders, cause it seems like we got a fight aheadin' our way. Never have backed down and ain't gonna start now. I'll go give my Winchester a good goin' over." She walked into the house.

"She's a strong woman, Otis. One to ride the river with."

"She sure is, and we've been down the river and back a few times. I remember the time she faced down a bear down by the east branch and shot that feller right between the eyes while he was comin' at us and my rifle empty. She didn't back down then and never has."

Over dinner that night, the conversation bantered here and there, but in a distracted sort of way, as all their minds were on the problem at hand. Otis Henry suggested they get hold of area ranchers to see how far this has spread. They would meet in town one week hence.

Parson spoke: "I reckon that will help us see how far this has gone and who's been approached. We need some information."

Otis spoke, "We need to find out what's going on. We need someone to go there and see and hear. Oh, for the days of the cavalry….they were the eyes and ears of the army. But we need a scout, someone who is sharp and not easily scared. I'll send one of the boys over to Cedarville to just sort of mosey around…another over to Royton."

Ella spoke. "Otis, best send Bill to Royton. That's where you said might be a hotbed, and he's less known than the others."

"You're right, Ella. Though might be I ought to send you." He grinned at his wife of so many years. “Been a long time since you been down thataway.” He saw the look in her eyes. “I’m jokin’, Ella!”

“Otis Henry, I declare you have a mind that beats all, comin’ up with ideas like that. That’s exactly what I’ll do! I’ll go down there myself and see the lay of the land. They’d never bother me, and if they do, well….I’ll do something. Sides, I need some material for some new curtains.” Seeing the look in her husband’s face, “Don’t you fret none, Otis! I’ll stop at the C bar C and see Dorta. She could use some female comp’ny. I’ll take some old horses and wear my old dress and take the old buckboard.”

“Ella, I’d feel better if you had one of the boys along.”

“You know as well as I do that someone for sure is bound to recognize the boys. They’ll be looking for the men folks, but the womenfolk they won’t pay no attention to. Now, Otis, it’s settled. I’ll go tomorrow. Drink your coffee.”

Married this many years to Ella, Otis knew there was no reason to try and argue with her. Besides, he knew his wife could handle most situations as well as a man – maybe better.

Otis winked at his wife. Parson grinned.

Chapter 24

As they spoke, several miles away Bill Henry was riding by moonlight. After working on the fenceline, he had been on the trail to home and decided to take a side trip to the bluff west of the ranch. It was an area rippled with gullies and near the North Fork. He knew the daylight was not long enough to look seriously, but he wanted to scout and see if anything obvious showed itself. Besides, he often found a night ride to be a time when thoughts came to him that were often chased away in the daylight by the constant busyness of life. It was different at night.

Now, as he rode silently, he listened to the night and thought of all the times before he'd gone East, when he had ridden in this same manner, home by moonlight or even less. There had been good times back then, though it seemed he had reached a point where he hadn't seen the good, got frustrated with the day to day, and then had left. Perhaps it was the romance of youth; perhaps just not having anything to compare his life to; perhaps rebellion against a life that he was expected to follow without question. It was what it was, he thought. No sense in trying to figure out why he did what he did. Too many people spent their lives reliving the past and never got around to living in the present.

Coming through some boulders in the trail, Bill pulled up. Some sense told him he was not alone. He slowly reached down and rubbed his horse, whispering soothingly. He sat quietly. He knew that often the greenhorn of the west didn't wait long enough, and this could have fatal results. Everything in him said someone was there, just beyond the boulders. A slight noise off to the left of the trail, his mind worked rapidly – it was a ruse, and he spun quickly to his right, drawing as he turned. His eyes burrowed into the darkness. He almost jumped out of his saddle when he heard a voice behind him.

"Don't make no sudden moves. You're the Henry boy what left and comed back."

Bill made no move, but responded. "Yes, I am. Who are you?"

"They call me Dooley in these parts. I got no gun on you, but didn't want you to risk a shot. I'm friendly. Go ahead and turn around."

Bill reined his horse around, and saw, a

dozen feet away, that ghastly apparition he'd seen in town.

"I heard you wandered these hills."

"I do, and I know everything what's going on. I stopped you cause you'se a man what thinks and wonders what's a goin' on. There's something you need to see.

"So you're saying I should just up and follow you?"

"Yup, leave your horse over yonder and follow me." With that he turned and headed off towards the trees. Bill swiftly tied his horse and shucked his Winchester, following Dooley. For a seemingly crazy old man, this Dooley seemed self-assured in the woods, making very little noise and weaving skillfully through the branches.

He didn't lead far before he stopped, put a quieting finger before his lips and led Bill to the brow of the hill. Following Dooley's lead, he got to his knees and crawled the last few feet, to bring their eyes over the top.

Down, below, approximately 200 yards away, was a fire and a group of 15-20 men. They were eating and bantering. They were as tough a bunch as Bill had ever seen. Bill recognized Nose and a couple others from town. They were close enough to hear the voices, but too far away to make out what was being said. They watched for almost an hour before slipping back down the hill to their horses.

Whispering, Bill turned to the apparition at

his side. "How long they been there, Dooley?"

"Off'n'on for several days. Tonight's the biggest passel yet. Like they's a'waitin' fer someone."

Bill looked at Dooley. He was as amazed at Dooley's presence as well as the group of men over the hill.

"Where are their horses?"

"To the west, behint them trees." Dooley looked towards him in the dark. Bill could see his smile.

"Think you could distract them a mite, Dooley, something natural sounding while I let loose the horses?"

"'Spect so…you hear a catamount an' you can figure these eastern boys will wet their britches."

"Give me some time to get in place."

Bill worked his way carefully down the hill and around behind the trees. He was being extra careful not to break any twigs, staring often at the ground in front of him before moving ahead. There was just enough waning moonlight to see darker shadows to step around. Working up behind the trees he sensed, rather than heard, a guard. He heard a yawn, allowing him to place the man. Was there another? He waited, listened and neither saw nor heard evidence of another man. He kept the guard placed in his mind as he waited for Dooley. He could hear the men talking round the fire.

Suddenly the night was shattered by the

wailing cry of a mountain lion. Very natural, very loud, very close. All voices stopped momentarily. The guard turned towards the fire, Bill stepped forward and knocked him out with his gun butt, then crouched and waited a moment. The men were starting to speak nervously, and he could picture them all looking the other way towards the sound. The sound came again, further on.

Bill slipped in and cut the picket ropes. Not able to resist a little extra, since he knew the men were preoccupied with Dooley's catamount, he slipped his knife under several saddles and almost severed the cinch on the off side. Should make for some trick riding, he thought to himself.

The horses, crazed themselves by the sound, ran off in the dark. One man gave the alarm, but then the catamount wailed again and the horses picked up speed and disappeared. Bill hurriedly made his way back to where he left Dooley, not worrying about the sticks as the men were making quite a ruckus.

He startled as Dooley suddenly spoke from just a few feet away.

"Better be movin.'" How did such a big man move so quietly?

They rode together down the trail for a time, then pulled off to the side where they could see both directions.

"Dooley, you got an idea what they're up to?"

"Nope, not bezactly. They'se a passel of strange ones around, though. Most of them seems eastern, with them differn't hats. I ain't takin' kindly to how many of the rogues is runnin' in the hills. I spect they's tryin' to hornswoggle folks hereabouts like they done in Royton.

Chapter 25

He was up early in the morning, as he wanted to get some strays rounded up that he had seen in his riding. He loved the peace of the mornings, especially when the birds began to sing and the squirrels and other animals started their days.

It was so different out here, he realized. In Boston, you didn't see the animals. Oh, there were a few, but not in the numbers one saw in the West. Out here, it was a virtual cacophony of sound. The occasional sound of the wind in the branches added a beauty that he just couldn't get enough of. He had been to symphonies in the finest theaters, from some of the greatest composers in the world, but none compared to the music of nature, and the quiet peace that he felt in his soul when he was in the hills. Even the events of late could not disrupt this feeling.

When he returned to the ranch mid morning, he went for a cup of coffee.

"Morning, Ma!" He hollered. No answer. She must be outside.

Pa came in. "Heard you yell. Ma's not here. Gone to Royton."

"Royton? That's where there's been trouble."

"You came in late last night, didn't get to see you. Parson was here. There's been another death. Red Bowen over to the Cummings place. Gut shot by some riders up to one of the line cabins. Parson and I decided to send your ma out as a scout." He grinned. "She was as excited as a she-coon in a crawdad hole."

"Pa, that's too rough of a group for her to face alone."

"We thought of that, son. She's riding the old wagon, old horses and old clothes. Nothin' to stand out. Just get the lay of the land. She'll be back by sunset. There's still decency in the west – she's a woman and she'll be ok."

"Pa, these men are ruthless." He then explained the group he and Dooley had seen the night before, and what they had done. Otis Henry grinned at the telling.

"Son, you ain't forgotten some things. One of the ways of battle is to keep the enemy guessing. Let them be so lookin' out in all directions that they can't concentrate in any direction in particular. Then hit 'em in the spot of your choosing.

“Pa, I’m concerned about ma.”

“Son, your ma is Ella Henry. They may be tough, but your ma’s no fool and she’s fought worse than that crowd can muster. I remember the time she had a coon treed and money was tight. Well, your ma shinnied up that tree with an Arkansas toothpick and fetched that she-coon with nary a scratch. Big enough to feed us nigh on to a week. Son, your ma can handle herself. She’s the best scout we could send

Ella Henry also liked the sounds of the morning. She had a hard time hearing them, though, over the sounds of the creaky wagon. Blast this old thing, she thought. Why hadn’t Otis greased the wheels?

At least she could watch the sunrise. Beautiful this morning, with deep streaks of crimson and the blue looking radiant. She always told people, if they didn’t believe in God just look at the sunrise and sunset. Weren’t no better paint than the paint God used in the sky.

She was excited for the day. Not only was it a day away but it was a day that reminded her of the past, when they would send outriders and scouts across the ranch. She recalled the days of the Winchester held across the saddle, when pistols rode loose in the holster, and danger all around. She was glad for the changes, but there was something about the old wariness that kept a person sharp and tuned to their surroundings.

This ride and its importance gave her a sense of thrill she hadn't had for a long time.

She came armed, of course. She had a shotgun under the seat and a Colt in her handbag. She had used a shotgun many a time in the old days. It was a gun inspiring respect. Point it at most people and even the most belligerent became friendly mighty sudden. Men may risk a bullet from a colt, 'cause there's always a chance for a grazing shot, but a shotgun does no grazing – it plain tears a man in two. She hadn't told Otis, but she also had her derringer in the pocket of her dress. In her heart she really was ready if something happened.

She rode into Royton three hours after leaving the ranch.

A mite more crowded and grown up than she remembered, she quickly noted that there were quite a few scraggly-looking men lounging around. Some appeared western but several wore bowlers and clothes not common in the west. Eastern thugs, she thought to herself. As she watched one group of several men, a young lady walked by and the men only half-interestedly parted to let her go by. Then they gaped and catcalled. The young lady nervously walked on.

Ella thought to herself: Land a'Goshen! What's happened? Come to where no decent woman could walk the streets. In the old days, that kind of behavior would have resulted in a shooting!

She brought the wagon to the dry goods

store and the millinery. Climbing out, she realized suddenly that Homer Fitz, the proprietor, was there to help her down. He said loudly, "Careful, Mrs. Lane." She looked at him and met his eyes, which looked wary and pleading. For some reason he had not used her name. Better to play along.

"Thank you, Mr. Fitz. I wonder if you might fetch my bag for me?"

"Delighted to," he said.

As they went into the store, they passed through a couple of rough characters standing seemingly nonchalantly outside the store. They looked blandly at Ella as they went by.

Inside, she smelled the smells of the store that she so enjoyed. The coffee beans, the ladies soaps, the rope and leather and the oil of the guns. She had enjoyed these smells since she was a small child going into the store with her father. She was partly lost in her reverie, when Homer spoke up.

"Ella, what in tarnation are you doing here? It's not safe."

"I come to find out what's going on, Homer." She winked at him. "I'm sort of scouting." She grinned. Homer had been a friend for many years and could be trusted. "What's happened?"

Homer cautiously glanced toward the door. The men outside were joking with each other and facing the street.

"They've got us over a barrel, Ella. Came in

about 3 months ago, just sort of causing a little trouble. Next thing you know, they've got us all hornswoggled. Demanded payment to keep safe. Anybody tried to leave was beaten – beaten bad. We're trapped. Have to give money every week to be left alone. So far the women haven't been bothered, but I'm not sure how long that will last. These men are getting pretty daring – used to having their way. Bunch of no-accounts who never amounted to a hill of beans and now feeling high and mighty."

He grabbed a paper and pretended to write as one of the guards looked through the window. The man looked away, satisfied that it was just store business inside.

"I heard the blacksmith bought it."

"That's true, Ella. A finer man you never knew. He refused to pay. Lord have mercy – we're into a big problem here."

"Who's the boss?" As Homer opened his mouth to answer, the door opened and one of the thugs entered, immediately spitting a long stream of tobacco juice on the floor. Homer and Ella both looked.

"Can I help you?"

"Ain't seen this lady around. Finnegan wants to know where you's from, lady."

Ella looked forlorn. "I'm from in the hills down south. Just a little place, but I done lost my man and I come for some comfort from my friends before I head east. My young'uns tell me I got to come live with them. I know it's true, our little place never did pay, and now it's played hob with Buell and kilt him." She began to sob. The thug appeared uncomfortable with her tears.

"Well, don't stay too long. This town ain't the place for you to be." He turned and exited.

Ella turned to her shopkeeper friend. "Oh, I'm good, Homer! That lily-livered snake took it all!" She smiled and covered her mouth and started to snicker. Homer looked at her sharply, then to the door.

"Careful, Ella. The second one might not be fooled so easily."

"How come the town ain't fightin,' Homer? Seems like the passel of you could read them from the book."

"We're all scared stiff! Ryland Kirk up to the barber shop pulled his Spencer out and told them to get out of his shop. Someone grabbed him from behind and they drug him to the street and beat him beyond cruelty. He was all but dead, then they let his wife get him and drag him home, but they wouldn't allow no doctoring. It's been 3 weeks and he's still abed. Likely never be the same."

Ella was aghast. "Lord have mercy!"

"Everybody's just scared to make a move. And we're not able to be together enough to plan anything. They've got us cinched tight."

The door rang, and another couple came in. Homer changed. "Now, Mrs. Lane, I'm so sorry about your husband," and he led her to the back of the store. He whispered, “People are scared to talk. That couple are known to tell Finnegan anything they know. We need to get you out of here.”

“Homer, tell me who’s the boss.”

“Don’t know, but this Finnegan is his man and is meaner than a pack of rattlers. Rattlers will bite, but he takes pleasure in it and looks for the opportunities for it!” The other couple came around the corner. Homer continued, “It’s ok, Mrs. Lane, I know your kids will take care of you. Living back east is not all bad.”

“Thank you, Mr. Fitz. Your words have helped soothe my heart. How can I ever thank you. But I won’t be able to pay my bill?”

“That’s ok, Mrs. Lane. Just send what you can when you can.” He escorted her to the door.

The men at the door parted, but with reluctance and false deference. The action of cheap toughs. Ella Henry seethed inside, but kept the act going.

“Mr. Fitz, give my best to Elmira. I won’t forget you.” She winked at him as she took the reins.

Ella decided to take a loop around the town. She saw the men gathered in little groups. All seemed peaceful but there were no townsfolk walking. Just the strange men. The saloon was going strong, despite the early hour, and as she passed a couple drunken men stumbled into the street and leered at her. She felt her handbag and was comforted by the feel of the Colt. As she came back by the dry goods store, she saw the couple from in the store talking to a group of the men, and one turned and watched her with squinted eyes and started to come down off the steps, making as if to stop her. She made a point of looking only out of the corners of her eyes, pretending not to see, and dabbing her eyes with her handkerchief. The man stopped and the last she noticed he was back with the men.

Whew! That's a nasty situation, she thought to herself. The poor people bottled up and even some traitors in the midst.

Boss Carter liked to do the odd job himself. It satisfied something deep inside him. This was just a small job, eliminating a little man who walked around the corner at the wrong time and saw him speaking to one of his informants. Can't have witnesses for such things. Carter grabbed him so quick and wrung his neck before the man had time to cry out. The informer was wide-eyed and knew then, if he had any doubts, as to how his life and family were in the control of Carter. Carter looked at his informer by way of threat, glaring into the man's eyes and, seemingly satisfied at his silence, dismissed him with a rough wave of his hand, as if he was swatting at a fly.

Boss Carter dragged the body down the alley to the waterfront. He found some odds and ends of metal from the dock and stuffed them roughly into the man's clothing, giving it weight. He rolled the body over the edge and watched it flop into the water and sink to the bottom, somewhat fascinated by the twisting of limp and lifeless limbs.

Horace “Boss” Carter had always liked that which made other hearts squirm. The son of the village butcher, he was accustomed to working with knives and seeing blood and gore. Yet, there was something more than usual in his delight. Others had tended to stray away from him since he was a young child. He enjoyed torturing small animals and even the toughest boys around kept their distance after hearing him laugh at the squealing animals.

Others suspected his involvement, giving him sideways looks, when a few of the local pets were found missing, but it was when a local drunk was found dead and mutilated that fear arose. His father was approached by the town council and strongly urged to send his son away. George Carter had been scared of his son for years, recognizing that he was just not right in the head. Now he was faced with telling his son that he needed to leave. He did so, shaking while giving Horace $50 and a horse and saddle. He actually felt relieved with his son gone. Horace traveled north, winding up in Boston, where being in the wrong place at the right time brought him into contact with Hook Logan, the kingpin of the powerful underworld of Boston’s shipping and waterfront. One of Hook’s men had attempted to rob him and had underestimated the agility of Horace Carter. Caught, Carter bound and gagged him and had begun to systematically torture him, when he found himself surrounded by men with clubs. He prepared to lunge, but suddenly a man stepped forward from the group. It was his first meeting with Hook. Hook saw what he was doing, the coolness and efficiency of the man and hired him on the spot. Carter used him to climb the ladder. Within a year, Hook appointed Carter as Boss of a neighboring district. There was a cautious respect among the two of them, as even Carter, in all his coldness of heart, sensed a man who could also be cruel and cunning. Though it almost seemed that they bordered on friendship at times, the aloofness and aloneness that kept criminal masterminds alive prevented them being anything more than associates. And even Hook sensed the deep cruelty, defying even his own, that resided in Horace Carter's heart.

Over time, Hook found that he himself slowly gave ground to the astuteness of Carter, his cleverness and deal making punctuated by cruelty and ruthlessness and absolute disregard for life. One day one of his men referred to Carter as "Boss" and Hook knew it to be true. Hook knew the lay of the land and saw also the opportunity for power as the right hand of Carter. After all, there was less heat and more time to enjoy the fruits. So Hook deferred to Carter and assumed the role of right hand and the organization settled into a profitable and well-oiled existence. To Carter, Hook Logan was indeed special and there was a respected friendship there, yet in Carter's mind Hook was more like the friend one finds in a loyal dog. He gave him the scraps, took him for walks and occasionally cuffed him good, but still the loyal dog would wag his tail and do as he was told.

And yet, when Hook Logan went to prison, Carter had a moment of regret - almost hurt - but just for a moment. Then the reality of the loss of a right hand tool of the trade sunk in and all human feelings gave way to the loss to the organization and the need to rebuild and go on and replace Logan with no more thought than a man replacing a lost dog.

He had noticed Finnegan. Cold and fearless, content to have the power of a second in command. Finnegan was reliable and preferred not to have the headaches that fell to Boss Carter.

Now, Finnegan was in charge of the new business venture in Colorado territory. He enjoyed his power. With a fine corner room in the Hotel at Royton, his windows gave a fine view of the street. He could sit back from the window and smoke his cigarettes, drink his special bottles of eastern whiskey and watch the goings on. Outside his door was always a man to do his bidding.

Boss Carter, even from far away, knew that Finnegan was skimming a bit extra off the top for himself. His eyebrows raised as he recalled himself doing the same from Logan. He enjoyed realizing that Finnegan didn't know that Carter was aware, that he also had his informants in his own camp. Let Finnegan think he was getting away with it! He really was, but only because Boss Carter allowed it. It gave Finnegan more of a sense of power over others, which would be needed later. As long a Finnegan didn't step over a line. If he did, well then…

Chapter 26

Out of town a mile or so, she came around a bend to see a man sitting in the trail. He was reasonably tall, dressed as the average cowhand. He had a yellow bandana around his neck. She had no time to grab the shotgun, but reached into her handbag.

"Ma'am, I'm friendly – no need for the gun. There's a pack of men coming up the road to take you back to town. We've got to unhook the team quick and get you mounted and take off over the hill."

"Who are you? How do I know you're telling the truth?

He raised his hat, and she saw his face. She knew men and she could see he was genuine.

"Name's Stacker. I know your son, Bill"

She hurriedly dismounted, grabbing the

shotgun and her handbag. The stranger unhooked one of the team and quickly rigged the other horse to pull solo. Then he slapped the horse and yelled, sending it running up the road with the wagon.

"We'll let them follow the wagon a bit further, better chance to put some distance between us. Here, Mrs. Henry, you take my horse."

"Sonny, I don't know who you are, and I don't know your horse, but I can tell you I will ride my Bessie bareback and will accept no arguments. I appreciate what you're doing, and I am trusting you as a gentleman." She accepted his help in mounting. He had rigged a hackamore on the horse.

"Ok, ma'am, off we go." He led her behind some brush and back down a short canyon before they heard the sound of pounding hooves. Then they started up the hill, gradually drawing away from the trail. Finding another game trail, they went quickly over the ridge. She kept her shotgun over the saddle and never let this stranger get beside her. They stopped for a moment.

"Young fella, who are you and how do you know me? I ain't takin' to running off with strangers. Don't get me wrong, cause I appreciate what you're doin,' but I need some answers."

"Mrs. Henry, you'll have to trust me."

"I ain't never heard Bill mention your

name."

"I said I know your son; I didn't say he knew me."

"Son, you make about as much sense as cabbage in a coffeepot."

"That's all you need to know for now. Right now we got to get you home in one piece."

After riding for an hour, the man called Stacker pulled up behind some trees and looked down their back trail. There was dust. They were being followed. Ella saw it, too, and realized they had a rough road ahead. Bessie was a good horse, but not the swiftest. Those men likely had faster horses. She saw Stacker looking at the dust through a telescope. She'd only seen one other in her time.

"Couldn't tell for sure, but looks like five, six riders."

Stacker led her over various outcroppings, doubled back a few times, but always moving quickly. Bessie was an old horse, but she was game and seemed to enjoy the free riding. Of course, Ella Henry did not amount to much of a load. After a couple hours, Stacker slowed again pulling up in a copse of trees overlooking the ridge.

There was no sign of anyone on their trail, but Ella noticed Stacker looking ahead.

"Think they're up there?"

"I've got my suspicions. If we run into anyone, you get down and let me do the shootin."

"Young Man, I fought beside Otis Henry many times. I've shot Indians and I've shot rustlers and occasional no-account varmints, both two and four legged. I can shoot straight and I can make it count. I ain't in the habit of actin' a'feared. And this is my own shotgun - I ain't afraid of what it does."

"Ma'am, I don't want to see you hurt."

"I've seen my own blood more than once. I'm still here, and I'll do my share."

Stacker couldn't help but grin. "You'll do to ride the river with, ma'am. How many weapons you carryin'?"

"The Colt, the scattergun and a hideout. I got extra shells for the scattergun."

They rode for another mile, and suddenly Stacker put his finger to his lips as they pulled up. Dropping back beside Ella Henry, he whispered, "Trail narrows up ahead. I've got a feelin' about this. Anybody that jumps out will be worth shootin.' Ma'am, I'd use the scattergun first."

Ella Henry had slung her handbag over her shoulders, and the opening with the Colt was ready to her hand. The shotgun was a short barrel and she held it in her hands along with the hackamore. With a nod at Stacker that she was ready, they moved on down the trail. They had gone no more than 300 yards when 4 men sat in the trail, guns at the ready.

"You all hold up. Who are you, mister?"

"What's it to you?" Stacker knew he had

Ella behind him, and he was concerned with her safety should the lead fly. He needed to stall for time, hoping to get the men off balance.

"Mister, why don't you just ease that hogleg back in its holster or we'll just set the lead flying in your direction. We spent the past few hours tryin' to find this old lady and we're takin' her to town."

Ella whispered, "move aside." Stacker sidled over to the right, acting as if his horse was jittery. The men's eyes were on Stacker. They hadn't paid much mind to the older lady.

"You got no respect for a woman?" Ella hollered. The men's eyes turned suddenly to her and she let go with one barrel after the other. Three men fell and Stacker shot and winged the fourth as he barreled into the trees. Stacker and Ella Henry glanced quickly around. Ella wasted no time, but replaced the shells in her shotgun.

One man lay unmoving, with a buckshot blast dead center. Ella had seen it before, but usually it had been an Indian running towards her. It was not a pretty site. One other was badly injured, the other superficial.

"Suppose that's it?" she asked.

"Likely, but if not they got something to think about. Good shootin,' ma'am." They ran their horses over the next hill, guns ready again, but there was nobody. They slowed to a walk.

"Ma'am. You were right smooth back there. You done rode the river before."

"Thank you. Felt good. Been a few years

since we had to deal with anything like this. Sort of makes me feel young again."

An hour later, still daylight, they met Otis, Bill and Matt with Gard and Sim on the trail at the edge of the home meadow. They said the wagon had come in and they were heading to look for her. Otis smiled at his wife and asked if she was ok. He looked at the unfamiliar rider.

"I'm fine, Otis. Might have been a tad bit different if Stacker here hadn't come along."

"Stacker, is it? Not familiar to me. But I thank you for what you done. I owe you."

"You don't owe me anything, Mr. Henry. It's just what a man does."

"You have a family?" Ella asked.

"No, ma'am."

Ella spoke up, "You'll have dinner with us and stay the night." It was more of a statement than a question. Stacker smiled.

"Be my pleasure, ma'am."

Later, after dinner, talking around the table, Ella looked hard at Stacker. "How come you know my son but he don't know you?"

Stacker paused, searching for the right words. He had to come to a decision. Finally, just when the others had begun to wonder, he looked at Bill. "I work for a man named Russell Long."

Bill, though used to the surprises of the courtroom, was startled. Russell Long was his law partner.

Ella Looked at her son, having seen the reaction. “Bill?”

“Russell Long is my law partner back in Boston.” He just sat looking at Stacker.

Stacker finally grinned and spoke. “Long hired me to hang back and sort of look out for you. I sensed you were staying around today, and then I saw your ma head out towards Royton in the old rig. I figured I’d just sort of mosey over that way. I been checking things around. I ‘spect it’s not safe to show my face there again.”

“You can stay here at the ranch.”

“I’d rather not. You all know who I am, but there’s many that don’t. I’d like to stay off the known trails, if you know what I mean. I sort of get used to stayin’ off in the hills, watching and waiting. Just know that I will be there.”

“Do you know who’s behind these happenings of late?”

“There’s a man on the scene named Finnegan. I suspect only he knows who’s behind this. They refer to the man behind it all as “the Boss.”

So, Bill thought, they had a boss back East. Who he was is unknown. Finnegan. Bill worked through his memory. The name was familiar, but also common among the Irish.

Stacker added, “A lot of the men are from the east. Derby’s and eastern style clothes. Not sure what the connection is, if any. So many of the men out here are from back east. This group seems new to the territory. I suspect a syndicate from the east."

Chapter 27

The next few days found Bill riding the further reaches of the ranch. He and one of the hands, a fella named Brewster, walked their horses down a branch and to the edge of the rim where Bill knew of an old trail he'd found as a kid. It was hidden and a mite rough, but it used to get a rider and horse to the rim.

As they turned off into a clump of brush and found the trail, Brewster grinned through his mustache, revealing crooked, tobacco-stained teeth. Laugh lines coursed his face. Brew, as he was often called, was known to laugh easily and had brought a lot of needed fun to the hands in the 7 years he had ridden for the Henry's.

"Ain't never had no idea this was here. Handy thing to know."

"Found it when I was a kid, and sort of kept it under my hat, thinking the same thing."

The trail was rough and not as clear as years ago, but an hour or so of careful riding brought them to the rim, with a vista that took both riders' breath away. The valley stretched as far as the eye could see, with mountains in three directions fading into different hues as they receded in the distance.

Brewster commented, "One of the things I like about this ranch, aside from your ma's cookin', is all the places like this, where I can look out over all creation. Times I think about movin' on, but then I see something like this."

Bill grinned inside. Ma's cooking was sure and steady and guaranteed to satisfy a working man's appetite. Many a bedroll cowboy stayed at a ranch for just a season or two before moving on, seemingly growing no moss under their saddles. Unable to settle, or something deep within them always wanting to see over the next hill, they spent their lives moving and restless, until they suddenly grew old, and sought a place to live out the rest of their years.

The Henry's not only fed well, but also paid better than the average wage, and made the hands a part of their lives. That was ma's doing, as she tended to mother any hand that came down the trail and, amazingly, she got away with it even with the most independent riders. There had been several through the years who stopped and just never seemed to leave. They became part of something they had not experienced – a family. It bred intense loyalty.

Bill Henry demanded that each work hard for the ranch and not have any problems with Tetch and Sim being former slaves making the same wage. Any problems with either of the former slaves was a guaranteed invitation to leave the ranch. The group that stayed had a deep bond as the Henry's invited loyalty

Of course, it helped that the Henry boys were all decent, firm and expecting a days work for a day's wage. They were neither cruel nor overbearing, and worked side by side with the hands on even the most menial jobs, winning with loyalty what others only held by demands. A Henry son never shirked from building fence, seen as greenhorn work on many ranches, or mucking out stalls.

In fact, Bill grinned inside again, he had been living in high society for so long, with his needs and whims met with a few dollars or the ringing of a bell, that when Pa suggested he muck out a couple stalls his first morning out, Bill was at first taken aback. Pa must have known his son needed to come down a notch. Nothing like horse muck on your face and hands to take away any vestige of Boston high society!

"I think this was part of the reason the folks settled here. Ma would not have tolerated a place with no beauty. Pa had to honor that in Ma, but I think pa liked it as much as she did."

As they rode on along the rim, they sat

silently, riding with only the thoughts that riding men have, for it is a time of musing, pondering and occasional dozing. Today they kept their eyes moving as they checked things out in the farther reaches of the ranch.

Bill had had a conversation earlier that morning with his pa about the strange doings in the country. Word had spread that some of the other ranchers had been pressured for money from some new outfit. Otis had been concerned, as he always was, about his "neighbors" as he called them. Bill knew that underlying this was a concern for when such a group might approach the Henry ranch. Bull Henry would never give in, and wanted to get any information he could on the situation.

Brewster had ridden on ahead, and suddenly stopped and dismounted. Bill rode up and could see tracks leading to and from the rim. He rode to the rim and looked out. Over to the west was a clear view of the ranch in the distance, to the right the main trail to the southwest, towards Royton and Carlsville.

Brew straightened up, "Looks like 5-6 riders here at times. Often just one. Looks like they're watching or waiting. Wonder what for?" As a seasoned hand, he knew that this was not a good thing. His smiling features showed concern.

Bill looked at the rim where various men had been sitting. Based on the evidence: worn grass, cigarette butts and even a bottle, the men had been here for extended times. Two items interested him, and may not have been noticed by someone else, but his well-tuned mind picked up on them: One man here had been well-paid, as evidenced by half-smoked cigarettes in one small area. No average cowhand would waste tobacco. The other item was the bottle. It had a subtly different shape to it that Bill recognized from back east. It was not a bottle that he had seen out here. It was the sort of whiskey that was preferred by someone, more expensive than the usual, and certainly nothing locally available. It showed no wear and tear of a long-carried bottle, so likely had been shipped from a distance, perhaps from East somewhere. The lack of wear and tear could indicate a ready supply. It was off to the side from the cigarettes, as if tossed aside by a right-handed man.

Someone here had come from the East and was used to some of the finer touches, with enough supply not to be concerned with throwing away half-smoked cigarettes.

"Let's track them a ways and see where the trail leads," Bill said.

As they rode, both men alternated between watching the trail and watching ahead and in the distance. They need not have said anything, it was just the way of tracking, and they settled into a pattern of one of them watching the surroundings while the other watched the trail and looked for anything that might tell them something more.

At one point they found where the group had

dismounted in a copse of trees and built a fire to make coffee. Nearby was another, more common bottle of the rotgut, cheap saloon whiskey of the seamier side of life. There was still a mite in the bottle, indicating someone pretty slathered, as no self-respecting cowhand or ruffian would waste a drop.

Again the half-smoked cigarettes also. He suspected the cigarettes and the finer whiskey belonged to the same man, who must be the leader, as in this location he had obviously sat off to the side, on a rock some distance from the others. Men tended to cluster together in these situations, and aloofness was not tolerated, unless that man were dangerous and the others avoided confronting him.

So, Bill mused, we had a man who was the obvious leader, likely feared by the others, who drank a more refined whiskey, obtaining it who knows where, and smoking his cigarettes only halfway. The leader was likely from the East. He looked more closely around the rock and saw well-defined boot tracks, not trail-worn. So the rider had cash in his pocket, or had just gotten new boots. Likely the former, he thought.

Finnegan?

"Ground still warm," Brew said, kneeling by the fire. "Three or four hours likely, if'n they left good coals going when they left. Otherwise..." He stood and looked around at the hills around them, "...they might be closer"

Bill loosened his pistol as he also looked

around.

"Might be waiting for us, Bill."

"Could be. Let's ride on, but sit loose in the saddle."

They rode on, especially alert for anything, only keeping half an eye on the trail, natural instincts kicking in that came from deep within. Survival instincts

The rider rode along the familiar trail, seeing the same things he'd seen for many years, making his weekly ride to New Haven. It was a pattern of his, like clockwork. He smiled and stretched in the saddle. He was no spring chicken any more. He had been concerned lately, what with all the going's on around. He had been riding the other day and saw a group of horsemen headed back from Otis Henry's direction. They seemed eager to stay out of sight, working their way through the trees. He had set his horse quietly and watched, knowing that it was usually movement that caught the eye. Sometimes a man could be sitting in the open, blending partly with his surroundings and never be seen. But if that same person made a sharp move all eyes would be drawn.

Some others had shown up a few days earlier at his home place, and spoke of needing money to keep him safe. Art Tucker happened to have seen them coming and was holding an ancient 8-gauge double barrel shotgun. As they pulled up to his house he just naturally pointed it in their direction. He had told them in no uncertain terms that he was not open to their proposition and they left with barely veiled threats.

He was going to go to town, then swing by Otis Henry's place. They had both been in the war and knew each other.

As he came over a rise and down the hill he was crossing a small meadow when there was a loud shot and Art Tucker dropped to the ground, dead before he hit.

Chapter 28

He came in to town like many others, astride a horse and with the marks of a long trail behind.

He was a man known to few, yet known to so many. He had been on this trail before, known by his whispered name, yet none knew who he was if they stood next to him. He preferred to be thought just a traveling cowhand.

Vernon Grantler never quite understood why he chose the profession of killing. It was something he had seemed to enjoy since his earliest recollections. No life ever seemed sacred to him, and pulling legs off insects as a small child seemed natural enough for many, but Vern took it a step further, torturing the insect with a sense of fascination. As he grew into his teen years his stepfather, whom he had no use for, grew sick and, one day, when his mother had to go to town, Vern took arsenic from the barn and fed it to his stepfather as a hot tea. When the man gagged, Vern forced the rest down the sick man's throat. By the time his mother returned, his stepfather was dead and Vern was miles down the road.

Somewhere outside Phoenix he was camped and a stranger stopped for the night. Vern had a hunch and feigned sleep. As the man rifled Vern's saddlebags, the knife slipped so easily between his ribs that Vern twisted it to see the look on the man's face. After that, somewhere he heard of some rancher wanting a nester killed and it was so easy.

Vern was cold and unfeeling - and efficient. It was a job to him, and his hapless victims, well, it was like stepping on bugs - there would always be more, so why worry about one. Besides, he needed the money. Along the way, he became proficient with a rifle – a rifle he took off a horse he'd found wandering in a meadow. It was obvious that the horse had been riderless for a time, but a little tracking took Vern to a body riddled with holes and not a pretty sight in the summer heat. The sign told the story....a hired killer who pushed his luck a bit too far and had been surrounded by a posse. For whatever reason the horse had been separated from its rider and the fine rifle was a part of the deal. The artwork and workmanship was stunning. A special scope was carried in the saddlebags. He practiced in the mountains and soon used it as a tool in many situations.

He didn't live a lavish lifestyle. He wore no fancy clothes. He looked like every drifting cowhand, except for his cigars. He had always wondered about them as a kid, liking the smell and the sense of style, but never made it a habit until one of his "jobs" turned out to be a fancy-dressed gentleman and when he was checking the body for valuables he found a large packet of cigars. He found the habit to his liking so always picked up a supply wherever he could. It was the one pleasure he afforded himself. More than once a cowhand at a small-town bar looked at him when he lit up a fancy cigar in a place that generally tended to a poke and papers and where fancy cigars brought questioning looks. A "get out of my face" look usually stopped all looks and any budding inquiry. Those that persisted in questioning, well, there were gullies and boardwalks where bodies would not be found for a few days until the smell and the carrion revealed something was amiss. By then he was far away.

He wasn't poor and he wasn't rich. He had a bit tucked away in an account in a bank back east. He'd stop now and then and wire money back; never big amounts, in order to avoid the scrutiny. He lived simply...but there were always the cigars.

He smiled and puffed contentedly.

He had received a notice at a dive in Topeka

that someone he had done business with before needed his services again. Repeat customers always helped. The packet contained names and the ever-necessary cash, which he counted and tucked into his shirt pocket.

The first man was easy.

He wondered what this second man was like. What did he do for a living, what did he do to offend someone such that he, Vern, was hired to kill him. He also wondered whether he would whimper when he died.

He went to Tagget's saloon and let a room, stashed his gear, went downstairs and ordered a meal and a bottle. The next part of his job was to watch and wait.

He lit a cigar…

After a couple of hours Bill and Brewster reached a fork in the trail where the main party had gone down the finger trail to Royton. The dandy of the bunch had taken the other trail….toward New Haven. Or some place in between. Bill suspected he was heading for the once-peaceful town.

"Nothing 'tween here and Royton," Brew said. "I 'spect that's where they're headed. Heard of doing's down thataway."

"You're right. But I'm wondering about this other rider. He's the leader of the bunch." Bill related his thoughts to Brew about the evidence. Brew looked at him and grinned.

"Have mercy! You pick up on a lot. I'da

never put all that together. So you think this man ain't the usual hired man?"

"Nope." He looked down both trails, empty as far as the eye could see. "We know where that group is headed. I'm thinking we might meander to New Haven and look at the lay of the land."

"I reckon. Been a couple weeks since I been to town. Marge's pie sounds good," he ventured. "Not that it holds a candle to your ma's."

Bill grinned, despite the moment. It seemed the better part of the men in the saddle in this part of the country had a crush on Marge. The quickest way to a man's heart is through his stomach, he said to himself as they turned toward town.

Riding into town, Bill paused. Grinning, he told Brewster, "Want a drink first, or straight to Marge's?"

"Looks like a good crowd at Marge's. 'Spect we should wait till it's a mite more quiet."

Chapter 29

Dismounting in front of the saloon, they both paused to give their horses a drink, noticing the brand on the nearby horses. Triple-C. The new outfit from near Royton. Giving each other a knowing look, they slapped some of the dust off their clothes and pushed through the batwings. Looking around, they saw the saloon was pretty slim on customers. They stood to the bar and ordered whiskeys. Turning, they noted a man at a table in a far corner, facing the room. A table to one side was filled with strangers. Their clothes were eastern, and the men rough looking. Must be Triple-C. One of then, being well into his bottle and catching Bill's gaze, stood up. They were settled in, as if they had been here a while.

"What is it y'be lookin' at, cowboy?" His Irish brogue was derogatory. Bill turned back to the bar and whispered to Brew, "trouble coming. I'll handle it – you keep it even."

Both heard the chair slide back roughly from the table. They continued to nurse their drinks as unsteady footsteps approached.

"I be talkin' to ya, feller."

Both men turned from the bar and looked into the eyes of the Irishman. They saw the glazed eyes. He was a man used to getting his own way, for he was muscular, with the scarred knuckles and broken nose of a fighter. The table had silenced as all the men turned to watch. Chuckling was heard.

"Is there somethin' aboot me looks y'don't like?"

Bill had learned over the years the best way to stop trouble was to start before the other side was ready. He knew where the conversation and the drink were headed, so he almost casually straight-armed the Irishman in the throat. The man went down, clawing at his throat and gasping for breath. The other men stood suddenly. Instantly, Bill's gun was in his hand and the men sat back down.

"Finnegan won't like this, mister."

"You can tell Finnegan I don't go for lack of manners. Had a long hard day and just came in for a drink to wash down the dust. I want to have my drink in peace. This is New Haven, and your boss is not in charge."

One man grinned. "He will be afore long. Who might y'be, stranger?"

"I believe you are the stranger here, mister. As for my name, maybe I'll just leave you pondering on that."

"Mister," He motioned for the men to stand. They started to spread out. "I think we be needin' to show ya who's who around here." He began to advance, pulling his coat away to reveal a pistol in a shoulder rig.

"Whatever your name is, you make a move towards that gun and you'll be meeting your maker before the sun goes down."

"Y'can't be gettin' us all."

"No, but you're the first."

"Y'act like y'be used to wearin' pretty important boots, mister. I think we's gonna be takin' 'em off ya."

The wings slammed open to the side of the men. To a man, they all shifted their eyes to the door. Bill did no such thing, knowing he'd find out soon enough who was there. Besides, he had heard Brewster pull iron and knew he had his back. It's never good to turn from a current threat.

It was Walt Larrimore. Bill eased when he heard the voice.

"Boys, what on earth is goin' on here?" He glanced briefly at Bill, saw the intensity and faced the Irish toughs. "You boys causin' grief?"

"No, sir, sheriff. Not a'tall. Just a mite of a

misunderstandin'."

"Then I think it's time you all went home, or wherever you're restin' your heads. We got no time for this here mess. Now…put the guns away! They'll be no fightin' here in my town."

"Me thinks they's gonna be some changes," said the man in front, followed by grunts and nods by the others.

"Not tonight. Now, since you don't seem to hear too well, instead of puttin' the guns away, let's just say you drop 'em? He lifted his shotgun and pointed vaguely in the men's direction. To even the simplest of minds, a double barreled shotgun pointed in a particular direction brings instant obedience. Yet, despite the fear registering in their faces, they looked to their front man.

"Finnegan ain't going t' like this, sheriff."

"You tell this Finnegan to keep a rein on his men and quit disturbin' the peace of my town." His aim centered on the leader. "Now, do I have to say it again, or do you'all need to spend a night behind bars?"

The men stared at the twin barrels and slowly dropped their guns to the floor.

At that moment the batwings swung again and a man entered. He was dusty, but dressed with eastern styling, with a derby hat. He was not a muscular man, but there was a presence in his piercing eyes and manner. He had a pinched face and narrow nose and the kind of ear that caused observers to double-take, because they stuck out almost straight from his head, giving the appearance of cupped hands where there were none. He had a carefully-groomed mustache. He paused after he entered.

"Sheriff, is there some sort of problem?"

Walt looked at the man. "Who are you?"

"Name's Finnegan."

"You know these men?"

"They are in my employ."

"Well, we don't take kindly to rudeness here in these parts. We expect respect and will not be pushed around by every wannabe tough. These men seem to think they have some special privileges."

Bill glanced down and saw the man wore almost new boots, covered with trail dust. Crisp, sharp heels.

Finnegan looked coldly at the sheriff and chuckled. He took a few moments to light a cigarette, puff a few times, then removed it and gestured around. "Well, there have been changes of late in this country. Seems like the usual order of things is changing…or so I've heard."

"Lay your cards on the table, Mister."

"I've noticed that it's been getting rather dangerous in these parts lately. A rough element appears to be gaining a foothold and, well, it's been a bit distressing. Perhaps you need some select men around to help keep the rougher element at bay. I would strongly recommend it. We have a hundred men and more on the way. We can make sure you stay safe without any problem. I believe out here you would call that being neighborly. Of course, there would be a financial understanding." His eyes glinted as he replaced the cigarette and puffed.

"I recommend you get on your horses and leave town."

"As you wish, sheriff. But remember I made the offer. I absolutely cannot guarantee safety without an understanding."

Bill spoke, "Watch your horses, they can be hard to catch if they get loose in this country."

Finnegan glanced sharply at Bill. His eyes squinted. Then he turned to the door. Gesturing with his hand, he said, "Be in touch."

The men filed grimly out the door, the looks from their eyes showing they had lost this battle, but were far from beaten. The last two picked up the fallen man and hauled him out. Walt knew he would see them again. He followed them out the door and watched as they mounted and rode out of town. He turned and walked back through the batwings, where Bill and the Brewster stood finishing their drinks.

"What just happened, Bill?"

"Don't know, but that trouble down south seems to be spreadin', and my hunch says they are part of it."

"That's just a small part of the day's problems, Bill. Couple hands rode in about an hour ago with Art Tucker over the saddle. Single high caliber through the chest. Nasty hole. They found him out by the Royton trail, likely a'headin' this way. Art always came in about this time every week, have a drink and some conversation, then head back to the ranch." His voice was saddened.

Art Tucker. Hadn't been here as long as Otis Henry, but not much less, and very respected. Kept mostly to himself, but made his weekly forays into town. No kids, but a prime ranch along the river.

"Any motive that you know, Walt?"

"Not sure, but Art told me he'd been threatened and they wanted protection money. Of course, he told them what they could do with that idea. Bud never would back down to nobody."

"High powered rifle?"

"Appears to be, Bill. Like a professional job."

"Something big is going on, Walt. First Royton, then some of the outlying ranches and crossroads and now spreading. It's all connected somehow, and I think Art's killing is a part of it all."

"Bill, what was that about the horses?"

"Haven't had a chance to tell you. Me and a friend found a camp of the toughs up in the hills. Their horses got loose."

"I see…." He looked at Bill with a half smile.

Listening in the corner, Vern Grantler showed a hint of a smile as he tossed his drink.

Chapter 30

Later, riding home with Brewster, they were both pretty silent at first.

"This don't make sense, Bill. Confound it all, this was a peaceful place to live and pretty much without trouble. Oh, the occasional missing beef, a brawl now and again. Now this, and it seems more than just normal bad. Art Tucker was a good man! I 'member when we was trying to make it through to Box Elder canyon a few months back for a wedding and we stopped and Art switched us off horses so's we could keep running and make the wedding. A bit on the rugged side, but a heart of kindness. Who woulda wanted him dead?

"I don't know," Bill mused. "but things are

serious now, and we can't ignore it. I can't figure it yet, but something is nagging at my mind – some clue, something that is right in front of us."

They rode the rest of the way in silence.

Boss sat at his desk, chewing on the butt of a long unlit cigar. Even Boss Carter had times of relaxation - it's just that they were rare. He was pondering his next move.

Why is it there had to be laws? Why not just survival of the fittest - me? The world would be a lot better off with the strong and powerful telling the weak what to do. The weak ruin a country just as they do an army.

Boss Carter remembered the war, remembered other strong men losing their lives due to the weakness of others. The weak ones up and running from the battle, leaving the strong to perish through sheer lack of support. What a waste. He had vowed never again to be subject to weak men or weakness within himself.

So he'd come east - Boston - after the war and built an empire. The strong ruling the weak. It'd been years now. His strength had been almost undisputed. He ran whiskey, he ran guns, and he had a hand - a big hand - in almost every vice in a hundred mile range. Those who defied him or denied him found themselves floating face down in the river or just never being seen again. Now, virtually every order he gave was followed without question and it had not been necessary to kill as much...yet he would not shy from it if it were needed. He would not be defied.

Yet, in recent months there'd been new laws, always encroaching on his empire. Too much law. He didn't need the law - what he SAID was law. Those who disobeyed rarely lived for a second chance.

The sniveling idiot who watched the Henry place. Why did he let him live? Was he going soft? No….he just had his usual second sense that the poor excuse for a man might be useful yet. If he failed again...well...the harbor'd be shallower in one more spot.

He despised weakness. In fact, he preyed on it. And he'd found new hunting grounds. The west. Colorado. Not so full of laws. The strong man still ruled in the west. He'd explored the idea carefully, and found a little intimidation brought a steady income and a new sense of power. Now to build a whole territory of intimidation and rule, and see the coffers fill. He admitted he did enjoy the fruits of his labors. The best of everything.

Someday he planned to plow his way to a position of respect. To become a mayor of a town and then governor. King of the range - his range.

And kill Bill Henry…and his family…and then live on the ranch like a conqueror.

One of the rare smiles lit his face.

There was a knock on the door.

"Come!"

It was Jonesy.

"What."

Jonesy walked to the desk and set the telegram down. He then stepped back.

Boss Carter read the telegram and his eyes lit up.

"William Henry!"

Boss Carter was almost apoplectic over the news. His sworn enemy, who had brought the collapse of an entire wing of his empire. Found!

A year earlier, Boss Carter had decided to hedge his bets and plan for a new base of operations – a new empire. He had chosen the foothills of Colorado because it was still newly established, yet far enough along to have pickings. He had gone through elaborate pains to scout the area and to find the town of Royton as a base of operations. When William Henry had succeeded in court against Hook Logan, causing the damage to his empire here in Boston, he had made a decision. He would move west in another year and get away from the constant headache of the law. In the west there was very little law, with much opportunity to become the law himself, unquestioned – a king of the range.

Over the last few months he had sent Finnegan to do his bidding. It was difficult to build an empire, much less run one, from so far away. He knew he needed to be closing up shop here and tying up loose ends and heading to his new empire.

He needed to move soon, as he had been

informed that evidence was now being piled up to arrest him. His sources said it was still a couple months away, but why push it? So the time was now.

He was a man with no attachments to Boston…it was just a place to him, a place where he could have power and be feared. He loved being feared. So he would move west and do the same in a fresh new land. First, get the lay of the land….

Then, of all things, to finally locate his enemy who - by happenstance – was in the same area.

"Blast it!" He yelled at the top of his lungs. Jonesy cringed, knowing the results of Boss's rages. Boss turned deep red, struggling to control himself, lifting his bulk slowly out of his chair. He turned to glare with intense cruelty at Jonesy, who instinctively drew back. Suddenly a different look crossed Boss's face. The glaring redness disappeared and he sat slowly down, his gaze somewhere off in the distance.

"Jonesy! Did your man tell you if Henry had family out there?"

"Aye, sir. I believe it be his momma and papa."

A grin – not the average grin – but a greedy, ruthless, conniving grin lit the face of a man who rarely smiled.

The father, and mother, of William Henry. What an opportunity. To nab the parents, then see William Henry come cowering on his knees, begging. He chuckled. No mercy would be given, but intense pleasure as the look on Henry's face as he watched his parents die! And then Henry himself.

"Culligan!"He yelled towards the door. The door opened and a small man peeked in, hesitantly.

"Enter!"

It was time to close it down here in Boston and go West. He rubbed his knuckles with anticipation, lost in his imagination of what methods he might use. He had always been creative in that realm, and he felt a twinge of what might be seen as joy in his heart.

He was absolute monarch of his realm. He enjoyed the power and the look of fear on the faces of those who came before him. The man who entered, Culligan, was a man of utter efficiency. He and Finnegan were important to the running of the organization. Each had their set of skills. Finnegan was ruthless, yet good at organizing. Culligan, on the other hand, was a tool for destruction. He never failed.

He thoughtfully wrote a detailed telegram, then passed it to Jonesy.

"Take this to the telegraph office. Get out!" He yelled at Jonesy. The man hurriedly slipped out the door, leaving Boss Carter and Culligan.

"Culligan," He spoke softer than usual. "I'm closing down here and moving West. You coming along?"

Culligan smiled. He was efficient, yet he had a strange attachment to the Boss. The Boss was his idol. "Aye, Boss. I'm wit ya. When we goin'?"

"Starting in the next couple days. But I need you to do something. Something very important to me."

Culligan grinned a snaggle-tooth grin. "Anyting, Boss."

Boss handed him a sheet of paper. "This is a list of our informants and a couple others in our organization that are no longer useful. They are a threat to us. They need to be no more. Can you handle it?"

Culligan looked at the list, and grinned again. "Aye, right away."

"You've got two days. Meet me here in two days. Don't be late. I need you out west."

"Aye, Boss."

After he left, he got back to work. He had debts to collect – he'd do that himself. If they couldn't pay, well…..the river hid many things. A lot of details to take care of.

He grinned. There was joy in his heart.

Chapter 31

Shortly after dawn, Bill was out riding again. He was checking waterholes and was straightening up from a drink himself when he heard the distant pounding of hooves. He looked and saw Becky approaching across the meadow at her usual full speed. He had a moment of wry sentiment for the horses she rode. She certainly put them through their paces.

"Well, if it isn't the Prodigal! I thought I recognized you."

"What brings you over this way, Becky?"

"I covered a lot of territory yesterday! I thought you'd want to know they'd had some trouble over to Clarksville."

"What kind of trouble?"

"Well, seems like some outfit roughed up the townsfolk and helped themselves to the store and threatened to burn the town. One of them had a big nose."

"Same men that were here?"

"Seems like."

Bill looked off into the distance as he thought.

It did not matter where one settled or what one did with life, there were always those around who sought what others had, for whom life was never settled and who lived on the bounty created by others. It existed in Boston, it existed here, and it existed everywhere this side and the other of the distant mountains. It was a fact wherever there were people.

Many people sought what was always around the bend in the trail, never satisfied nor wanting to contribute, merely seeking whatever they found – even if it already belonged to someone else. They would take, and then they would move on around the bend again. Most times they left behind destruction and a hardship for those who were there first. Often their actions destroyed the livelihood of others.

There were those who felt they had courage, but whose life showed their courage only when others of their ilk stood beside them. Men whose courage was really a deep cowardice, a lack of confidence in themselves, so that the only feeling of worth they could get was through intimidating others and destroying that of others. Or they were under the control of others and lived in fear of what would happen if they failed. It gave a courage of sorts, for when someone threatens you it often can give a resignation to do what might not naturally be done.

He remembered Boss Carter and the weak hirelings who strutted and felt important because they worked for a ruthless man who was feared. Through a sort of warped osmosis, they felt feared because of the machine they worked for. They had no inner sense of importance – it was only because of Boss Carter's strength.

He guessed there were Boss Carter's and Hook Logan's and all their minions in various forms no matter where you lived. Still, few would be as cruel as those Brahmins of Boston's underworld.

This was in direct contrast to the businessmen and others who came to build, to become a part of the fabric of the land. They thought of themselves, yet others also. The basic premise of all business through all the passage of time has been the same: find a need and fill it. When this need in others is attended to, then oneself naturally is well taken care of also. For where others pay for a need, the one filling finds their need also met.

His natural gifts began to work at gathering details.

Big Nose was the boss, but he was a two-bit captain and not of the type that could run the whole group in the long run. This was more than just a passin' through band of outlaws. His mind was telling him something. This had the looks of something bigger, a power play.

Yet, there were no known animosities among the area ranchers. Oh, there were the minor disputes common to such country, but usually they were resolved over a beer at the saloon or over a cup of coffee in a ranch house. There was something deeper here. Pushing around simple, peace-loving people, taking their sense of safety away from them. Was that their intent? To take away their security? What would that get them, he mused. Well, they would want to regain that security. How? They'd be willing to pay for it….was that it? These same men, or whoever was behind it, would then extort the townsfolk and the ranchers and live off other people's fears. Hmm...could be.

"Hello?" Becky interrupted his thoughts as she saw the far-off look in his eyes.

"Sorry." He grinned. "A habit I have when I get to thinking. I've been known to sit through an entire play and never hear a word when my mind starts working on something."

"Well," she grasped his arm lightly and looked him in the eye. "When you have a young lady in your presence, you're supposed to have your mind on her." She looked at him intently - more intense than many women, and with a different look than the flighty husband-seekers back in Boston. They gazed at each other for a few moments, as if seeing each other for the first time. It was Becky that averted her eyes and, looking off at the hills, spoke softly, still holding his arm. She could feel the muscles and enjoyed the aura of gentle strength that Bill brought to her. Yet, beneath that gentleness was something else….

"Saw a stranger lookin' over your pa's ranch this morning."

He was startled. "Where?"

"Over at the base of that gnarled pine on Baldy. I couldn't be sure, but I kinda wonder if it wasn't a horse I saw at the store with those men you run off." She had a serious look on her face as she turned and looked right into Bill's eyes.

"Do you have any idea what's going on here, Bill?"

"Becky, let's look at the clues. What do we know so far? Let's start with the men at Wilsons. They were men used to having their way. But they weren't all smart – which means they are led by somebody. Big Nose was the leader of that group, but he said his boss would not like what happened. So there is somebody bigger behind this."

"You're right, Bill. And that someone must be fairly ruthless, because these men are ruthless. They have killed, and not killed in a normal, western way, but with cruelty. They seem intent on power at all costs, and they are working their way slowly into control."

"They have several of the small spreads already paying, for obvious reasons. It seems strange, though, that none of the small ones came to the big ranchers to ask for help."

"Things have changed here since you left, Bill. As things settled even more over the years, the close alliance of the ranchers has sort of fractured. I think they're not sure the big guys will come to help. Or they were threatened not to."

Bill hurriedly walked to the side of his horse and looked at Becky before he mounted. "Becky, can you ride to the ranch and tell them what you told me? I want them to be on guard."

"Won't take long if I ride fast!" She smiled and gave him a saucy turn of the hips as she mounted and immediately whipped her horse into a trot.

Bill smiled as he watched her cross the meadow.

He came up the back way on Baldy and came out near the spot where the stranger had been watching. After scouting the position and not finding anyone, he knelt and looked at the ground. Someone had spent several hours here, and there were several cigarette butts, smoked to the very end. There was an excellent view of the home place.

What were these men up to, and what reason did they have of watching the ranch? Were they targeting Otis Henry? Did they want the land, or was it protection money? Where did these men come from? They were cruel, ruthless. If they were going to extort money, why not just send an emissary to the ranch house with their demand? This observation seemed different.

As he stood looking over the valley that had been the family ranch for his whole life, he had a deep anxiety in his heart. Finnegan had mentioned a hundred men, with more on the way. That was an army out here. It was feasible to get forty or fifty cowhands together and attack, but they couldn't risk failure in a battle…the morale would plummet and the Triple-C would have the upper hand.

On the other hand, he wanted to know who was behind all of this. His mind and experience said there was a man behind this, a man greedy and cold. If he could find out more information.

There was a sudden sharp crack of a pistol and Bill felt the whip of the bullet as it just missed. He leapt into the brush and quickly moved a dozen steps to one side of where he entered. He stood still and heard nothing. He did not know how many men were there, but possibly only one. He moved slowly through the brush and worked his way slowly to look over the trail opening behind the observation point.

He saw a man looking intently at where Bill had entered the brush, gun in hand.

Not too trail savvy, Bill thought. It was a known tactic of the trail to move from the point of entry when fleeing gunfire. He stooped carefully and chose a fist sized rock. Rising carefully, he chucked the rock to the brush on the other side. The man whirled at the sound and shot. The man was obviously of the eastern bunch. Peering through the brush to the man's horse, he saw the Triple-C.

So, it was the Triple-C observing the ranch! Anger welled up inside him.

Chapter 32

Working his way through the brush and boulders, he reached a point behind the man. He was 30 yards away, too far to risk a dash to tackle the man. Unless he distracted the man. Looking around, he noted that the man's horse was grazing nearer the trail opening. Slowly moving closer to the horse, Bill deliberately threw a handful of pebbles at the horse.

Startled, the horse whinnied. The man turned and ran over to his horse. Bill crouched and leapt at the man, causing the man to drop his gun and lose his breath. Bill stood quickly, pistol drawn.

"Who are you?"

"You ain't m' boss!"

Bill glared, "You obviously are not aware of the gravity of your situation." He grinned.

"What's dat posed to mean?"

"On your stomach, hands behind your back!" The man was slow to comply, but did as he was told.

Bill pulled some piggin' strings out of his pocket and tied the man securely. Then he dragged him by the shirt collar over to the edge of the bluff, making sure the man's head was over the edge.

"That's the gravity of the situation. You either tell me what I want to know or you go over the edge. Gravity will take you to the bottom. Looks to be far enough to crack you open."

"Whatta ya want?"

"I want to know who is behind all of this protection organization."

"I ain't gonna tell."

"Ain't or can't?"

"He'll kill me!"

"Who will?"

"Finnegan or the Boss."

"Well, the way I see it, you've got a couple options. Either you don't tell me anything and you go over the edge, or you tell me what I need to know and then I give you a head start out of the country. You can be gone before Finnegan knows."

"You're bluffin."

Bill walked to his horse, returning with a

coiled rope. looping one end to his pommel, he tied the other around the man's ankles. Then, giving a little slack, he then shoved the man over the edge, so that he hung by his ankles.

"Stop!" The man was frantic.

"Are you going to tell me what I want to know?"

"I can't!"

"I hope your shoes are tied tight, if they slip off the rope won't hold any more. Maybe I should see." He reached for the man's shoe lace.

The man screamed. "Pull me up! I'll tell ya's. Please!"

Bill clucked to his horse, who then backed slowly away from the bluff, drawing the man up on firm ground.

Bill stood over him. "Why are you watching this ranch?"

"Was told to."

"Why?"

"Dey's checkin' it out."

"Mister, I think you need to go back over the edge. You're not talking much." He grabbed the man's collar and drug his face back over the edge.

"No!"

"Then talk!"

"Pull me back!"

"I think you need to stay there, just to keep your tongue moving!" He squatted near the man's face. "Now. Let's try again. Why are they watching the ranch?"

"Dey's got special plans fer this place."

"What plans?"

The man paused, Bill started to stand up. The man spoke. "Boss wants this place."

"What for."

"Boss wants to live here."

"What about those who already live here?"

"He says dat dis place won't have nobody alive. He says dey's all gonna be dead."

"Murder? They've been wanting protection money…why is this place different?"

"Dey's sumpin personal wit de boss."

"Where is your boss and who is he."

"He just got here on da stage from Boston."

Realization and fear rose in Bill. He reached and grabbed the man's shirtfront violently and the intentness of his stare bored through the man. "Give me the man's name. Now!"

"Carter, Boss Carter."

Chapter 33

Indeed, earlier that morning a stage had driven into Royton. Finnegan and his closest henchmen walked thru the dust cloud to the coach. As was usual in frontier towns, the locals gathered to see who might be arriving. A circle of the Triple-C kept them back. Finnegan opened the door, the dust cleared and out stepped an enormous man with a cigar and a bowler hat, rivulets of sweat coursing through the dust of his face and neck.

"Welcome, Boss." Finnegan said. It was not a warm greeting, but the words of a man accustomed to acknowledging a superior because he has to.

Boss spoke, but his voice croaked with dust.

A man next to Finnegan laughed. Instantly a powerful hand gripped his shirt front and another punched him solidly in the jaw. All those present heard the bones break and the man crumpled to the ground like a sack of field stones.

As townsfolk gasped in horror, Boss Carter wiped his hands on his trousers and relit his cigar.

"I trust my rooms are ready, Finn?"

"Yes, Boss. Hannigan! Decker! Get the Boss' bags." Two men hopped to do as told, with impetus from the incident they just witnessed. Boss followed Finnegan, who led him to the hotel. As they entered, Finnegan curtly told the clerk, "Key to the suite!" The trembling man shook as he turned over the keys and saw the look of command in the newcomer's eyes.

"Dey's good whiskey upstairs to wash the dust down, Boss."

"I would hope so."

While Bill had been with Becky, other happenings were filling the conversation with Marge's lunch crowd. She listened from the kitchen as the talk buzzed around this morning's confrontation between a pack of mongrel Triple-C hands and Bull Henry and the boys.

Apparently, Bull and three of his sons had been out on the road to town for supplies when they were approached by a mounted group of riders, dirty and not looking like friendliness came easy. Bull, ever attentive, sensed rather than saw them and alerted the boys.

As the men rounded the bend, Otis and the boys were spread out. Chad had the wagon on the trail, Otis nearby on his horse, and the other two boys further out. Big Nose pulled up and walked his horse over, not missing the defensive posture of the Henry clan. Nor the rifles just casually pointed in the direction of the riders.

"You the Bull Henry we hear about?" Big Nose spat, narrowly missing his own horse. Otis Henry was not impressed. The man was clearly trying to intimidate him. He sighed inside, feeling the old war-horse rising within.

"Speak your piece. You obviously ain't here for a pleasant social call." Big Nose, used to thinking he was more than he really was, reared back and glared angrily at Bull Henry.

"Henry, I got a message to give you." He looked back at the five riders behind him, like a Sampson making sure his hair was intact.

"You ain't the bull of these hills no more, Henry." He grinned. "There's some mighty rough characters running around and we're takin' on the job of protecting the ranches here about. Of course there's a fee."

Bull Henry's ire was building with every word from this dirty, irritating wannabe tough guy. Bull Henry had not gotten his reputation easily. He had fought - white men and Indians - faced arrows and bullets many times. He knew some men lived their lives to prey off others, and he knew that once the gate opened to such there was hell to pay. He was grey now, but he wasn't about to cower to any man.

He was concerned for his boys, but manhood required some tough lessons. His boys were not afraid of this, and if this group of mongrel upstarts wanted to dance, he was gonna give them the dance of their lives!

"Mister, this here Sharps is pointed right at that ugly big nose of yours and at this distance it'd be a right interesting place for a hole. Why don't you and your fellow weasels get while the going is good." As if on prearranged signal, all of the Henry's guns cocked at the same time, the sound magnified by the tension. The boys were young, but they had the grit of their father.

Big Nose was seething, ready to make the foolish plunge and reach for his gun, but one of his hirelings, a wayward cowhand and probable rustler, seeing the intent, said, "It ain't worth it Zeke, there'll be another time."

The tension held for what seemed like an eternity, as various scenarios played through their minds, and each man became hyper-vigilant, eyes wide with intensity, each man focused on a target - or being one. At such a time the threat magnifies, as increased tension results in touchier fingers on triggers.

What was actually only seconds passed and Big Nose relaxed and his hand moved slowly away from the grip of his pistol.

"Ok, Mr. Bull of the woods. We'll not finish this now, but without our protection, you have no guarantees about what might happen. Before long you'll pay our fee...and more.

He reined his horse over and turned, the others following him. In moments they were cantering down the trail.

"I don't think we've see the last of that bunch, pa." It was Matt, and there was no fear in his voice.

A grizzled, unshaven man sat off to himself in Babbet's Saloon in Royton. He had a look that made people glance twice and walk away wide-eyed. It was a bitter look; the look of a man unsatisfied and disappointed with life.

Finley was, indeed, disappointed with his life. Like most other men, he grew up dreaming of making his mark on the world, of a house, kids and a beautiful wife. Then came the war. He joined up with the Union and learned how to kill, with any remorse fading over time. He became cold and callous watching his friends die or be crippled from the ravages of war. When the war ended he could not go home….home was no more, his parents killed by confederate foragers as they sought to protect their home. The bitterness never left him. He returned briefly and, after spending a few minutes at the graves, fists clenched, he rode off – never to return.

He went west. He lived a wayward life, with off and on stints on the wrong side of the law. He saw killing, he saw robbery, he saw…he saw things that should have torn his guts out. But he was hardened. He often drowned his frustration in drink, but that never took care of it, and actually made it worse.

There were times he longed for the days of his youth when the future looked bright and cheerful. Most often, though, he longed for the days of his service in the war, when there was friendship made of common living and common cause and the good of the unit. Once or twice over the years he had come across fellow soldiers of the 49th. There still was that special bond. Once, when in the midst of robbing passengers of a stage, he recognized a fellow soldier of the 49thCavalry. He said nothing, and did not lower his bandana from his face, but he would not take any of the man's valuables. The man had looked at him, sensing.

Oh, to have those days of comradeship back again.

He took another drink. It seemed he spent a lot of time drinking now…and he didn't like this bunch so he stayed aloof. Needing a job, he heard about an outfit starting in the Royton area and he found himself around all these eastern thugs and wayward cowhands.

As he nursed his drink, he mostly listened to his own thoughts, but occasionally a word from some table would catch his mind and he would listen.

As he sat today, he was thinking once again with bitterness of the passing of years when his mind latched onto a conversation…

“I heerd Boss Carter came in this mornin.’ I heerd he is nobody to trifle with and has killed with his bare hands…”

“You hear how he nailed old Smithers at the stage? They say Smithers didn’t do nuthin’ but laugh.”

“Well, he ain’t gonna laugh no more. His jaw’s broke somethin’ awful!”

“I hear that Boss has some sort of personal grudge with someone in the area.”

“Heerd that, too. Somebody name of Henry. Son of a rancher in the area. An’ they say this old man is tough – used to go by the name ‘Bull’ in the war. Was some sort of officer.”

“Bull Henry. Ain’t that impressive?” They all laughed and slugged their drinks. “He won’t last long once the Boss decides to go after him.”

On a table nearby sat a half-filled bottle and a partial glass of whiskey, the liquid still moving from the last drink…

Chapter 34

They all looked at Bill.

"Boss Carter is a criminal mastermind, a man of unbelievable cruelty and physical power. The criminal world itself fears him. He destroys those who oppose him. I have been working to topple him for a couple years, and I was just able to topple one of his main lieutenants. That's why I came out here, to get away from his reach for a while."

"So you think he's out here?" His father was concerned.

"It's him."

"Why is he out here?" asked ma.

"I don't know. But it's time to find out. I'll send some messages back east. Stacker, I wonder if I might get you to take them in the morning. They don't have you connected with us at this point. And they may be watching the telegraph office and I think you'll know how to handle it."

Stacker nodded.

"You think he's looking for you?"

Bill paused. "In reality, it is not logical that he came out here for me. There must be a reason he left Boston, and it is just coincidence that he is out here. He is here to create another empire. The law must be getting too close for his comfort. Times are changing and he knows it and he is likely seeking to build his empire where interference would be minimal. He is taking control of towns and ranches, bringing a sure cash flow, and the power he craves. It seems that our paths are destined to cross until one of us is no longer."

Otis Henry leaned forward. "We can get the ranchers together and drive him out."

"No, pa. That won't work with Boss Carter. He's a man who is used to running an army. He had hundreds of men in his pocket and under his thumb. If you crossed him, he had many whose sole job was to kill. He is utterly cruel and would torture you in the slowest possible fashion.You'd need an army. Carter needs men. Somewhere in this picture he has to have his army."

Finley rode into New Haven shortly after dawn, watching warily as he rode up to Marge's. He glanced around as he dismounted and loosened the cinch, seeing no sign of the men from Royton. Without express orders to be here, he would be suspect. It really didn't matter now, except that he had not wanted to ask anyone in Royton where the Henry ranch was located, so he rode over to New Haven.

He had ridden in the night until he was clear of Royton and knew he wasn't followed. He'd had to leave his bedroll to avoid suspicion. He'd seen that it was easy to join the force at Royton or North Fork, but to leave was another thing. He'd had to use all his learned skills to escape detection.

He walked into Marge's and looked carefully around. Only a dozen or so tables, it seemed a pleasant place. In the corner sat a man, nursing a cup of coffee. The man glanced at Finley, taking his measure as westerners do. He chuckled inside as he realized he wasn't much to look at and looked probably pretty unsavory.

A pretty woman came out and glanced his way. She frowned slightly, but asked, "What can I get you?"

"Eggs if you have 'em, and beef, ma'am."

"Comin' right up." She quickly brought a cup of steaming coffee.

He sipped the coffee carefully and spoke. He, too, had taken the measure of the man in the corner.

"I don't see any of the men from Royton out there."

"They like to sleep late." Parson shifted in

his seat.

"They cause much trouble?"

"Getting a bit pushy. What are you fishin' for, mister? Are you one of them?"

Finley glanced up as Marge brought his breakfast. She also had been listening.

"Thank ya, ma'am." Glancing at Parson, he said, "Used to be one of 'em. Till yesterday. Now I'm lookin' fer an old friend. Figured I needed to see him."

"What's his name."

"I knew him as Colonel Bull Henry."

Parson paused…uncertain. "What business you have with Henry?"

"Mister, I been around a bit, an' I can tell me asking about him has you bothered. I ain't trying to hurt him. I'm tryin' to warn him. If you can tell me where his ranch is, I'd be much obliged."

Parson waited a few moments.

"Colonel Henry is in danger. I need to get word to him, an' I'd rather take it myself. I served with the Colonel in the war."

"Ranch is a few miles northwest of here. Follow the river and take the right fork through the valley. Take you right to the home place."

"Much obliged, mister."

In the hills outside New Haven, a satisfied smile crosses the face of a man experienced with such looks. The rifle is finely made and specially designed. He has never missed. He rises, places the rifle into an ornate saddle case, mounts and rides off towards Royton. He reaches into his coat pocket, casually produces an apple and bites into it with deep pleasure.

Tetch was riding to town with the buckboard for supplies when he saw the horse at the edge of a canyon mouth a few hundred yards away. It was just standing, reins hanging. Turning the team over, Tetch covered the ground and slowed as he neared, so as not to scare the horse. He slowly dismounted.

"Whoa, boy," he whispered as he approached the horse. The horse shied a mite, but then whinnied softly. It appeared to have been standing a long time. Tetch knew a horse taught to be ground tied might stand half of forever where he was left. Blood on the saddle caused Tetch to pull his gun and look around carefully, what with all the going's on lately. He searched the ground for tracks, seeing that the horse had come a ways before standing at this spot. Backtracking him, he found the body. He looked around wide-eyed before he noticed the flies. The body'd been here a while, so likely nobody around. Kneeling, he turned him over.

Nate Tyler! Nate was a local man who worked odd jobs, from helping on ranches to making deliveries from Wilson's. He was well-liked and was never anything but kind. Tetch looked around carefully and found where someone had come up to Tyler – probably to see if he was dead. Backtracking with all senses alert, he found a copse 500 yards away where the killer had waited. A large caliber shell lay to one side, partly covered by dirt, and a small stub of a cigar was ground into the grass.

Working his way back to the body, Tetch brought the wagon over and carefully loaded the body and headed to town.

Finley rode up to the Henry ranch a couple hours later. As he approached, he saw activity and knew he was watched. A black man stepped forward, Spencer casually resting in his arm.

"What can I do ya fer, mister?

"I'm looking for Colonel Henry."

"You know him?"

"I do."

"Your name, suh?"

"Finley. Private Finley."

A voice came from the door of the house. "Finley! Well, I'll be!" Otis Henry came out the door and down the steps. "It's fine, Sim!"

"Hello, Colonel."

"Light and set, Finley." He walked up to Finley and the two shook hands. Otis Henry look intently at the man in front of him. He spoke kindly, "The years look like they've been rough to you, Finley."

"Ain't been much of a picnic, Colonel."

"What brings you here?"

"Well, Colonel, I ain't gonna lie to ya. I been in a bit of trouble here and around and found myself of late with an unsavory bunch in Royton. Them eastern thugs. Yesterday I overheard that you was in the area and that they were gonna come after you sooner or later. Well, sir, you know the bond of the 49th. So's I injuned out of there and come here to warn ya."

"That means a lot, Finley. I appreciate it. You know anything about their plans?"

"No, I jus' know they seem to want to take over the territory an they've got a lot of men – least a hunnert."

Otis Henry looked at the man, seeing the changes of the years, the hard trails, the disappointment, the homelessness. "Dinner's near ready, I expect you'll accept my wife's hospitality?"

"Oh, I can just eat out here with the hands, Sir, if'n ya don't mind. I ain't been in a house fer many years."

"Well, here we all eat in the house. Sim here will show you where to wash up."

"Yessir."

As Sim showed him the washbasin and towels, Finley eyed him over.

"Was you a slave or was you in the war?"

"I were a slave. Been with the Henry's fer lotta years now."

Finley glanced at the towels. "These is clean towels?"

Sim smiled, "Missus Henry likes the men to be clean! She treats us same as family."

Finley sloshed water on his face and gingerly took a clean towel and felt it on his face, perhaps wiping more than he had to.

Chapter 35

Several times over the weeks Becky came by the ranch. Otis was making comments about the lack of work getting done – tongue in cheek – while Becky and Bill walked the near meadows or rode together. Otis Henry had known Becky since she was born and had watched her grow and become the feisty cowgirl she was. Some said she was a bit too big for her britches and advocated reining her in a bit, but Otis always treated her like a lady and was pleased at the respect Becky gave to those who respected her. Otis looked now with joy in his heart while Bill and Becky rode out together.

In spite of the anxiety he was feeling over the recent events and what was to come, he was a happy man, seeing his son home and with this fine young lady. He had to admit in his heart that he'd love it if Bill had reason to stay.

Ella Henry looked out the kitchen one day at the sound of pounding hooves. It was Becky again....she chuckled. Ella Henry saw in Becky a vision of herself in her younger years, riding fast and free over the land. She could still run a horse when need be, but need be didn't happen very often and she didn't do it if she didn't have to.

Becky, on the other hand, was fast and loved riding hell bent for leather anywhere she needed or wanted to go. Such a difference between her and Bill....but why is she thinking that? A smile crossed her heart – she and Otis were quite a bit different at the start – still were – but they had grown more alike over the years. Her wild side had been checked by his logical, methodical, down to earth ways. And her eagerness for adventure had softened his resolve a bit. Still they had meshed well over the years, and built a dream together.

She watched as Bill came from the near barn to greet her, wiping his hands on his jeans. The look he gave Becky....Ella Henry smiled again.

As they cantered out of the ranch yard, Bill found himself enjoying the company of this exuberant and vivacious ranch girl. She was unlike the women he had known back East. Where so many he knew back in Boston had a shallow exterior and were even more shallow and selfish below the surface, Becky was genuine and exhibited a depth and vision inside her adventurous and friendly exterior. She knew how to dress to accentuate her beauty, but never in a suggestive or vain manner. She was a wild bronco of sorts combined with a calm rootedness in her family and those for miles around.

Becky had been raised in the territory, and though her parents were successful like the Henry's, she knew the struggles of the building of the ranch and the changes in the land and people. She had the freedom to ride whenever she pleased and, to the chagrin of her parents, she refused to be accompanied by one of the ranch hands.

They had given up on her being escorted, as she made a point of outrunning them and throwing them off her scent. She had some of the best horses in the territory, thanks to her father's breeding and business, and she instinctively knew and was attracted to the wilder, exuberant horses. She rode far and wide and never seemed to grow weary of the saddle. Her friendliness and easy-going personality endeared her to many, and she became privy to all the secret trails and shortcuts through the hills. She was a lady through and through, but it was said that Becky could go farther in a day than any rider and she was known to range as far as Royton and Cedarville and return the same day no worse for wear. She seemed to know anybody and everybody and had no enemies anywhere. The hot-blooded bachelors for many miles around were eager for her hand and sought her company, but rarely did she accept an invitation, as she was of a different breed and refused to be tamed or to take second fiddle. She could ride and she could shoot and she could track and she could think. It scared many of the young men away.

With Bill she found someone different. She found herself quietly attracted to him. They had ridden together off and on in years past, but they were kids then. They all rode as friends back then, but she saw that Bill was different than the average friend from childhood. He had been dissatisfied, tired of the seeming toil of the land, and she had not been surprised when she heard he had up and left. She knew then that he needed to seek his own way.

He was a different person now. He was content, mature, self-assured, possessing an awareness of himself and others. He had been very quiet at first, watching more than talking, but he had opened up over the weeks and they had ridden together several times. He came closest to keeping up with her than anybody, and he seemed to appreciate her uniqueness and neither did nor said anything to squelch it. She liked riding with him, sharing thoughts and ideas.

Yet, she felt there was something else, a reserved quality that at first bothered her, but soon she came to see it was him keeping his own counsel, a quality of the life he had lived in the East. He had shared some of his experiences, and she grew to understand how very different he was from all those years ago. He was steady and of the fabric that was the foundation of the land.

Gradually, she noticed, as did he, that he was growing more comfortable in the land of his youth. He was relaxing; he was laughing more and the vigilance was less obvious. He was becoming a part of the land and the land was becoming part of him.

That day they followed the creek south from the ranch proper and to the hills bounding the Henry land. Around every bend in the trail there was something new, from deer to marmots to vistas of breath-taking beauty. At one outcropping over a valley, they paused and sat their horses to take it in.

"Did you ever miss this while you were back East?" Becky ventured.

He didn't answer for a few moments. He looked at her. "I think I did. Yet I was unwilling to see it. I was so eager to forge my own way that I refused to accept any contact with this land. I can remember those times when I was alone in my thoughts and recalled the ranch, the family, and some of my old favorite haunts." He looked again across the valley, and became quiet for a time.

"You seem miles away. Where are you?" She probed quietly.

Again the pause. "I'm back about 10 years ago, looking at a pert young lady that even then knew the land and had her own mind." He smiled and looked at her. His look did something to her that she was not used to – she blushed.

"Becky, the land is beautiful. It seems like we can ride all day and around each bend in the trail, over each ridge is something new and beautiful. But as God is my witness, you are the most beautiful sight I've ever seen." Her jaw dropped as she turned red. She had been spoken to by shy, uncomfortable cowhands mumbling niceties, but Bill was looking her in the eyes and something stirred in her that had hitherto been dormant towards men. It was a yearning. There was a comfortableness with Bill that she was unused to. She was drawn to him, as a friend and as a woman.

He still looked her in the eyes. She was excited in a new way but didn't know what to say.

"Why, Bill Henry. I bet you've said that to a dozen Boston belles."

"I never said it, because I never felt it – until now." He reached out a hand and she instinctively reached out to meet his hand. Yet she was shuddering inside with the newness of the feelings that she was having. Just before their fingers met, she came to herself – she shook her hair, gave out a wild yell and spurred her horse down the trail.

Bill, recovering swiftly, grinned and spurred his horse after her. She galloped across a meadow and he was spurring his horse to catch up when he heard a shot. He looked ahead and

Becky had pulled up. As he cantered up, they looked at each other.

"That was close," she said.

"Sounded like over the ridge." He was suddenly aware of how far they had ridden. "We're near North Fork. That's where I hear that lot of riff-raff is holed up."

"We need to get closer."

"Becky, I need to get you back."

"Bill Henry, if you think you know me, you're sure an old mule. I can take care of myself and, besides, I know a trail that will sneak us in the back way."

"Is there anyplace you haven't ridden?" He asked with a grin.

"I know these hills better than any man around, Bill, 'cept for one."

"Who's that?"

"I ain't answering questions right now. Let's go." She headed along the brow of the hill, under the cover of the overhanging pines. Where a ghost of a trail headed away from the gunshot and away from the ridge, she turned and started uphill. They rode for a half mile or so, going easy and eyes roaming all around. The trail was difficult, and they finally got off and walked as the trees became denser and made riding all but impossible. Even the horses had to duck. Eventually, Becky paused and, with a finger to her lips, whispered.

"May be someone on watch up ahead. Not sure, but it's a likely spot. Better tie the horses."

She led him into a dense thicket where they loosely tied the horses and began to work their way upwards to the rim. Bill noticed with pleasure that Becky was no tenderfoot, and glided virtually silent through the woods. Soon Becky slowed and they looked carefully around as they crawled the last few feet and looked over the crest into the valley beyond – the valley of the North Fork. It was a beautiful valley, with the Fork flowing in the valley after a fall from the precipice, forming a pool in the small valley. Below they could see a large camp, with tents scattered here and yon and men sitting and standing around fires. Some were bathing in the pool, others seemed gathered in small groups, likely playing cards.

There were a few women near a larger tent, likely prostitutes for the men. The entire camp gave the sense of planning to be here a while.

As they watched, some men came out of a tent set away from the others. Out side this tent were men, obviously guards. One of the men who exited looked familiar to Bill in some way. He looked hard and the man turned. It was the man with the nose from Wilson's! He nudged Becky and whispered his realization to her. As he said it, they both turned their heads sharply at the sound of a stick breaking not too distant. A hundred yards away was a jumble of rocks, hidden from their view by the brush – which also hid them from view of the rocks. Must be a sentry, Bill thought. He looked at Becky and motioned for them to leave. They worked their way slowly backwards, carefully avoiding sticks and other potential noises.

As they reached the horses, they untied them and quietly walked back down the trail. It wasn't until they were a significant ways down that they began to talk.

"How many did you guess were down there?"

Bill said, "I'd guess near 75. That must be their base of operations."

Becky grinned. "That the way you say it out east? Out here we say that's where they're holed up."

Bill grinned in return. "Either way, we've stumbled upon a rats nest. With a group that size, they can back up their threats and even field a good size force if they meet opposition – I mean" He grinned at her "if someone stands up to them."

She stopped and turned to him. "You know, you're kinda cute when you speak Easternese. If it weren't for the seriousness of the situation, I might even be tempted to let you kiss me." They gazed at each other for a moment, then Becky wrinkled her nose in a grin and turned and led the way.

They rode quietly for a mile or so. Then Becky spoke.

"What do you suppose they're up to, Bill?"

"Well, with Boss Carter in charge, it won't be something small. They look as if they are seeking control over the territory. They are threatening and extorting. That group in the valley is large enough to fight a small war, and they seem like the men to do it.

Chapter 36

The same afternoon, a rider rode up to Grantler's camp. Allen was just a local cowhand for Otis Henry, checking on the tendril of smoke he'd seen. Grantler, for all appearances was just another cowhand making a pot of coffee. Allen thought he'd just get a late afternoon cup and report the stranger to Bull, but Grantler knew he was fishing for information. He saw the cowhand's gaze hesitate on the rifle scabbard on Grantler's horse. As they laughed over some comment or another, Grantler stood and offered to fill Allen's cup. As Allen reached his cup upwards, he was scalded by dumped coffee and died with the coffee still steaming on his shirtfront, now mixed with red.

After dragging the body to a gully, Grantler

went back to camp and dug through the man's saddlebags, finding a bottle of whiskey. He drank a few slugs and stared at the fire, then crawled into his bedroll, now enhanced by the other man's blanket. He slept without fear or worry. He would hide the man's horse in the morning and later sell him on the trail after doctoring the brand.

His dreams were different than those of normal men. He had been given orders - and a healthy packet of money - to kill Otis Henry. He was dreaming of snuffing the life out of this "Bull." He had spent the better part of an afternoon in the saloon listening. He'd learned a lot about the area. Get some of the cowhands a mite heavy on their drink and much comes out. He'd found over the years that a little saloon spending upped his information. Bull Henry was quite the man, and with a lot of experience. Maybe not as easy as the average cowhand. In his dream he was wrestling a Brahma bull to the ground where he plunged a knife into its heart. There was a smile on his sleeping face.

As Otis rode, he pondered the happenings of late. He was concerned with what he'd been hearing. Ranches all around had been approached. The saloon owner over to Cherry Creek was found beaten to death. He'd refused to pay money to that pack of coyotes. They meant business. If people refused to comply, they were given a 'convincin', and if that didn't work they received worse. This enemy did not just kill, but took pleasure in cruelty. They had also found their land claims filed on. Once they were filed, a pack of these men would move on to the land, build a ramshackle building, and set a man there with a rifle. This was a different brand of trouble that he'd ever dealt with the years past. He'd fought Indians. They were a calculated opponent. He'd fought in the war. Again, very clear lines of who was who and the battle settled the matter.

Otis Henry was a man of the old days. He was a man who understood the ways of strength and weakness, the clear decisions made by battle and the idea of winning or losing. He did not understand illegalities and extortion. It was foreign to him. He knew it was only a matter of time before they approached him again.

One of his cowhands, a boy named Allen, didn't come in from a circuit a couple days earlier, but his horse wandered in about breakfast time the next day. Trailing backwards, they came to a point where the tracks disappeared and a windstorm that night had not helped.

Then, Tetch had found Nate Tyler drygulched. Allen probably died the same way. They had ridden the circuit and found nothing yet, except where some traveler had stopped for the night. Perhaps it was the killer.

Bull Henry had seen lots of action during the war. He'd seen many men fall, most never to rise again. He'd faced the fears of battle common to all men; he'd faced bullets and had been wounded - once by a minie ball and once by a misguided bayonet. Misguided because he'd shot the reb 'tween the eyes at the last second, but the momentum of the reb kept the bayonet moving and he'd caught the spent thrust in the leg. He had a healthy respect for battle. He knew the value of force, and he knew how to assess his enemy. He'd risen to the rank of colonel and was respected in the conclaves of General Grant. He was no fool.

He'd thought long and hard about what was happening in his surrounding valleys. He knew the ways of man and he knew that some unknown evil man had decided to make a living by extorting the ranchers and townsfolk. He also knew that this person, whoever it was, was absolutely ruthless. It was coming to a showdown eventually. But the evil was upheld by a pack of hardbitten men who thought nothing of beating a helpless man to death, and did it as a pack. From what Finley said, there was almost an army hold up in the hills.

The townsfolk included those ready and willing to fight - former soldiers and mountain men and the like. But too many others were scared. And these good men had wives and children now and were scared for their families. They had been threatened in a way they'd never faced before and didn't know what to do. He'd heard the men at Royton had tried to stand up, but they were just beaten later when they were caught alone.

He himself would take it on, but it was a restless evil that even he didn't quite know how to deal with yet. And his still healing wound was an issue. He knew he'd almost bought the farm getting those rustled cattle back.

Dad burn it! He wanted to take care of this, but it was too widespread! He might succeed in protecting his own ranch, but they would have to watch their backs at all times and eventually one of them would bite it. He was like the others - he now had more to lose than just his own life. The evil would continue to grow and fester, and more lives would be lost and the vise would tighten. There was no solid law yet outside of the towns, and there was not enough time to work through the legal system

No, there needed to be a cleaning of the house, and it wouldn't be easy - these men were some of the toughest he'd ever seen. The dregs of society, but very good at being mean.

Otis Henry prided himself in his self-reliance, but like in wartime self reliance wasn't always the key. Sometimes force had to be faced with force.

Finley had casually said it'd be nice if the 49th were here. As he said it, he had a look in his eye.

As the 49th had mustered out at the end of the war, the men had vowed to come running if each other had a need. There had been a few of the men show up at his ranch over the years and he had helped them. After all, he was their former Colonel. But they also had said to him that he was to contact them if he had need of them. These were men he trusted with his life. But that was a lot of years ago and they had settled lives now and many likely had families. Still, it would be a full scale blood bath here within a month or so.

As he sat his horse at the edge of town, he suddenly and decisively turned towards the telegraph office, and with such moves come the hinges of fate.

A small man with a too big mustache sat at the telegrapher's desk.

"Hello, Frank." He said to the man.

"Oh, hullo mister Henry! What can I do for you?"

"I need to send a telegram." He grabbed a form and began to write. He finished and turned the form to the small man.

The small man looked at Otis Henry and hesitated.

"What's the matter, Frank?"

"No telegraphs are to go out without permission of Reeker."

"He a part of that pack of coyotes been hangin' out?"

"Well…"

Otis Henry whipped out his pistol and cocked it and placed it to the head of the telegrapher in one swift move. "Frank, send that telegraph, and send it now. And remember, I can understand Morse code." The man hesitated. "They'll hurt my family, Mr. Henry."

Bull Henry laid the barrel hard along Frank's head and he collapsed to the ground. Otis Henry sat at the stool and tapped the keys. Down the line the message traveled:

RALSTON ADAMS,
SPRINGFIELD,MISSOURI:
BULL NEEDS 49. NEW HAVEN,
COLORADO. SOUND REVEILLE

Chapter 37

In a law office in Springfield, a young aid knocked at a mahogany office door.

"Come in."

The aid entered an office with luxurious furnishings. Years of talent and hard work had given success and comfort.

"Telegram, Mr. Adams."

Receiving the paper, he unfolded it, reading the words of his old commander. He leaned back in his chair, thinking. Bull Henry in trouble - their beloved commander. He began to mentally calculate, then scribbled out a note and called his aid.

"Johnson!"

The door opened. "Yes, sir?"

He handed the note to the young man. “Send this to…” He opened his desk drawer and pulled out a list of names and towns. “...all of these names.”

“Yes, sir.”

Two days later, on a backroad of Illinois, a half dozen or so men cantered their horses along the tree-lined country lane. all were showing touches of graying hair, some bearded. For one of them, the years had given prosperity and a hearty appetite, and his horse was much larger than the others. All shared a commonality–they rode with a sense of seriousness.

They came to a crossroad, where another two to three similar men traded nods and a few words, then fell in and the cavalcade cantered on. A train whistle sounded in the distance. The horses moved to a gallop.

Similarly, at various locales in the midwest, groups of men with the same look in their eyes traveled west. Some met at train depots and boarded trains… All heading West.

A few curious folk ventured to question them, and received a curt reply, “we’re the 49th Indiana Cavalry. We stick by our own.”

These men came from various walks of life. There were farmers, lawyers, shopkeepers, blacksmiths, preachers, engineers. The intervening years had accentuated the various differences, yet there was a similarity, a common bond that transcended all aspects of their lives–

they were veterans of the Civil War. They were, more specifically, all veterans of the fighting 49th. They had spent the defining years of their lives fighting alongside one another. They had experienced the baptism of fire, the comradeship of those whose lives were so intertwined and the events so significant that everything from then on through the years was compared in importance to those times. They had seen their friends die; they had held the hands of comrades in blue with the rattle of death in its final cry. They had stanched each other's blood and carried one another off the battlefield. They saved each other's lives on the field of Antietam, on the wooded hills of the wilderness, at the deadly shrine of Gettysburg. They had proven their mettle and had become melded together with a forever bond.

The loyalty of the veterans of former military outfits was legendary, and it showed in these converging groups. Some were much older than the others and were, perhaps, a little slower in mounting their horses. There were a missing arm or two and an eye patch here and there, giving each a scary cast in the site of onlookers–especially children.

It was a proud gathering of men, with handshakes, hugs and harassment–but above all–love and loyalty. There were occasional moments of silence as news of comrades' deaths came to light. You see, in youth there has always been the sense that they would live forever, but these veterans had lost that fantasy on the battlefields, where they saw the reality. Yet, once the war was over, they felt almost invincible, as nothing could faze them when compared to the horrors of war.

The loyalty caused some issues on the home front. One of the men received word as his wife was preparing to give birth. The call was urgent, and two men on horseback waited outside. As he glanced from the door to his wife, the internal battle raged. His wife's eyes glared wide amidst the pain as she saw the torn looks back and forth. In the end, his wife was left pushing alone as marital responsibility gave way to the loyalty of the outfit.

Others left jobs, left courtrooms, left farms and headed west to meet up with fellow veterans of the fighting 49th.

It all began with a simple note sent over the wire to a select list of men, who then spread the word further.

FIGHTING 49 URGENT MEET TOPEKA
APRIL 10

There were many who could not come, due to health or other circumstances. They stood with wistful eyes looking west, their hearts torn. If possible, they helped others with carefully hoarded dollars, knowing there would be horses to purchase at the railhead. Some gave cherished weapons, hats, and always words of encouragement.

And so they gathered at Topeka. The agent at the railhead depot was amazed, as were the hotel proprietors. The eating houses were filled to capacity, profits skyrocketed for a week. Horses had to be brought from outlying ranges to meet the demands.

Within just a few hours they were gone. A blanket of silence seemed to cover the town. There was a collective sigh, some with relief, some with a smile as they counted their earnings.

It was a beautiful summer day, with cattle roundup over for many of the area ranches. New Haven was used to such days, with stray cowhands hanging lazily about town with the first extended free time in weeks. Some dozed, some conversed and some just sat.

It had been a month since the last conflicts, and it seemed that the problems had disappeared. Some realized, possibly correctly, that the roundup was on and it must be allowed to happen. Also, there were some larger groups of cowhands together at times and violence would have resulted in death.

One cowhand sat at the corner of Wilson's Store, silent and morose, To the casual eye he was dozing, his feet up on the hitchrail - but his eyes were not drowsy like the others. Jonesy was there for a purpose. As he tried to look like a cowhand dozing without a care, his hands clenched and unclenched with nervous energy. A tightly strung man, he was perhaps not the best choice of men to sit still yet he was the most reliable the Boss had. Whereas other men would quickly doze in the heat and aimlessness, Jonesy's nervous energy, his tightly coiled internal spring, kept him wide awake.

His eyes shifted as he detected a rider coming up the street. He lifted his brim and squinted at the approaching rider to close off some of the glare of the bright sun as it reflected off buildings and windows and the dust of the streets. As the rider approached, Jonesy lowered his hat brim again and feigned dozing. As the rider approached, the watcher could almost imperceptibly be seen to startle for, in that one glance, he sensed triumph in his life. The description, the way the man sat, the brand….it had to be Bill Henry.

Bill's eyes were also active in the shade of his wide brim. He saw the man at the rail, and noticed the almost imperceptible reaction and noted an intentness in the demeanor that betrayed the falsehood of casual cowhand. He had already, from down the street, seen the hat brim lifted and lowered.

Pulling up to the hitch rail a dozen feet or so from the watcher, he got down and looked briefly at his observer. He, too, registered recognition. He'd seen that face before. Always a man to remember faces and names, Bill searched his mind's catalogue of such things. So many recollections were based upon situations encountered, and he was unable to place the face with a name. It would come to him. His mind would be active at every possible moment to find a name and, as happened many times, it might be in the wee morning hours.

When Bill came out of the store the man was gone. East of town there was a subtle hint of dust in the air, such as would indicate a fast-moving horse.

Bill had been active in the past few weeks. Several wires had been sent to contacts back east, using great care in coded words. Bill had found that Boss Carter's empire was starting to crumble and evidence indicated that he was slowly but surely phasing out parts of his empire and that men and supplies were heading west.

To Bill, it seemed that the area here was not chosen because of he, Bill, being present. It seemed more likely that Carter had chosen this area for other reasons, as a secondary plan when he saw part of his empire crumble. The fact of Bill and his family being located here was just a coincidence that then played into Carter's sense of vengeance.

He needed to find out more, to find Carter's exact location, find his Achilles heel.

He had no fairy tale endings in his mind, He knew that Boss Carter was feared even among criminals back east. He was cruel beyond imagining. The only way to stop him was to destroy him.

He would go to Royton.

Abilene was a place which saw the best and the worst that the west had to offer. Saloons and fleshpots and theater and fine dining, separated by very little. When the herds came in, the men who had been on the trail for weeks received their pay and cut loose for a few days, many heading home at the end as broke as when they arrived.

Macomber's was a middle of the road saloon just off the main street. It wasn't fine china, but it wasn't a place where a man needed to watch his back all the time either.

At the bar a group of cowhands stood nursing their drinks. The batwings opened. The men glanced in the mirror to see their ramrod walk in.

"Howdy, boys." The men nodded. The newcomer stood to the bar.

"What's the latest?" He asked.

"Guess there's quite a fracas getting' ready up in Colorado. Some gent from out East trying to take over some ranches."

"Glad we're not there. I'm ready for a relaxing ride home."

"They say there's some old soldiers marching that way. Meeting in Topeka. Goin' to help somebody named Bull Henry."

The men looked around to see their ramrod walking to the door.

"Tell Mr. Anderson I'll be back as soon as I take care of something."

"Where you headed?"

"Topeka…to join the cavalry. That's my outfit."

Chapter 38

Bill rode warily into town. Royton was larger than he recalled, with the usual hotel, 5-6 saloons, general store and emporium, barber, and miscellaneous other establishments. It was a cattle-buying center of the area, and there were side streets that housed the families and children of town and beyond that the houses with lesser reputations. There were several new buildings at the north edge of town that looked to be bunkhouses.

He surprised himself when he loosed the thong on his gun without really thinking about it. The old habits of the west were returning, combining with the senses of his recent years. There was within him a sixth sense of danger. There were few townsfolk in sight - unusual at this time of day. He was aware of eyes peering at him through storefront windows as he passed the emporium. The batwings of one saloon revealed curious men. There was a watchful silence and two men, unkempt and armed, lounged on the street outside one saloon.

He pulled up to a saloon that seemed less busy than the others. As he tied his horse he looked around, trying to move his eyes rather than his head. He paused to look over the batwings before he entered. It was quiet with a couple cowhands and a couple of derby-clad eastern toughs drinking together at a table. A man with a faded yellow kerchief sat by himself off in a corner, seemingly looking at nothing but his drink. Bill smiled inside to see Stacker. As he walked in, he made a point not to acknowledge Stacker. Stacker preferred and needed to remain an unknown.

At the bar he ordered a whiskey, standing so he could see the men in the mirror while pondering the situation. To nobody in particular he said, "Town seems a bit tense." Heads turned in his direction.

The bartender dusted the bar and found a spot right in front of Bill, which he polished with rapt attention. He spoke quietly.

"Tense ain't the word for it. You're not from around here?"

"Yes and no. I'm curious."

"Not a whole lot to be curious about. The whole town is scared."

"Of?"

"Well, mister, I'm not so sure I'm free to say," he glanced at two of the men together at a nearby table. One of the cowhands, Bill had noticed, shifted so he could see better and riffled through a deck of cards while trying to look disinterested. Bill grinned to himself. The man, who was unshaved and seemed to have no regular interest in it, had long sandy hair and deep-set eyes below massive eyebrows that seemed to sprout everywhere like a line of tumbleweeds.

"Questions ain't welcome in Royton, mister. Neither are strangers." It was the man at the table. His eyes remained on his cards.

Bill recognized the type. A kind of man who got his kicks feeling important, usually with some task that made him feel more important than his life actually permitted. Most likely this man fit the pattern and was set here by someone who owned his soul.

"I always had a problem with asking questions. Never could help myself." Bill chuckled as he said it. He watched the stranger carefully in the mirror.

"Questions ain't healthy here." Sandy seemed to have some idea he was essential to the running of the world.

"Sorry to upset you. Who's in charge here?"

"Depends on who you ask."

"But I'm not supposed to ask questions?"

"You makin' fun of me, mister?"

Bill's anger at the two-bit wanna be started to rise. He was known as a very patient man, but there were times when his ire built quickly. Now was one of those times. He held it in, reminding himself of the mission. "I'm not having any fun at all. You having fun?"

Sandy started to rise. Bill had always believed in attack. He was shrewd in the courtroom, attacking his opponents from various directions to keep them off-balance. He grabbed a bottle off the bar and spun over to sit with the cowhand. Sandy was shocked, staring at Bill across the table, but slowly lowering himself to his seat. He didn't know what to think.

"Have a drink?" He asked Sandy.

"Why...sure....?" As Sandy brought the drink to his lips, Bill spoke:

"Whose flunky are you?"

Sandy choked on his drink and shoved his chair as he stood up. "What's that supposed to mean?"

Bill calmly lifted his own drink. "I simply mean that a gentleman wannabe of your intellectual deficiency is not likely to be persuasive to many of the opposite ability."

"Mister, I don't know who you are or what you just said, but I think you're playin' me."

The other men had leaned back in their chairs, watching this bold stranger play with Sandy. Nobody would move until Sandy called the play. He needed to saddle his own broncs.

"I don't have time to play, thanks. Never was much good at cards." He poured a drink without looking at Sandy, and filled those of the others. Finally Sandy sat down, unsure of this stranger.

"If a man wanted a job here, where would he go?"

"Finnegan's the man to see."

"Is he hiring?"

"Yup. A bit better than cowhand wages, but the benefits are great. No branding, no riding line shacks in the snow, cheap drinks."

"Couldn't be hiring that much. I didn't see many around."

"Oh, he's got them out in the hills. Building an army." The others looked at Sandy.

"Bob, watch your mouth. Boss doesn't like a loose tongue."

Bill ignored them, pressing Sandy. "So he needs fighters?"

"Yup, needs men willing to fight. Gonna be a big one in a couple weeks."

"Bob, shut up!"

"I might be looking for a job. Where might I find this boss and Mr. Finnegan?"

One of the others spoke up. "Mister, don't know what you want, but if it's a job, Finnegan can be found at Babbet's Saloon. Boss ain't here right now, be here in a few days."

"Might be you're fishin' for information for another reason." He reached for his gun, pointing it at Bill.

"I just want to know before I ask for a job. Easier to not get hired sometimes than hire on and try and leave. No offense meant."

The man behind the gun pushed back his chair and stood. "I got things to do," he said, and headed to the door. The others stood and left also.

Bill went to the door and watched as they walked partway down the street, then ducked in Babbet's Saloon.

"Mister." It was the bartender. "You best be movin' quick. If'n they send somebody over to check you out, there may be trouble."

"How many men here will fight this bunch?

"Mister, they got us over a barrel. Just a handful of guns amongst us now, and we can't leave town. It's a mess." He glanced at the door. "We need help."

Bill glanced at Stacker, walked out the front, mounted his horse and took the alley between the buildings. Glancing towards Babbet's as he went around the corner, he saw a handful of men exit and turn towards him. Then he was around the corner.

When he reached the back, he tightened his cinch and, cutting behind some buildings, he galloped his horse like a cowhand heading out for a job. A couple men with rifles, seemingly positioned as guards, hailed him, but he just raised his hand in greeting and rode on. Obviously they felt secure, for no one took a shot. He couldn't see what was going on in town, or if anybody went to check them out, but he knew another visit would not be as easy.

Chapter 39

As he built distance between himself and Royton, he took care to stay off the main road. Likely he would be followed. He had asked too many questions.

He found himself getting more tuned to the land than he had been. When he returned to the ranch, he had felt out of place. Now, after the weeks in the saddle and away from the rush and crush of Boston, he found himself more at ease, more relaxed in the saddle, more noticing of the details of the land. Back in Boston, he was focused on the people and the courtroom and the intricacies of legal wrangling. Here he was becoming ever more attuned to the intricacies of nature and the open range and the mountains.

He cut down a short draw and took what

appeared to be a deer trail through the brush. Deer would duck under many branches, but there weren't many trees at this point and the trail wound swiftly up through the brush, following the contours of the mountain. He reached an outcropping and came near enough to look over and remain out of sight.

A small dust cloud was coming from behind, too far and too dusty to make out details. Whoever it was had not reached where Bill turned off the road yet, so he couldn't be sure it was actually someone following. He didn't want to take the time to wait, since he wanted the distance if he was being followed. He continued up the trail, taking care to leave as little trail as possible.

Where was Stacker?

About a mile further he set his horse behind some brush and watched the distant trail behind. Sure enough… dust… He was being followed. He moved ahead carefully, yet swiftly. Whoever it was needed to work out the trail. Unless this was an experienced tracker… Such men thought ahead, trying to put themselves in the minds of the hunted, anticipating moves and directions. If so, then the danger was more imminent.

He rode higher and higher, taking a route over Fesser's Bluff instead of the swifter way home.

Suddenly he pulled up. Fresh tracks! Coming off Fesser's Bluff and headed northeast towards the ranch. Of course, it could be coincidence. What would be the purpose of being on the bluff? What would someone who had been on the bluff be doing headed towards the ranch, if that was indeed the destination?

He glanced down his back trail. No sign of dust. He grinned wryly to himself. Wouldn't Russell Long get the humor of the hunted also becoming the hunter. If the one ahead of him was bent on mischief, then he needed to prevent that, yet he also chafed inside to wait and see who was behind Him. Judging by the trail, he who was ahead was about the same distance as whoever was behind. Interesting predicament, he thought to himself. His mind began to work on a solution even as his other senses watched the trail.

The rider ahead was a fairly big man, based on the size of the horse. The right front hoof toed in. He pulled up. The rider had stopped, maybe to watch his own back trail. Bill looked back and mentally tried to calculate his own speed and what the observer would have seen. How much dust had Bill raised? The rider had dismounted, the boots confirming he was a good-sized man. The marks also showed he was wearing large Mexican spurs. One boot heel was worn more than the other.

He glanced down the back trail. Was that dust or just haze? He moved on, figuring the rider ahead was maybe an hour away. Vigilance was the key here. If the rider ahead had seen him he might be running into trouble. That rider likely had sensed being followed, else his profession made it imperative to stay out of sight.

Bill considered backing off the trail and waiting….but not yet. He rode cautiously ahead, scanning the trail and the hills ahead, aware of areas that provided cover. Despite the danger from behind, he wanted to know what the rider ahead was up to.

He made frequent stops to check his back trail and to scout ahead around narrow turns in the trail. His curiosity grew as he realized the rider out front was making a beeline towards the point where someone had spied on the Henry ranch. Was this the same man whom Becky had seen? He'd found no cigarette butts as he'd ridden; yet a cautious man would not leave careless markers on the trail. Especially if he knew he was followed. That angle had to be considered, as Bill's eyes ranged across the slopes ahead, all senses alert, and then quickly he turned in his saddle and scanned behind.

What on….the sound of the gunshot ricocheted off the rocks as he fell from his horse. He instantly rolled off the trail into the rocks. He was in a hollow, out of sight to all but those above. He put his hand to his head. He felt as if a hard rock miner had used his head for sledgehammer practice. Blood ran down his face. It was a graze wound, but he had taken a stiff jolt, and his recollection of the sound told him it was a high powered round. Not the average rifle.

That meant whoever shot was not the average gun hand, and likely knew the art of hunting men. Bill knew he had to choose his next move carefully. His head throbbed beyond imagining. He desperately knew he could not give in to the pain. He must focus on staying alive.

He forced himself to think. His wound and the sound seemed to indicate a flatter trajectory, putting the hidden gunman somewhere at a lower level. Not above him - yet. He took his bandanna and tied it around his head. He was dizzy. He knew he could not let the dizziness take over.

Everything in him screamed at him to get away. Just like in the courtroom and other situations, he could not stay in one position. He must be able to maneuver. If he stayed where he was he would be trapped and the gunman had only to gain the ground above to pick Bill off like a sitting duck! Whoever it was might already be creeping upward to find a vantage point above him.

Bill knew he needed room to move, to evade and attack. Quickly he assured himself that his gun was still on his hip. His rifle lay on the ground where he fell - out in the open. His horse stood 20 yards away.

Where was the hidden gunman? And who was the stranger following him and where was he now.

He raised his head above the rocks and glanced where he guessed the shot had come from. Splinters of rock showered his face as the gunman placed another high-powered round very few inches from his face. Bill hugged the inside of the hollow. He had to get out of there! That shot had come from higher in the rocks than the first shot. I might only be minutes and the gunman would have a sure kill. Bill glanced around. Up the hill a few yards was a rock - not big enough to hide behind, but as a momentary shelter to get to higher ground.

Plunk! A round slammed into the earth by his side. The gunman was getting higher. He knew that the man would have to glance where he was walking, so there would be fleeting moments of opportunity. He had to move now!

Expecting to feel the slam of a bullet, he rose swiftly and ran upwards as he heard the sound of another gun firing, this one from behind him.

Bill quickly raced across the open and dove behind a small outcropping. He stooped, looking rapidly from side to side. He now needed to be wary of two gunmen. He crouched lower and crawled into a gap in the boulders.

Who was the other gunman? After a few minutes, he heard the sound of hooves on stone in the distance. It must be the first gunman, riding off. Blast it! He wanted to know his opponents! The danger would remain until this enemy was identified.

A voice hailed from beyond the rocks. “Don’t shoot, Henry! I’m comin’ in.” Bill crouched and raised his rifle.

It was Stacker! He came into the rocks and crouched next to Bill, who squinted through the pain.

"Saw ya comin' up the trail through my spyglass. Then I saw this other fella up in the rocks. Looks like you'll live, but we better get out of here. You sit tight while I fetch your horse."

A few minutes later Stacker returned with the lineback. "Went back of them boulders where he was holt up. Found this." He held out a crumpled envelope. It was addressed to a Vernon Grantler.

Stacker helped him onto his horse, then led off into the rocks. They wound and twisted around until Bill was not sure what direction they were going. Stacker seemed very sure of the direction, so he let him lead. Finally they turned around a boulder and immediately were before an upthrust, which created an overhang. Stacker dismounted and helped Bill down.

Stacker took the horses to some hidden place under the overhang, returning with twigs and sticks and almost immediately had a small blaze going. The dry wood made almost no smoke.

He poured water into a cup and placed it over the fire. A good western man always had a cup he could place over the fire. Never knew when a cup would come in handy - to share a cup of coffee or to boil water to bathe a wound.

After the water heated, Stacker bathed the wound gently.

"Vernon Grantler...ever heard o' him, Henry?"

"No, but he's not the average cow hand. Must be a professional killer."

Bill mused. How did a man get into such a profession? All of society is raised with the commandment "Thou shalt not kill." Yet some choose the path of this man. It wasn't necessarily the upbringing. Lots of good mothers raised bad sons. Sometimes it seems that no matter what, the sins of life seem to take control and they head down a path to worse things. Some realize it and turn around, while others seem not to recognize the signs - or maybe they enjoy the path. Most people who go bad have many opportunities to turn it around. He remembered a Sunday School teacher who taught them Bible verses. "He came to seek and to save that which was lost." Well, this man was lost...no more chances to turn it around. He wondered what kind of thoughts go through the mind of a man such as Vernon Grantler as he lay in wait to kill.

Then, someday, the roles are turned and Grantler would become the dead man. They, themselves, will someday lay clutching at the earth as their own lifeblood runs out. They will just disappear from the face of the earth. Animals, decay, erosion and time take all reminders. Suddenly such a man would just never show up again. Any family would just wait, and time without contact would just stretch longer and longer until they didn't think on it much. They'd think something happened but never really know - but deep in their hearts they would finally guess it. He wondered what the family knew. Did Grantler's family know he was a killer? Or did they believe whatever story he told them? Everybody likes to think the best of their loved ones.

Stacker went out to look around. It was obvious that they'd be camping out tonight. The sun was low in the west and it was no fun to travel a mountain trail in the dark. Bill had not planned on a night out, so Stacker passed him some jerky. They built the fire up and lay close to ward off the chill.

"Better get some sleep, Henry. My horse is half wild and will wake us if needed."

Chapter 40

His head felt better as they rode the daybreak trail. There were no indicators of being followed. Even so, they kept their rifles across their saddles. They watched their horses carefully, as horses smell and hear one another quicker than a rider. Many a traveling man has slept soundly on the trail, trusting his horse to let him know if danger approaches

It was near mid morning when they reached the pine covered outcropping looking over the sweeping valley of the ranch. Known as Sampson's Porch, it was a favorite of the family. Bill never failed to feel awe when he realized the beauty of the valley and the solid wisdom of his father in choosing this valley.

This morning, though, his thoughts were far different. As they dismounted quietly in the rocks, they found where a horse had been tied. The tracks were recent, probably last night. The rider had returned and led the horse towards the cliff face also. Warily they followed the boot prints towards the face of the cliff. They crept to the hollow. Sure enough, there was no one, but quite a few cigarette butts, and some were older than others. Whoever it was had been here more than once, perhaps several times.

They looked over the edge of the bluff towards the ranch. Far below in the fertile valley of the Henry ranch, they watched a rider moving fast towards the ranch in the far distance. As the crow flies it was about 5 miles, but another mile would be added by going down the bluff, and it was a slow descent, so maybe an hour or so riding to the ranch from here.

Had the rider known he was followed, prompting the ride down the bluff? Or was this part of a plan?

As they watched, they heard a sound like raindrops on their hats - the distant popping of guns. The ranch was under attack.

They jumped for their horses. In mid jump he heard the sound of a gun, Something hit him in the hip that sent pain jarring through him, and he felt himself falling, falling. There was a jolt and something jarred his side. He was hurt – bad.

He felt his face and his hand came away bloody. His side, too. He didn't know what happened, or whether Stacker was alive or dead. Whoever had shot would be looking for him.

With his every being telling him he needed to get away, he eased to an elbow, fighting the pain that gripped him. He looked around and saw he had fallen off the rim of the bluff, maybe 40 feet above. How he had survived the fall he didn't know, but he knew he was dead if he didn't find shelter. He felt for his gun. Still there.

He saw a cleft in the rock wall, with a space behind. He clawed and crawled in and blackness came over him as he passed out.

Things were bleak at the ranch. The day before, the ranch was attacked.

Matt Henry had been lingering at his chores, enjoying the sounds of the horses chewing contentedly and the sounds of the birds in the trees. He was always freshly amazed at how many sounds there were. It was like an orchestra, and there was a pattern to the sounds. He put his bucket down and leaned against the doorpost of the barn. It was Sunday, and the ranch took a bit of ease in the afternoon. Some of the men were in the bunkhouse playing cards or napping.

He wondered what would happen in this and the surrounding valleys. Would this evil take over? What was to happen? He knew there would be gunfire. He had never used his gun except to hunt and to better his brothers shooting the occasional can or branch. Would he be able to shoot an actual man? Deliberately? He wanted to voice his thoughts to pa, but hadn't had the chance. He wanted to ask what it was like to aim a gun at a man with actual intent to shoot. His dad was a tough man, able to be gentle, but always ready to use force for the cause of justice. He had more than once ridden out with other ranchers through the years to straighten things out. He had not hesitated to head after the rustlers with Old Man Slater. He had fought in the war. He had become a leader of men. Men came to the ranch to prop a leg on a fence rail and ask Otis Henry for his ideas and opinions.

Would he have what it takes to be as much of a man as his pa?

And Bill. What a man he had become. They were a mite worried over him right now, as he had been gone 2 days. They had done some looking, but saw no sign of him. They had to trust he was on the trail of something.

His mind jarred to a halt! The sounds of the woods had stopped. Something was out there. Slowly he crept to the corner. Peering carefully around, he saw several men running towards the ranch buildings.

He ran toward the house, yelling, “Attack! We’re under attack! Pa!” The oak shutters in the house began to slam, the bunkhouse suddenly did the same, the door opened and his pa yelled, “Here, Matt!” Just as Matt rushed through the door there was a burst of firing. He felt a sting in his side and fell to the floor. He felt hands pull him further in and the door slammed.

Shots filled his mind as he came to a few minutes later. He felt a knot on his head.

Looking around, he saw ma come and kneel beside him. His side hurt. He felt a bandage.

"Matt, you been hit, but not hard. Bullet tore a ditch in you, but you'll be ok. We need your help." Sensing his emotions as only a mother could, she put her hands on his shoulders and told him, "Matt, we need to defend our home and each other. Those men outside intend to kill us. It's ok to shoot them. It needs to be done."

"Ok, ma."

Sudden shots rang out and he looked to see his pa levering several shots out the firing slits. The cabin was built like a fort, as it really was intended when Ella and Otis first built it. It was meant to resist Indians and whatever element of white man who tried to take it. The bunkhouse was also built the same way, and the two were placed such that they could see each other and communicate through facing windows. There was an excellent field of fire if there were enough to man all sides of the cabin. Thick oak shutters with gun slits were already fastened.

Matt got to his feet, wincing with the pain. Grabbing his Winchester he looked at his pa. His pa looked at him. It was a look that urged Matt to do his best. It was a look of concern, intense awareness and paternal love.

"Take the back bedroom window, Matt. Make every shot count. This isn't the average attack….they intend to kill us."

Matt nodded and moved quickly.

"Otis, you think they'll try and fire the

house?" Ella was always aware of the possibilities.

"Don't know, but this is a cruel bunch. We need to hold them off till help gets here. You ready, Ella? Been a lot of years since we had this happen.

"I'm with you all the way, Bull Henry!" She saw him smile at the name. It was a reminder that he was a fighting man.

Shots rang out, and they could hear Matt in the back, levering his rifle. Buck had one side and Chad the other. Ella moved around, getting coffee on the stove, and began frying bacon. She wanted her men-folk to eat and this looked to be a long day.

"Pa?" It was Matt, speaking loud enough to be heard inside but not outside. "There's a good half-dozen out thisaway."

"How many you got, Chad?"

"Hard to tell, but at least that over here."

"Buck?"

"A few more over here. I see more around the bunkhouse. Looks like an army out there, Pa. Probably 30, maybe more out there."

"We've gotta watch that they don't get close, boys. Keep your eyes open."

A smashing volley sounded and shattering glass fell beyond the windows. The men returned fire, and at least one scream told them someone was out of the fight.

"Otis Henry?" Her voice was stern. "They done broke my glass windows. Those come all the way from St. Louis!"

Suddenly the firing became intense, with one or two stray shells coming in the slots and plowing into the walls opposite. Ella ducked as she turned bacon. There was a haze of acrid smoke already in the room. Ella pulled the bacon off to cool, then grabbed her Winchester and manned a window. She shot off a couple quick shots.

"Got one!" She said. A bullet splintered wood in her face.

"Lotta men out there! Who do we have here at the home place?"

"It's us here, then in the bunkhouse we have Tetch, Sim, Gard, Brady and Finley."

"Griggs?"

"Griggs went to town. There are a couple at the line cabin. Still no sign of Bill. Not sure where he is.

Otis and Ella had been talking about Bill earlier that day, knowing that he was investigating all the recent happenings. They had sent men out today looking, but with all the other happenings, knew they had to keep a force at the home place. Bill had taken care of himself all these years and would have to do so now. It was the way of the west.

"So we got five in here and five in the bunkhouse." Volleys of shots peppered the house. An occasional stray shot got inside, one hitting the fireplace and ricocheting to hit a lamp. Buck suddenly jumped, blood splattering his face as he hit the floor. Ella jumped to him. He was conscious but stunned, the bullet having creased the side of his head.

“Head wound,” she said to Otis. She ran for her bandages, putting liniment on before she wrapped the bandage. Though she was stunned herself at her own sons being hit, she was a woman of purpose and the old instincts kicked in. All business, she quickly helped Buck to a seat near his post and went room to room ducking as she filled coffee cups and passed out the bacon.

Chapter 41

Bill stirred. The blackness was all around him, but for a small light from the cleft. He heard distant voices, and he faded into unconsciousness again.

When he awoke, it was to the sound of a fire crackling. He opened his eyes and saw the glow on rock walls. Reaching to his head he felt bandages. Someone had bandaged his wound. He felt to his side and found a poultice tied there. Reaching to his hip…his gun was gone!

Where was he?

All was quiet. He looked over and saw his gun sitting on a rock across the fire.

Nobody around, his gun nearby. Was this a trap? If he sought to get the gun, would he be shot? That didn't make sense….after all, someone had bandaged his wounds.

He remembered crawling into the cleft of the rock, then fading into unconsciousness. He looked around. He must still be in a cave. Only this room was fairly large, enough to allow for an average man to stand upright.

How long had he been here? What about the ranch? Panic welled up inside him and he tried to rise, but fell back with the pain and weakness. What about his ma and pa and his brothers? He tried to rise again and fell back once more, his mind fading once more into darkness.

He awoke to the sound of quiet singing. He recognized the voice and turned his head. Dooley! He was bent over a pot stirring, but turned as Bill reached again for his head.

"Howdy, young man! For a while there I thought you was kilt!"

"Where am I? How did I get here?"

"You're in a cave... my cave. One of them. You comed in the back door. I seen what was agoin' on out yonder and ducked in the front door. Found you by the back door…one of them."

"We were near Sampson's Porch."

"You was. Even closer now." Dooley looked around him. "If'n ol' Sampson had found this cave, he'd still been alive! See, ol' Sampson was caught in a mighty fierce storm on the mountain, with lightning a flashin' and a strikin' all around him. He almost made it to safety. I found him -

he and I was partners. I found him the next day. I'd been in the same storm and stumbled on this cave. I explored it, found the back door where you was, crawled out and there was Sampson, looking mighty terrible. It was his clothes what told who he was. He was that close to this here cave."

"There was a man with me…"

"Kilt. Got him 4-5 times, looked like. From the look of the ground, they got down off'n their hosses an beat him." Dooley shook his head. "They's some mean folk a wanderin' these parts. I didn't bury him 'cause they might come back. Got his particulars for ya. I think they figured you fer dead."

Stacker! A good man. Lost because of him! What was going on! He had left the East to get away and spend time away from all the conflict. Instead he had walked right into it.

He lay back again.

"How long have I been here? The ranch was attacked. I need to help."

"Well, son, you been here a day. I ain't gone far, on account of takin' care of you, but from what I seen, your folks and those with 'em got away into the hills – up that draw back of the place. I been hearing lots of gunfire still, so somebody's a puttin' up a fight. I think they's other places was hit at the same time."

"I've got to get there to help."

"Son, you ain't doin' nobody no good today, mebbe tomorry. You took a good hit in the hip. I ain't sure if anything's busted inside you. Don't seems no broke bones, but you landed on your side pretty hard, too."

Bill glanced to where his gun lay. Dooley saw the look.

"I ain't keepin' you from your gun. It's there and it's loaded. Just didn't want you doin' somethin' crazy whilst you was out. I figure when you're strong enough to get to it, you're strong enough to have it back." He turned to the pot and began to hum.

Ma! Pa! What was going on out there? They got away, which means they had to abandon the cabin. What was it pa used to talk about? Back in the recesses of his memory he could hear it:

"Son, if we ever have to hightail it, go to 'the fort." The fort was a place about a mile back of the home place, up by Whispering Lake. They all knew where it was, and pa had them work on it once in a while. It was a circle of boulders and upthrust granite about 50 foot around, with a trickle of an underground spring that gave a bit of water. Over the years they had built a small cistern and filled the gaps in the rocks with smaller rocks and logs. They had cleared brush and trees around for a field of fire. It was a last ditch place to be, but could be held well. His pa always said that the best way to fight was to be moving, on the attack, but that some battles can be won by just wearing the other side down.

They would have gone to the fort if they could make it. Was anybody hurt? He tried again to get up, but groaned and lay back down, Soon he was asleep.

> "Cannon to the right of them
> Cannon to the left of them,
> Volleyed and thundered…"

Chapter 42

Through the afternoon they settled into a pattern: Shoot, draw back from the hole, peek and pick a target if possible. They needed to keep the attackers from getting close. They kept their eyes roving and shot at anything that moved from cover. Otis Henry had taught his boys well, and they knew their way with a Winchester.

Gunfire deafened the afternoon as the attack intensified.

Ella checked her weapon. Keeping her thoughts to herself, she knew that this was an attack more intense than many, and she knew that it might get worse before it got better.

Hours later there was no sign of letting up.

All at once they heard a yell, repeated as it took affect. "Hold your fire!" The defenders peered into the darkness.

"Henry!" None recognized the voice.

"Who are you?" Otis yelled.

"We've got too many men for you. Throw down your guns and come out"

He looked to his sons and his wife of many battles. The reality of the battle was there before him, but he had never surrendered.

"Chad, while they're distracted, see if you can get some contact with the men in the bunkhouse. Careful at the window. Tetch's been through this with us; he'll likely be thinking the same thing.

"Matt. How you doing?"

"Ok, pa. I guess it's easy to shoot when it's like this."

"We'll give you one more minute!" came the voice outside.

Otis looked at Buck. Buck looked back at him. "I'm ok, pa. I've got a fierce headache but I can shoot."

"I'm proud of you, boys. You're standing strong. Ella, I ain't sure we can hold them off. I just wish we knew what they wanted." He moved to a window slit. "Who are you and what do you want?"

In a tone that sent chills up their spines, "We want you."

Chad returned. "Tetch's been hit but not bad. The others have scratches. They're running low on bullets."

"Ella, much as we love our home, we can't

hold out against an army. Come dark they'll overwhelm us with numbers. It's only a matter of time before they fire the house."

"Pa!" it was Matt. "We can't give up! You heard that voice. I think they'll kill us."

"He's not talking giving up," Ma said. "He's talking new battle plans."

"Boys. Get all the ammunition together. Get some blankets and such. Ella." His wife was already in action. They had talked and planned of this before.

"Come dark, we make our move."

"Boys…the tunnel." They looked at their pa. They hadn't thought of the tunnel in years. There was a crude tunnel from the bunkhouse to the house, then from the house to a spot about 50 foot into the woods. It was dug shortly after they had arrived, meant as a last-ditch effort under dire circumstances. It had never been used. It was barely big enough for a good-sized man and none knew the condition of the tunnel after so many years.

Otis went to the window that overlooked the bunkhouse. He saw Tetch watching. Otis cracked open the shutter and pointed downward and Tetch looked confused, then his eyes widened with recognition. He disappeared from view.

The voice outside yelled. "You coming out?"

"Never!" Yelled Bull Henry. The gunfire commenced with a purpose, more intense than before. Bullet after bullet smacking the wall or coming through the slits. They stood away from the shutters. There was a big boom of a Spencer and a bullet came through the front door.

Ella pulled up a rug before the hearth, revealing the door to the tunnel, the ring inset in the floor to avoid a bulge. Buck joined her and grabbed the ring and pulled. The door was heavy and moved sluggishly with age and lack of use.

"Never used this before." Ella was musing as they kept themselves low. As it opened, Ella put a lantern in the hole. Soon, Tetch appeared, covered with cobwebs.

"How is it, Tetch?" Otis asked

"Better shape than I thought. Passable. I'd forgotten about this. Can't say what the other leg looks like. Give me a few minutes to check." He ducked down and continued in the tunnel.

The firing continued.

A while later, Tetch appeared again, looking like a mole breaking new ground. "A mite crumbled in spots, but we can get through. The hatch budged at the other end. I nudged it up a mite and it looked clear." At that moment, a fresh fusillade struck the door. It seemed they might try to hit the hinges or latch and get the door to fall. But it was built well, with the hinges on the inside.

"Who all is in the bunkhouse?"

"They's me, Sim, Gard, Brady an' Finley."

Finley! He'd forgotten about Finley. An excellent soldier and excellent shot.

"We'll leave after dark. Wait for my signal."

"Yessir." Tetch nodded and ducked towards the bunkhouse.

The next few hours passed in a blur of gunsmoke and desperation. As the sun set, Otis Henry nodded to Ella. She began to cook a mess of bacon and ham slices. She smiled at the thought of the attackers outside smelling the meat frying and them without food. She slapped a couple more thick slices into the pan.

"Henry!" It was the same chilling voice as before.

"What!"

"How many men did you have yesterday?" There was a pause. "Well, you have less today. My men shot two of yours last evening over at that place called Sampson's Porch. Your numbers aren't looking good. You need to surrender. I promise I'll be kind to your wife and give her a ticket out."

Otis Henry grimaced. Which two? Bill had not returned. Had he lost his son? He looked at his wife, who was holding her mouth aghast. The others wore shocked expressions.

Then something came over the face of this patriarch of the family. He stood tall, and a determined expression crossed his face.

"What about the boys?"

There was a wicked laugh. "Well, first thing I'm gonna do is have a few words with your son, William Henry. Then we'll go from there."

They all heard. He didn't say anything about Bill being killed! He may still be alive.

"Who are you?"

"Boss Carter…the new man in charge around here."

Otis Henry responded by placing a bullet near the corner where Boss stood. The men around could see the shocked look on Boss's face turn evil as he yelled. "Flush 'em out!"

The firing commenced with a vengeance.

Those inside did their best to not get hit, while trying to return fire. The attackers knew to aim for the shutters and the slits. It kept those inside almost ineffective. It was now fully dark.

Bull Henry moved to the shutter overlooking the bunkhouse and cracked it a bit. Bullets blew splinters wickedly from the wood. Bull Henry wiped them from his face. He signaled to Tetch.

Before many minutes went by, Tetch appeared in the tunnel.

"The others is comin' in a few minutes, sir. They's gonna fire a few more rounds."

Soon Sim and Gard appeared and came into the room, covered with dirt and cobwebs.

"Pardon the mess on your floor, ma'am." Said Sim with a grin.

Ella smiled.

"Where's Brady and Finley?" Otis asked.

"They're shootin' a few more times to keep them jumpin.' Be here in a minute."

Brady showed a couple minutes later. He looked quizzical. "Getting' hot out there. You know, worked for you all for 15 year and never knew about this tunnel. I declare!" A few moments later a wide-eyed Finley appeared, shaking his head in wonder. Otis Henry looked around.

"Ok, grab the gear and let's go. Tetch, you go first; Ella, you next. It'll take some work pulling the gear through."

Otis helped his wife down. She had put on some men's jeans.

"Move fast. They'll find we're gone soon enough."

More shells smashed through the door. They sensed movement outside. The men entered the tunnel in turn.

Otis Henry glanced around the room with anger. He brushed the dirt into the hole, arranged the rug as best he could to cover the hole when he closed the trapdoor, and lowered himself into total darkness.

In the not too distant hills of Colorado, a half-day's hard ride from the Henry ranch, tents were pitched and horses were picketed, sentries out. A camp of men, sitting and telling yarns around the evening fire, talking about the days of yore and the thoughts of tomorrow. Men who had sat and talked the same way many years before.

One man squatted on his heels amongst the others. "Recall that time at Antietam? If it weren't for Colonel Henry, well…who knows what woulda happened."

"A good passel of us wouldn't be alive today."

They all quieted. It was a contemplative silence about a moment impressed in their memories forever. At Antietam, faced with overwhelming odds and looking to be overrun, Colonel "Bull" Henry had appeared at the edge of the ravine they were holding. They trusted this man and his presence in their midst gave strength. He rallied the men and did the opposite of what was expected. He sounded the charge and the men responded instantly. Former downcast faces turned upwards, courage and valor rippled through the ranks and the men turned their anger to the enemy. The enemy, perhaps overconfident, did not expect a sudden charge with the venom of this one. The running wall was invincible and the confederate line wilted and ran in fear before the crazed, screaming Union tide.

Corporal Mason broke the reverie. ""I'll never forget that charge."

"Till my dyin' day it'll be burned in my memory."

"We'd of bin overrun if he hadn't come along."

"I'd follow him to the jaws of hell." Heads nodded in agreement.

As they drug at their memories, they heard a fast horse approaching in the darkness, and soon Mahoney, one of their scouts, rode in.

"Where's Walter?" He asked.

"Just over there a mite. What's up?"

"No time, I gotta report." He rode away. They heard the creak if saddle leather as he dismounted a ways off. They heard a few indistinct words, then excited directives.

"Get the men mounted! The Colonel needs us."

Chapter 43

"Hold up," Otis's breath was raspy with effort.

Otis Henry was struggling hard up the wooded hillside. He still hadn't recovered fully from his wound of months before, and, he had to admit, he wasn't young anymore. Ella was doing a bit better, but Matt was helping her along.

There were ten of them. Gard, Sim, Tetch and Brady were all solid hands, been with them for years. Finley was new, but a proven soldier. Matt was struggling, his wound bleeding again. Couldn't help that till they reached the fort. He'd be ok, barring other wounds. Chad unhurt. Buck nursed a headache. Tetch also had a flesh wound, but not serious. The other hands had scratches at the most.

Suddenly he heard a yell. The firing had stopped a few minutes earlier. He heard more yells. The attackers had discovered their prey had flown the coop. They'd be on them when they found the trail. Hopefully no one would find the tunnel, and the trail would take some doing to locate, as it was so far out from the cabin. Besides, even men of that nature knew better than to come up a hillside in the dark after men with guns.

Another yell. Had they found the tunnel? Likely, as that was an excited yell. The rug must not have fallen over the trap door as well as he'd hoped.

"Better move along, we're about halfway. Chad, you go ahead and see if there are any varmints between the fort and us. Give the fort a look-see, too. We don't need any surprises when we get there."

Moving ahead, they were all glad for the bit of moonlight they had, but they also realized if they could see so could those coming behind.

Just before they went over a shoulder of the hill, Otis told the rest to go ahead, but for Matt to stay with him. They peered over the edge. They could vaguely see men crisscrossing behind the house, looking for trail. Then a yell.

"Over here!" The shapes began to converge.

"Get ready to shoot, Matt. Unless I miss my guess, this ain't all woodsmen and they're gonna do something stupid and light a match to see the trail. When they do, you've got to nail him….Matt this shot will be a warning."

Sure enough, before too many minutes, they saw the flicker of a flame as someone stooped near the ground then slowly stood up. Matt fired, the match flickered out as they saw the man fall. They ducked as shots rained around them.

"Good shot, Matt. That'll buy some time. They won't rush up the hill. Let's go"

By the time they caught up, the others had reached the fort. They cleared it of fallen limbs and patched any holes they could see in the moonlight. Otis Henry assigned each man a spot, and settled in himself. Ella Henry was to be ready if anyone got inside the circle. She had brought her Winchester.

"How we doing on bullets, Matt?"

"'Bout a hundred apiece."

"Good."

"Ella, you get any food?"

"A mite, Otis. A good passel of jerky and some other odd and ends. And the bacon and ham I fried. I'll pass out some biscuits and beef.

Otis smiled at his wife. She smiled back and dug in her sack, pulling out her pistol, followed by wrapped food. They needn't worry about water. He urged them all to eat and drink while they could.

"I don't think they know about this place, or theyd'a had someone here waiting. When they come, watch for my signal. We'll need to use that moment of surprise and make every shot count and put the fear in them.

Griggs was headed back from town, He had been courting the blacksmith's daughter, Betsy, and had a pleasant evening. Dinner with the family, a snort of whiskey afterwards in the barn with her father, followed by a walk in the moonlight and a time to sit on the porch together. He smiled…letting his horse take the lead for the last couple miles as he dreamily went over the evening. It was almost dawn.

His reverie was broken by the distant sound of gunshots. Lots of them! He spurred his horse on towards the ranch. When he neared, he could make out many muzzle flashes, way up the ridge behind the home place. Warily he slowed his horse, shucked his gun and came up behind a copse of trees a quarter mile southeast of the house. He came close enough to see dozens of horses and some wagons.

His mind reeled with the realization that this was an attack by a significant force. The battle was on the hilltop, meaning the family had lost the house and retreated to the fort. He stopped for a few moments and thought. Then he dismounted, crept his way up to a bunch of tied horses, looking carefully around. He saw no guards, so untied all the horses he felt he could and, taking two extras, filtered back into the darkness. Mounting, he spurred the horses to town. This would be a hard, fast ride and he would switch horses and let the used ones go.

Up on the ridge, Matt peered at his father in the darkness.

"See anything, Pa?"

"No, with the cloud covering the moon, it's awful blasted dark out here. I can hear those tenderfoot derby-toter's climbing through the brush, though. They sure don't know anything about the woods."

Matt was seeing a new side of his father – careful, observant, commanding all rolled together. He watched as his father walked the perimeter, checking on each man and whispering encouraging words. A commander! Despite his fears and tension, Matt was eased by his father's presence. He sensed the same from the others. This must be what his father's men had felt like all those years ago in the war.

They heard the noise getting nearer as the men started reaching the top of the hill and gathering and talking amongst themselves.

Otis Henry walked the perimeter and approached Tetch. "How ya doing, Tetch?"

"Doin' fine, suh."

"Any sign of them anywhere but the hillside?"

"None."

"You watch the north and east, Finley the west. The rest of us will prepare for a frontal assault. We'll need to take the wind out of their sails quick."

He gathered the others toward the hillside.

"When the shooting starts, we need to make them think twice. I want you to choose your shots carefully, shoot through the holes twice and then duck, as they'll likely shoot for the muzzle flashes. When they get tired of the searching fire, we'll do it again. We know the field of fire, but they don't. At first they'll cower, but then later they'll start trying to flank us. That's when we've got our work cut out for us. Make every shot count.

Otis Henry touched his side. He hurt, and his age didn't help, he thought wryly. Yet, he was also exhilarated. It had been so many years since his senses had felt the sharpening of battle. He felt good, felt younger as he took note of each man's position and mentally calculated their supplies.

He looked out over the rocks. Even though it was dark, he knew every inch of the hillside. At the top, it was not flat. The attackers would face not only the fort in the rocks, but a varying slope between, making running difficult. Over the years, he had cleared most obstructions that might benefit an attacking force. As peace had settled in the region, he had even contemplated letting the hillside grow over. Now he was glad he had kept it up. The hillside was bare for 200 feet on both the uphill and downhill sides. The flanks were half that. The flank was a potential weakness, but the slope made it difficult for a man to run, one leg being downhill.

He never wanted to have to use this fort, he

thought to himself, but now he was glad it was here. He walked over to his wife and looked tenderly at her.

"Sort of like the old days, huh, Ella?"

"It's been so many years, Otis. But the senses are still there and I ain't gonna shy from the fight. Neither one of us is spring chickens anymore, but we're smarter. Our sons are doing well, Otis."

"Yes...I don't know what this night will hold, Ella." She knew what he was saying and reached out and gave his hand a squeeze.

He gave his wife a kiss and moved to the wall.

Boss Carter labored up the hillside. He was a massive, brutal man, with an imposing stride on level ground, but climbing steep hillsides was different than walking the wharf in Boston.

Reaching the top of the main slope, he stopped and caught his breath. Finnegan came to his side.

"What's the plan, Boss?"

"The plan is attack! We've got enough men to overwhelm that bunch. Just gotta locate them. Can you see anything?" Boss lit a cigar as he saw many cigarettes lighting up along the slope. Little flashes of light flickered as men scratched matches and lit up.

"Can't see nothing, except it seems a little darker up there." He pointed.

Boss saw nothing. He whispered. "Get the

men moving. We'll locate them. They may have gone into the woods, so get some men along there."

A few moments later the cigarette glows moved upwards, glowing brighter as the men puffed with exertion.

Ella looked through a hole in the rocks. She smiled, despite the situation. Cigarette glows showed across the hillside as these greenhorn eastern thugs showed their locations by their habit.

Otis came to her side, grinning. "I see it, too! I've passed the word to shoot at the glows. We'll likely get two shots and then they'll get smart. Wait for my word."

Otis walked the perimeter and spoke to Tetch again, assuring himself that there were no signs of flanking movements…yet. He moved to the front. He whispered. "They're about 200 feet, you're shooting downhill so aim right at the glow and you should be about right. Wait for my command."

He gazed through a hole and readied his Winchester. There was a pulsating effect among the cigarette glows, brightening as each man drew air. Some pulsed more than others. Otis Henry took aim at a heavier puffing glow.

"Fire!"

The usual silence of the mountain was rent even further as the sudden thunderous clap of gunfire exploded on the invaders.

Chapter 44

Boss Carter walked up the hill, his cigar glowing bright with his exertion. His eyes peering, he saw nothing. Maybe they were long gone up the slope?

Suddenly the dark was rent with muzzle blasts and men in his ranks fell screaming. Before it all registered, there was another round and more men fell, including the man next to him. The man screamed and rolled around. He bumped against Boss Carter. Carter kicked the man viciously. The man continued to scream, but with less strength.

"Get down!" he yelled.

Boss got down and felt moisture. He felt of

it and realized it was the blood of the fallen man. He reached over and wiped it on the man's barely visible pant leg. The man was screaming no more and lay unmoving and lifeless.

"Blasted idiot!" He whispered loudly. He had no compassion for human life. The man had been inconvenient to him, and now that was taken care of.

Down the grouping of men along the slope, he saw a small fire, probably from a cigarette. He saw the men around moving to return fire. Another round of shots from the darkness and he saw the men along the hill hit and cry out.

The cigarettes! He hurriedly grabbed his cigar from his own mouth and threw it to the side. He yelled, "No cigarettes! You're making yourself targets!" Bullets peppered the ground near him, and a man nearby was hit in the shoulder.

Blast it! This was a lot different than the waterfront. The men were so used to lighting up, and he the same, that he had lost men through something so stupid! Well, lesson learned and he was ok. The other men were expendable and he, himself, was the only one who mattered.

A quick learner, he called for Finnegan. The man answered from very close, startling Carter.

"Want you to go along the hillside, tell the men to back up just over the crown of the hill for cover. Now!" Finnegan went and Boss wriggled his mass backwards 20 feet till he was over the edge of the hill. Others fell in around him. There was noise as the easterners rustled around going backwards, but there were no shots. Groans and cries still rent the air from the men who had fallen. Some had been drug backwards by men nearby. A few still lay ahead of the force on the hillside, crying and calling out.

Bull Henry walked the interior. He suggested Ella get some sleep, as he didn't feel anything was going to happen soon. He speculated that Boss Carter, unused to the darkness and not knowing what he was facing, would wait till first light to assess. He set up a watch schedule, telling them to pay particular attention to any sounds of movement. He himself would try and rest then stand the middle watch. He stopped by Finley.

"You tired, Finley?"

"I'm ok, sir."

"Fine, you take first watch, then wake me."

"Yes, sir."

Boss Carter had slipped below the edge of the hillside, far enough that he could light his cigar. As he cupped his hand around the match, he drew back for a moment as he saw the blood on his hand and sleeve. Then he grinned to himself. Coulda been me! My luck holds! It was that idiot that got it and I didn't need him anyway.

To him all men were throw away's, useful only in as far as they served his purpose. He had

had the blood of many men on his hands. It just happened that this time it was not of his planning.

Boss Carter puffed his cigar rapidly, thinking hard. He wished the wounded wretches would shut up so he could think.

He held his cigar low as he peered over the hillside into the darkness. He looked up and saw no stars. He could see nothing, and didn't know what he was facing. Ah, well, he thought, better just wait till first light and get a look at what's going on. Being impatient by choice, this was not an easy decision. He passed the word.

Many in New Haven heard the rapid hoof beats as they neared town and looked up from their pillows. Windows were dark with sleep. Griggs shouted and saw lanterns lit in windows and sashes raised. He trotted the street shouting.

"The Henry ranch is under attack! The Henry ranch is under attack! We need help! Meet at Marge's in 10 minutes!"

In 10 minutes there were a dozen men at the restaurant. Marge was handing out cups of just fresh coffee as the men finished buttoning shirts and putting up suspenders. All were armed. There were many of the younger set, watching as the older men seemed to become younger and take on importance as Griggs told what he knew and the men made plans. The youth would not have noticed, but their fathers' spirits were quickened as they rallied for battle and began to check their weapons again.

Wilson came in with a heavy crate on his shoulders. He set it down and began handing out ammunition to those present.

The Parson had been late heading home last night, and had bedded down in the Livery. He heard the ruckus and followed Ike out the door to Marge's. Even old man Slater was here, having been coming in for a morning meeting with a cattle buyer and decided to arrive the night before and stay at Tagget's.

As a few more came in, Tanner spoke. "From what Griggs says, they've left the house. Matt told me once they had a place to fort up on the hillside, up over the crest of the lower slope. That must be where they are. Now, it's dark and we don't know where the attackers are. We know there are lots of them."

"Let's go get 'em!" yelled one just barely into manhood.

The older men, seasoned in conflict in their younger years, turned as one to stare grimly at the young man. He wilted, turned his eyes downward.

"This isn't going to be fun. Somebody's maybe gonna die." He then turned to the men. We have to go slow, and Griggs suggests we come up behind them and some over the ridge up top. We need to wait near the house till first light, or we're just gonna stumble over each other and let them know we're coming. It'll take us a couple hours to get there. We'll need to go slow, stay unseen and avoid shooting. You younger fellas listen to what the older ones tell you. They've been through this before."

"Griggs, you take the bunch over the ridge, since you'll know the way. The rest of us will come in behind at the ranch house. Get your horses saddled. We'll leave in an hour."

Heads nodded in determined agreement as men went to get horses and weapons.

The smell of stew woke him up. Dooley was working over a small pot and Bill could tell he was better because the food attracted him.

"How long have I been out?"

"Long time. Hungry?"

"I feel like I could eat a horse"

"Well…I can't promise ya that. Never did cotton to horsemeat. But I got some fine tasting rabbit here." Dooley chuckled and hummed to himself.

Bill felt his hip. "What's the salve made of," Bill asked.

"Ya pro'bly don't wanta know."

"I'll take your word for it." Bill chuckled despite his headache. "I am glad. You saved my skin. Thanks."

Bill pushed himself to a sitting position. He felt stiff all over. He rolled to his knees and reached out a hand to the wall.

"Go slow, youngster…don't overdo it."

Bill gripped the rock wall as he forced his way to stand. "I can't lay around longer. I have to help my folks." He grimaced as he leaned against the cave wall. He eased himself over to a rock and sat down. His head still hurt, but wasn't throbbing as before. His side felt like he'd been kicked by a summer colt. But he could move. He got up again, reached over and retrieved his gun. Dooley was watching him carefully.

"You jest set there. Get some vittles in ya." He passed Bill a mug of rabbit stew. Bill tore into it as only a starving man could. Dooley grinned as he watched him eat. "Don't go so fast….there's more. A body should least taste fer they swaller!"

"Is this where you live, Dooley?"

"Oh, I plant myself hither and yon. Sometimes hither and sometimes yon. I likes to be in different spots. I has places for every season, an' every weather."

Dooley grinned as he saw himself being scrutinized.

"I might be crazy."

"Whatever you are, I'm glad to see you."

"Comes from bein' alone. The crazy stuff. I ain't sayin' I ain't crazy, but I ain't crazy all the time. I'm jus' crazy when I'm crazy." He chuckled. "Guess that sounds crazy."

Dooley got up. "I got's ta go check my doors. Make sure there's nobody thereabouts. Then we'll see what we can find out about yer folks."

Chapter 45

The eastern sky showed a touch of the birthing dawn as New Haven came to life.

As the townsmen gathered, they heard many hoof beats approaching and the cadence of the sound brought them to the street, where they watched in awe and wonder as at least 40 men, gray and grizzled and ghostlike with dust rode into town. They were used to dust-covered riders, but this was different. The lead horseman lifted his hand to halt in the street before the townsfolk. In the bright light of Marge's, where a dozen lanterns lined the porch, the dust began to drift, revealing a large column unlike anything ever seen in New Haven. It was as if the mists of time itself were parting and the past was emerging from another dimension. All appeared ghostlike and there were men in uniform, men in stylish coats, men in the standard clothing of the west. A tall, lanky, bearded veteran nudged his horse forward. He looked wraithlike with dust yet his eyes were piercing in the lamplight, showing all business. He removed his hat and slapped it on his leg, sending up a plume of trail dust and revealing a well-groomed head of peppered gray hair. He placed the hat carefully back on his head before speaking.

" 'Scuse me. Could you please tell us the way to Bull Henry's spread?"

One old man stepped forward, "What you want with Mr. Henry?"

"He sent for us. There's been trouble."

"I'll say! Lot of strange doin's lately. Otis has been good for us and good to us. The latest news came in early this morning. He's holed up on the ridge back of the ranch northeast of here. Some of the fellas hereabout is headed over this morning"

The veteran raised his eyebrows. His mouth pursed with withheld words.

"Thank you, sir." He said, and turned to others nearby. "Sergeant, have the men water the horses. We'll take a short breather for the horses. We'll be makin' time. Canteens to be filled."

"Yes, Capt."

"And Sergeant?"

"Yes, sir?"

"Send Murphy up here."

"Yes, sir."

The sergeant gave orders to others, and then led the column northeast.

The captain looked as Murphy approached. "Yes Walter–I mean Capt."

"Murph… we don't know what's coming with today. How are we on ammunition?"

"Each man has at least a hundred rounds, Walter."

The Captain lowered his voice. "How are we on medical supplies, Murph?" He looked grim.

The Sergeant's eyebrows lifted. "I brought along a fair supply, but I pray we don't need much."

"Thanks, Murph."

The captain started to turn. "Sir?" It was the town man. He turned his horse back to the boardwalk and looked at the man.

"Sir, pardon me, but who are you?"

"We're the 49th Cavalry. Bull Henry's outfit."

"But you're not all wearing uniforms"

"We haven't been together in this big of a group since the war." He grinned, "Some ain't the same shape they once were." He looked at the line of men receding in the distance.

"But the war's been over these 12 years?!"

"This outfit goes beyond war. The Colonel's in trouble and we've come. Whoever is responsible is about to find out what war is about. And the 49th." With that, he turned and rode to the column.

When he reached the column he came alongside 2 men near the end of the group.

"Mike! Rad!"

"Yeah, Walter?" The captain grinned.

"When you fill your canteens and water your horses, take a short stretch, then mount up. I want you to go northwest and scout it out. See if you can locate the fighting and determine where Col. Henry is. Rumor is he is holed up and possibly wounded."

"If'n he's hurt, Capt..."

"I know. We'll play hob. But right now we need to have you out there as our eyes. You don't need me to tell you to be careful. We need you to find out what's going on, but we don't want the enemy to know.

"Yes, sir, Walter."

Bill and Dooley walked carefully through the passage, heading downwards in a gradual slope. Bill was amazed that he had never found it in his years of exploration. Dooley had found it after finding the initial cave and trailing with a torch through all the passages he could find.

As they walked by torchlight, Dooley told him about exploring and finding connecting tunnels where water had gone over the years and washed out the porous layers of sediment and rock, leaving the passages. He told of the springs in certain places and the way the water could get knee high in some passages during a cloudburst. Some were dry and snug no matter what.

After 10 minutes, Bill was tired, but the thought of his family gave him the strength he needed.

"Last time I saw you, there was a horse under you."

"Yep, will be again in a few minutes. You, too. I done caught yer hoss after he run off."

Bill was amazed at this man who so many referred to as crazy.

They leveled off and came around a twist in the tunnel and suddenly stood in a large chamber, tall as two men and large enough to hold several horses. Dooley had contrived a stable, and there was Bill's dun, head perked up from the manger, looking at him. He walked over and patted him. The dun nickered.

"I checked him over when I brought him in. He was scare't but fine. Had to blindfold him to bring him in here. Didn't want a loud ruckus.
Once he was in, it felt like a stable an I throwed him some vittles an' brushed him an' he settled in."

The saddles were over a tree trunk suspended between rock formations, and they both hurriedly got the horses ready to ride. Dooley again blindfolded Bill's horse just in case he spooked, and they went through a short twist and turn passage and into the bright sunlight beyond an upthrust of rock. They stopped for a few moments to let their eyes adjust, and then Bill saw they were at the base of the Bluff. He shook his head in amazement and gingerly stepped into the saddle.

Bill glanced at the edge of the bluff above. He wondered if anyone was there at Sampson's watching. Dooley noticed his glance.

"There was someone up there on the bluff, but he ain't watching no more."

They took the ride at a gallop, knowing they needed to save the horses for a later burst of speed.

He and Dooley had split up about a mile from the ranch. Bill suggested the older man go to town and rally some help. There was sporadic firing from up the hillside.

Bill came in through the woods at the base of the hillside a quarter mile away and worked his way carefully upwards through the trees. His head did not ache anymore, but his hip hurt badly. His eyes were intent as he searched for any outlying thugs. He saw none for quite some time, then saw movement of a derby hat on the hillside above. He skirted away and went further to find a group facing out of the woods. They were in a line facing what would be the fort. They began firing, with return fire singing through the trees. Bill ducked, not wanting to be hit by friendly fire. He looked around and then tied his horse in a protected copse, then crouched and worked his way slowly up a shallow draw till he was at a point above the men flanking the fort.

Raising his head between two rocks, he was

able to look down the hillside at the fort.

There were men below and men all to the sides. He saw flashes of color in the Fort as the defenders moved about. How many times he had gotten tired of clearing brush when his father would talk about the need to keep this place ready. He and his brothers would just look at each other. It was hot and tedious work all on a hillside. Now he was glad for all the effort. His family seemed secure.

Nevertheless, the sheer numbers of the enemy would make a difference. If there was an organized rush, there were not enough defenders.

Bill realized he was an unknown to the enemy. If he could keep them guessing, then it might thwart a rush towards the fort until Dooley was able to get help.

Moving left a few yards, he picked a spot behind a tree, rose slightly and levered a shot from his rifle that took one man down. The others did not grasp the direction and kept firing at the fort. Bill levered two more shots, putting one man out of the conflict for good and another clipped in the shoulder. By this time, someone of the bunch figured they were getting hit from somewhere else and turned and began shooting into the woods. They were shooting blindly, and others began to do the same. Bill took careful aim and squeezed a shot that took another man down. By then he was spotted and bullets came in his direction. He eased back into the draw and went down the slope.

Dooley was galloping around a bend in the mountain, heading for town, when he spied men up ahead. He reined into the trees and patted his laboring horse as he peered through the trees at the men.

Parson! Wilson! Ike! It was the townsfolk!

He began to shout:

"Cannon to the right of them,
Cannon to the left of them,
Volleyed and thundered…"

The men stopped and he rode out of his hiding place.

"Dooley." It was Parson, who noted the laboring horse.

"I was headin' to town to round you'uns up fer the fight. I'm glad you're on the way, cause my hoss is used up. Bill's headed up the hillside east of the ranch. His pa is on the hillside."

"We're on our way. We got the word earlier. Your horse is used up. You better rest him a while. We're headed to the ranch to come in behind. There's more men with us – friends of Henry's."

Dooley looked to see a dozen grizzled veterans. "Lawd Almighty! Into the valley of death rode the six hundred! I'll be behind ya's. Let my horse rest a mite."

The men spurred up through the trees, led by the Parson. Dooley dismounted and let his horse rest, finding a seep to water him. He knew the horse desperately needed rest. He sat down on a log beside the trees.

Chapter 46

Sometime later, two grizzled veterans in blue rounded a small ridge and heard rifle fire. Pulling up behind some trees, they peered thru the brush. The sound was some distance away, possibly a mile or so, but the chance of perimeter riders was always there.

Then there came another sound to their ears, from not far away. They looked at each other with wonder as they heard the voice, loudly:

"Half a league, half a league,
Half a league onward,
Into the valley of death
rode the six hundred!"

They pulled further into the brush and

watched as the strangest man they had ever seen came into view around the bend. The rider walked his horse and came to a halt near the hiding place of the two veterans. He spit to the side of the trail and said, in a conversational tone, "You's too far from the action and bein' too careful. Besides, I been watching you fer some time. Ain't seen uniformed scouts fer a coon's age. Maybe we oughta palaver a bit before I pull the trigger on this scattergun." The two peered through the leaves and saw the Colt revolving shotgun pointing their way.

"Hold your fire, old timer. We're coming out."

"Make sure you ain't got no hand near where I might suspect there's a gun."

"We're treading careful mister…hold your fire." They came slowly out of the brush.

"You friends or enemies of Otis Henry?"

"Friends."

"Good." They saw the hammer eased on the shotgun. "Mr. Henry needs help."

"We're from his old army outfit, the 49thCavalry."

"Well, I guess two more might help him. You looked like you's rode the river a mite"

"There's more. We're trying to locate the way up the ridge."

"Follow me, I'll fetch you there." He cut through some brush and started traversing the hillside, his voice raised a mite, but not as loud as before:

"Cannon to right of them,
Cannon to left of them,
Cannon in front of them
Volley'd & thunder'd;
Storm'd at with shot and shell,
Boldly they rode and well,
Into the jaws of Death,
Into the mouth of Hell
Rode the six hundred."

The two soldiers looked at each other quizzically, both caught off-guard by this strange apparition. As they drew nearer to the sporadic gunfire, the buckskin-clad old man quieted and raised his hand to halt them.

"Up ahead, they's a draw. Beyond that there's a small meadow and across from that the Henry outfit is holed up. Betwixt you and the meadow's some no-good scalawags – but they ain't got the sense to watch their backs. Herd of buff's could walk up their back and they'd never know it. Too citified, no horse sense."

"What's your play in this, stranger?"

"Ella makes good pie." He grinned through stained and stubby teeth. He began to quote, softly as he rode away:

"Forward, the Light Brigade!
Was there a man dismay'd ?
Not tho' the soldier knew
Some one had blunder'd:
Theirs not to make reply,

Theirs not to reason why,
Theirs but to do & die,
Into the valley of Death
Rode the six hundred."

He turned to look at the scouts. "I'll take care of the scalawags – you figger you can lead the rest of you blue-bellies up this way?"

The men nodded and rode back the way they had come.

It had been a long morning. With almost the first light there had been gunfire, sometimes sporadic, sometimes heavy. Bull Henry looked around at his little cluster of an army. Not like the old days, he thought. What he would have done to this bunch of outlaws if he had a command!

"Henry!" It was the voice from last night. He ignored it.

"Henry, this is Boss Carter."

His voice sounded venomous.

"Henry, the great 'Bull' Henry. Well, you ain't so great now. We've got you cornered and we've got so many more men than your piddly little group. I got a near a hundred men here now. You don't stand a chance. I know you can hear me or, if you're already dead," He chuckled audibly, "then the rest of you can."

Bull Henry glimpsed the speaker through a hole in the rock fort, but just enough of the man showed for Henry to see he was a large man.

"Here's my new proposition, Bull Henry. I want you to send out your son, William Henry, and in exchange I will stop shooting. Then, you will agree to leave this valley and I will take over your ranch as my own personal home."

Henry and his family fumed! They also realized that Boss Carter had no idea that Bill was not here. That made it all the better chance that Bill was somewhere around! He also knew enough to realize Boss Carter had no intention of letting anyone get away.

"What is your answer, Henry? I'm a very impatient man."

Bull Henry looked around at his family, saw the grit and determination and family pride in their eyes. The hired hands, like family also, showed the same. He grinned, levered his rifle and, easing the barrel into an opening, shot fragments off the rock near Carter's face. Ducking, Carter became malevolent! How dare he!

Carter screamed, "Kill them! Kill them all!"

Not long later, Bull looked around during a lull in the firing. Most of the men had blood on them in some form or another, but only Brady had been hit seriously. A bullet had by chance come through a small hole and had hit him hard. Looked like a lung shot. He needed care, and Ella did her best for him as the men manned the walls.

Bull Henry, deep inside, knew this was a

lost battle. Yet there was no alternative to continuing. This man would kill them no matter what. He knew that and the others knew that. Eventually the ammunition would run out. The only hope was for Griggs or some other to bring help. He looked over and saw Ella lever a shot through a hole, then turn back to Brady. He could see Brady was done for. He was already breathing ragged and foaming at the chest and mouth. He'd seen it in the war.

Finley looked his way. He could see the grit in the man's eyes as he fought in the face of these desperate odds. Tetch, wounded but doggedly fighting on. Gard, Sim and the boys, all bloodied and red-eyed from dust and smoke and constant vigilance, held their posts.

He caught Chad's eye. They looked at each other a moment and a pride and unity showed between them before Chad turned back to lever another shot at the hillside.

On they fought.

As he paused to reload, he heard yelling. The others heard it, too. They all paused and heard firing in the woods to the east, but nothing was hitting the rocks. The yelling increased and Bull Henry risked a peek through a rifle hole and saw men at the edge of the woods turning and shooting the other way.

They had help! Someone above and behind. It sounded like a lone rifle. Could it be Bill?

He was hoping for more men, but Bill was worth a few and thank God he was there.

Already it was disturbing the ranks of Carter's forces as men all around turned to look at the sudden disturbance.

"Keep shooting," he said. "That may be Bill. Don't let them focus on him. He needs our help as much as we need his."

They began firing as those who had a sudden glimmer of a better outcome than anticipated.

Bill moved up and down the draw, popping up unexpectedly to shoot, keeping the other men guessing. Finally, running low on shells, he worked his way up the hill. Lead whizzed by his head and slammed into the ground next to him. Below, Boss Carter decided to take things into his own hands. Leading a dozen men into the woods, they caught a glimpse of Bill up the draw, and set off in pursuit.

Carter had a look of triumph and glee on his face, as he saw his longtime foe so close at hand. He guessed Henry was low on ammunition by his actions, and he pushed the men mercilessly. As they neared the crest of the hill and the edge of the woods, they saw Bill go over the top.

As Bill came slowly over the top of the hill, gasping hoarsely for air, he suddenly faced a dozen gun barrels.

"It's Bill Henry, don't shoot!" It was Parson, and the men from town!

Bill gasped, "A dozen coming up and will be

over this ridge in just a minute!"

Parson waved the men to spread out and all became tense as they faced the hill, hearing the gasping and cursing of the men toiling up.

As the men rounded the summit, they faced a barrage of bullets as the anger of a quiet town vented itself upon evil.

No man coming over that hilltop that day survived.

Boss Carter heard and sensed what was happening, and only his girth and exhaustion with the climb saved his life. He had fallen behind and was a dozen steps behind his men. He startled backwards and moved downhill more quickly than he knew he could. For the first time in many years he had felt fear.

He reached the other men and urged them onward, his malevolence returning. He had Finnegan take charge of protecting them from above as the townsmen took up firing positions higher up.

Boss Carter saw possible defeat staring him in the face. He had never been defeated. Something within him was breaking. It was perhaps true what some people said that he had a very light grasp on sanity, and that he broke that day. Witnesses of that day say that he became driven, screaming himself hoarse at men to kill Henry, even shooting his own men if any showed any sign of running. He was evil incarnate that day.

Chapter 47

Two hours of hell happened over the next few hours, as men from both sides fought for what they believed in. Carter's men fought to stay alive from Boss' wrath, and to stay alive to fight another day. The town fought for their way of life and for their friend. The soldiers fought for their commander. Those in the fort of rocks fought for life and for the keeping of their home.

It is unknown how many bullets covered the ground that day, but witnesses said that it reminded them of Antietam, or perhaps Gettysburg.

It was vicious. Both sides were strong and men fell, but there was no decisive action. Bill Henry fought with determination, Boss Carter fought with crazed insanity. All fought with thought for nothing else. It was an even match and hope for final resolution began to fade.

And then....

A bugle was heard by a few. They stopped firing and cocked their ears. Others slowly noted what was happening and stopped firing also, turning their ears to the western slope.

Bull Henry heard the sound.

Boss Carter heard the sound.

Firing virtually stopped.

Over the ridge came a sight that was never to be forgotten.

Unexpected.

Jaws dropped and men stood paralyzed with shock.

A force of cavalrymen, with wide, blood-crazed eyes swooped across the hillside.

Men screamed and leapt for safety as these men on horseback relived the days of yore and lived for the future and fought like wildcats. Guns belched fire and smoke and screams were heard across the field of battle. The toughs from back east had never seen such a sight and the sheer power of the charge was beyond their comprehension. They were used to having the upper hand. Little knots of men made stands that day. For a time they could hear Boss Carter screaming in the background, and the fear kept them fighting. Soon, however, even that motivation gave way to their fear of death, fed by the sight of their fellow toughs falling and the sight of blood everywhere.

Finally, those remaining of Boss Carter's forces broke and scrambled and ran pell-mell down the hillside, into the barrels of the latecomers arriving to join the battle. Dorta Cummings was there to avenge Red Bowen and showed no mercy as she fired upon the Triple-C men. Some tried to fight, some tried to surrender, all were caught in the fire of men angry at the threat to their families, angry at themselves and wanting to redeem manhood.

In the midst of it all, Boss Carter ducked into the woods, frantic with defeat, with insanity.

Bill Henry caught a glimpse as Carter entered the woods and scrambled down the hillside to follow. He couldn't let Carter get far.

Boss Carter was not as far away as he would have liked to have been. He was breathing heavily, his muscles arguing as he trotted through the trees. Coming around a clump of trees, he saw two riderless horses. He approached them carefully as his chest heaved.

The horses shied a mite, but seemed also glad to see someone. Boss Carter gained their halters with a sense of triumph. He turned suddenly at the sound of running behind him. Turning, he saw Finnegan pull up, bending to put his hands on his knees as he gasped for air.

"Thank God! Horses." He gasped. "Let's get outa here, Boss." He moved towards the horses but stopped as he faced Boss Carter holding a pistol aimed at him.

Carter glared at him, a wry smile at one corner of his mouth. “Too much distance to cover, Finn. I need both horses so I can switch and keep going.”

“But…” The bullet tore his heart open, and glazed-eyed he fell.

Boss Carter mounted and rode away through the trees.

As he rode, his thoughts went back to what happened.

Where did all those soldiers come from? All his plans! He had looked at every angle and he was to be on top, the ruler of the valley and all the valleys beyond for 100 miles. He was to live like a king, surrounded by his minions! It was all carefully worked out. He had always been able to work it out, to win, to be, well... Boss.

Absolute hatred welled up in Boss’ heart as he pushed the horses with crazed disregard through the woods and boulder-strewn clearings along the top of the bluff. Somewhere he lost the reins of the other horse. No matter. On he pushed.

He hated the man! Even more so, now that his plan to kill Otis Henry and family had failed. Blast it! Someday….someday he would get him. For now, he needed to get away, get where he could rebuild his empire and plan another way. And he would succeed! And he would get Bill Henry!

His horse was lathering. As he fumed about

what happened, he drove the horse harder and harder with his emotion, kicking the horse brutally. He was making plans for the future, such that he didn't see the drop off. Suddenly the ground fell out from underneath him and he toppled over the edge of the escarpment.

He wasn't sure if it was he or the horse that screamed, and he lay, broken, upon the rocks 30 feet below. A horse struggled beside him. In its death throes, the horse was kicking out, striking Boss Carter – but strangely he couldn't feel it.

He looked around. Why couldn't he move his legs? Why couldn't he get up? Hurry! Before the others found him! But try as he might, his body would not do what his mind commanded.

He thought he heard hoof beats. He twisted his head to look back up the escarpment. Henry!

Boss Carter saw his enemy looking down at him. He tried again to move but nothing worked. He had to move.

Looking up again, he saw Henry still looking down at him.

"Your bossing days are over, Carter. The death you've brought to so many has now come to you."

Though he wanted to curse the man, no words would come. What was wrong? His vision was hazy. Was it foggy?

The horse nearby had ceased kicking, but it didn't matter.

Boss Carter's glazed eyes lay open to the

sun…

Near the fort, the men of the 49th looked to their wounded. Just a few scratches and flesh wounds. The impact of the totally unexpected charge had completely routed the forces of Boss Carter.

Among the townsmen there were a couple bad wounds, but most were veterans and had looked out for their sons. Wilson took a hard one in the shoulder…he wouldn't be lifting supplies for a while.

It was the Triple-C that suffered the most. Unused to the west, unused to gunfights, they had run pell-mell over the slopes, and at least a dozen lay dead on the hillside. More lay in the woods.

Bull Henry was exhausted and barely able to get around, but insisted on looking to his men. His concern was eased somewhat when he found there were no deaths, no serious wounds in the men of the 49th. His own family had not fared so well. Sim had taken one hard in the side. Captain Bartner, the doctor of the outfit, was attending to him now. Matt's injury was bleeding again. Chad was sporting a bloody bandage around his arm. Brady was dead. One of the area hands had been killed. Dorta Cummings was bleeding from a leg wound, but feisty – which meant she'd be ok.

"Colonel, sir?" It was private Cab Johnson.

"Yes, Johnson."

"Captain Bartner wishes me to inform you that your hand, Mr. Sim, will likely make it but it's going to take a long time."

"Thank you. My respects to the Captain" He turned away.

"Sir?"

"Yes. Johnson?"

"The Captain wishes to see you, sir."

"Johnson, let's stop this military stuff."

"Yessir, Colonel. This way, sir"

Otis Henry followed Johnson, rolling his eyes.

Otis Henry came up to Captain Bartner on the hillside with a couple other men.

"Colonel Henry, sir, we've had quite the battle here today, but the troops came through well, considering. We've got several wounded, a couple seriously. Doc's looking to them now. We've rounded up the enemy. There's about 50 dead, lots of wounded. The rest are being held down the hill."

"Thank you, Captain"

Chapter 48

His orders were to kill ranchers and cowhands. He specialized in it. Usually, he killed his man and left. A week prior he had hit but not killed Henry. Best policy would be to leave now. This time, however, Vern Grantler had bent his rules. The money was better than anything he'd ever earned. A thousand in gold for every body he left laying in the grass.

Tyler and Tucker were easy targets. Of course, with a man of his skill, all targets were easy. Find their pattern and lay in wait.

Something inside him rebelled, though, at hanging around. He was on his way to pick up the gold where it was always left in the hollow of a tree. Forget the rest. Money bought a lot of things, but only if you lived to spend it.

It was time to leave. He had never missed and had never been caught, and never really scared, but something in this situation made the hair on his neck stand up. There was too much happening, and he had already stayed longer than his senses told him was healthy. With him it was always kill and ride, never staying around to even hear what others thought. He figured he'd stand a better chance of enjoying a rocking chair someday if he left the mystery open ended. Besides, there was that pretty little senorita down Boulder way….

As he mused and puffed the cigar, he rounded a bend in the trail, and his normally alert nerves were dulled with the vision of a sweet smile and a drink. Too late did the warning signs reach his senses.

All six men held their rifles leveled at his shirt pocket.

"Hold it right there, mister."

He sat motionless.

"Smith, go take a look in that there scabbard." A lean man slowly dismounted and walked over to draw the rifle out. They all admired the workmanship – one man even whistled.

"Could do someone in mighty easy with that gun, and do it from quite a distance." The lean man stepped back.

When a man faces certain death, things that seemed important fade quickly. He no longer thought of the apple or the senorita. In fact, his mouth was so dry…

"Mister, Art Tucker and Nate Tyler were good men and had families. You got anybody we should notify?"

He knew what was coming and his mind screamed as he reached for his Colt. He felt the impact of multiple bullets, and didn't know where to shoot. Something was on his face….no….his face was in the sand of the trail, and he felt something trickle across his face, blurring his vision. He lay, and it seemed that he couldn't move. He saw, but heard no sound as his rifle was broken against a boulder. Such a fine weapon… A cigar lay nearby….a brief thought and then a shudder as death claimed him.

Becky had ridden up to the Henry ranch full speed as usual. She had brought the women to help though, of course, they were a ways behind her. She pitched in and did whatever was needed with all the energy she had. Carrying water, bandaging, wiping brows, cleaning up the house.

Every once in a while she would catch a glimpse of Bill in the sea of faces and pause. Every now and then their eyes would meet and hold for a moment.

Later that evening, the Henry ranch looked like a military installation, men and tents everywhere, parties of soldiers sitting around campfires laughing and feeling young again.

Bill walked with Becky through the camp

and out to the meadow beyond all the noise.

The sunset was stunning with magenta's and blues brighter than any they remembered.

"It's hard to believe what has happened, Becky. It seems like some nightmare."

"Does it make you want to head back east again?" There was a touch of fear in her voice.

"I haven't thought much about that, Becky. The past weeks here have certainly been full of anything but peace of mind. And now that Boss Carter is dead, his empire will crumble. Those minions he left behind don't have the strength to carry the way. Once things are cleared up here, the house repaired and a myriad of things taken care of, then I'll have time to think of myself."

She turned to face him, grasped his hands in hers. She gazed at him intently. "Bill, either you stay or I'm coming with you."

"You would not be happy in the east, Becky. For all the reasons I've told you."

"Does that mean you're leaving?" There was moisture in her eyes.

He did not answer. Becky looked down as a tear coursed her cheek.

"I wonder if there's room for a lawyer in New Haven?" Becky's wide eyes bolted to his face.

"Bill, are you saying…..?"

Ella Henry rose wearily from the fire as she cooked. She wiped her hands and glanced off towards the meadow. She was just in time to see two silhouettes come together as one. She smiled and turned back to the fire.

The next few days were busy as the soldiers spent their time helping the wounded to get on trains or other methods of transport if they were unable to ride. Bull Henry bore the expense, in thanks to his men. He made sure his orderly got correct and current names and addresses for all the men. He later had a local smithy forge medallions for each, attached them to ribbons and mailed them to all the men who had come. On them was stamped:

VALLEY CAMPAIGN
COLORADO
1878
MANY THANKS
BULL HENRY

As many received the medals, they called their families together, placed their children and grandchildren upon their knees and told the story of the Valley Campaign.

About the Author:

Mark Herbkersman spent his high school and college years in Idaho. He holds a B.A. in History from Boise State University and a Master's in Counseling Psychology from Ball State University. He has been a Counselor, a seminar presenter/speaker, adjunct faculty at Butler University, pastor, chaplain and now author.

An avid reader all his life, Mark grew to love the adventure and clear morals of the classic westerns authors, with his favorite being Louis L'Amour.

He resides in Indiana with his wife, Marilyn, and their two daughters.

Remember:
Follow Mark on his blog:
markherb.blogspot.com
And feel free to email him at
askmherb@yahoo.com

Made in the USA
Middletown, DE
24 October 2016